I0732781

THE PERUVIAN EXCHANGE

JACK BARR THRILLERS

BOOK 2

NICK THACKER

THE PERUVIAN EXCHANGE: Jack Barr Thrillers #2
Copyright © 2022 by Nick Thacker
Published by Conundrum Publishing

This is a work of fiction. Names, characters, places, and incidents either are the product of the author's imagination or are used fictitiously, and any resemblance of fictional characters to actual persons living or dead, business establishments, events, or locales is entirely coincidental.

All rights reserved. No part of this publication can be reproduced, stored in a retrieval system, or transmitted in any form or by any means—electronic, photocopying, mechanical, or otherwise—without prior permission of the publisher and author except in the case of brief quotations embodied in critical articles or reviews.

WANT FREE BOOKS?

HEAD OVER TO NICKTHACKER.COM/FREE-BOOKS to download three full-length thriller novels!

CHAPTER 1

SANCHEZ

THE PLANE WAS GOING DOWN, and the pilot knew it.

Getulio Sanchez's Cessna had been traveling at approximately 120 knots when the rocket-propelled grenade slammed into its right wing. The explosive charge glanced off the wing before exploding slightly behind and below the plane.

But it had been enough to do catastrophic damage to the aircraft. The plane rocked to the side, rising a dozen feet in an instant from the explosion, but losing it just as quickly. Pieces of the flaps and spoiler on the port side of the aircraft disintegrated, falling down to the jungle below.

The pressure wave of the detonation knocked control cables inside the wing loose as well, no longer allowing the pilot to control the plane's position in the sky.

Three of the port-side windows blew inward from the impact, the frontmost window shattering and sending shards of glass into the side of the pilot's face. The pilot screamed and fell to the side, but recovered an instant later, only to find his plane beginning to spin wildly out of control. He grabbed the yoke and yanked it hard to the right, trying to compensate for the loss of control on the left side.

He checked the altimeter, seeing that they were losing altitude far too quickly for a safe landing attempt.

Not that there was any place for a landing to be attempted. The man looked out the side window, watching the jungle stretch by in all directions. There was not even so much as a plane-sized gap in the thick green canopy.

In an instant, Sanchez knew what was going to happen.

The well-trained pilot ran through a mental checklist, his training kicking in immediately. He had flown for the Colombian Air Force, had trained for *everything.* He knew how to force the small single prop plane into a stall and then recover, accidental barrel rolls, and even flying upside down.

But Sanchez had never tried to fly with a single wing.

Heat throbbed on the side of his face where he knew the shards of glass from the blown-out window had landed and were still stuck. Blood oozed from many of the cuts, dripping onto his left knee. The cold air whipping in from the high altitude did little to ease the pain, and as he tried to look to the left to inspect the damage on the wing, he realized his left eye was unable to move. Sharp pains shot up his optic nerve and around his occipital lobe as he tried to wiggle it.

He groaned in agony, his hands still clamped tightly around the yoke handles. He tried to force the plane to maintain its lift and heading.

To let go now would be suicide — it would immediately launch the plane into an unrecoverable barrel roll, sending it hurtling down toward the jungle canopy.

And yet... there was no other option. The pilot finally forced his head all the way to the left, his neck cracking with the exertion, and saw a large chunk of wing missing. Smoke ran in a straight line from behind it, the smoldering and charred pieces of fuselage that had caught aflame adding to the mix.

Sanchez knew it — the plane was definitely going down. He had trained for controlled crashes, not-so-gentle landings, hitting the ground with no landing gear.

But he was not sure what hitting the treetops at nearly full speed, head-on, would feel like.

He was not going to live through it, that much he could be sure of. Would it hurt? Would he black out, or would he feel every moment, as if hitting in slow motion?

He was about to find out.

The best Sanchez could do now was try to somehow hit the canopy at an angle — and speed — that kept his two passengers alive.

He heard shouts from behind him, where one of his two passengers sat. The passenger was either injured or scared, or both. But whatever the shouting was intended to accomplish — the pilot could not respond.

There was nothing to say. Nothing left to do but hope for the best. He began to pray.

The man to his right was staring at him, wide-eyed. He was another passenger, another delivery.

And the pilot knew he would not be making his delivery successfully today.

CHAPTER 2

JACK

JACKSON BARR, Jr. tossed the half-eaten protein bar to the floor and gripped the small handle above his head. It was mounted between the front windshield and the starboard side-panel glass in the cockpit of the small Cessna, but it felt as though it would rattle away and disappear.

Like the rest of the plane.

The engine was howling, the whine of it louder now than it had been at any moment during the journey.

He watched the pilot toiling against the craft's pull, knowing he would not be able to hold much longer. The wing was going to eventually give way, and the crumpled carcass of the rest of the aircraft would plunge straight down to the jungle.

Jack felt his stomach rising, and he tried to ignore the feeling of wanting to hurl by forcing himself to think of something else.

They had left from the tri-border region in southern Colombia, flying west-southwest on a heading that would take them directly to Iquitos, Peru. Their destination was a small strip of runway on farming land, well out of sight from the local authorities and cartel members.

But apparently, they had not remained out of sight of the *other* hostile faction in the region. The Shining Path — or *Sendero Luminoso* — had been Peru's most infamous terrorist group about three decades ago, rising to power and calling themselves the Maoist Communist Party of Peru. They had taken over villages, claiming them for their own, generally horrifying and terrifying locals with atrocious acts of violence.

And someone had armed them, as well. Rumor was it had been the Peruvian government itself. Some assumed there was a faction that was not excited about Peru's leadership at the time, wanting a new party in power. Jack tended to believe the answer was much simpler: guns had been easy to come by in this corner of the world at that time. It wouldn't take much to outfit a terrorist organization down here with enough fire-power to fight an army.

Over the past 20 years, however, the Shining Path organization had dwindled to almost nonexistent status after the capture of its leader, Abimael Guzmán. In the past five years, rumors had resurfaced about another group of radicalized communists with the same name — seemingly rising from the ashes of the once-powerful organization.

They were claiming to be the original Shining Path and had marked this entire corner of Peru as their own.

The Amazon tributaries flowed freely through the region, starting high up in the Andes and collecting speed, power, and other tributaries as they bound together into one great river. It was over all of this — Shining Path revolutionaries, tributaries, and the jungle surrounding it — that Jack and his partner, Rudy Estrada, had been flying.

A drifting sensation snapped Jack back to the present. He wished he knew what to do. He had seen the pilot play with the oxygen settings before, pushing it in and out as they rose in altitude, listening to the engine.

The explosion had rocked everyone, and Jack had smacked his head against the glass. It wasn't hard enough to be painful, and he had recovered quickly. Rudy, in the backseat, had been fine as well. The man had immediately jumped into action, pulling his pack over the front of his body and onto his shoulders, then looping the backpack with the chute inside over his back. He had shouted something, but Jack could not make sense of the words.

He was scared *shitless*. He had no idea what to do, so he mindlessly copied Rudy's actions and reached for his own bag. It was sitting directly behind him in the back seat, and it would be impossible to get at it and successfully pull it to him. He would have to move into the back of the fuselage to put it on.

As the pilot yanked hard to the right, he noticed that Rudy was holding out Jack's chute.

"Give me the pilot's, too!" Jack shouted.

Rudy frowned, then shook his head. Jack couldn't see his eyes from behind the man's dark sunglasses, but he understood the confusion on the man's face.

"Just give it to me!" Jack yelled, his voice louder.

The pilot continued fighting the plane.

Rudy shook his head again, still not agreeing with Jack's decision. Nevertheless, he handed him the third pack.

Rudy reached for the handle that would open the port-side hatch. Jack barely heard his words over the engine's roar and the plane's whine as it fought to stay afloat in the air. "Time to go, Jack!" Rudy shouted. "Get back here, now!"

Jack did as he was told, tossing the third chute onto his seat while throwing his own over one of his shoulders. He jumped over the navigation clipboard next to the pilot and landed in the backseat of the large Cessna.

He reached back to the other seat and grabbed his personal duffel — his lifeline. He wore both the chute and his pack now, putting the straps of the parachute on his back and the strap of his pack on his front side, over his chest.

He had just gained a hundred pounds, but it was worth it. The heavy bag on his back would save his life now, while the pack on his front would save his life over the next few days.

Rudy already had the hatch open a bit, and Jack heard the louder rush as air flew by the inch-wide gap.

"Are you ready?" Rudy shouted.

Jack swallowed. *No, I'm not ready to jump out of an airplane.*

He was new to fieldwork, a brand-new operative working alongside a seasoned veteran. Jack had been under the Directorate of Intelligence for twenty years, but he had never left the comfort of his desk when working for the CIA. Now he was under the Directorate of Operations, and his cozy desk was nowhere in sight.

Jack shook his head.

"Now or never, Jack," Rudy shouted.

Jack ignored the man, turning to the pilot. He could see sweat falling from the man's forehead, mixing with the blood and perspiration already covering his face. He looked as though he had been through a battle, even though the entire incident had happened over the course of only thirty seconds.

Jack reached over and pulled on the pilot's shoulder. He

leaned forward and spoke directly into the man's ear. "You let go, we start spiraling, yeah?"

The man nodded, leaning his entire body toward the center of the plane, as if trying to counterbalance the weight of the damaged wing himself.

"Let go and climb back here. I've got your chute ready."

The man stared straight ahead as the nose of the plane dipped below the horizon. They were picking up speed. He shook his head. "You go. I'll hold her steady."

"Jack, Now!" Rudy shouted from Jack's side.

Jack ignored the veteran operative.

He pulled harder on the pilot's shoulder, almost yanking the man's hand free. It was exactly what Jack was trying to do, and the man fought against it.

"Let's go *now*, or else we all die," Jack said. "This is our only chance to get out of here alive. You have to leave!"

The pilot seemed to consider this for a long moment — seconds Jack knew they didn't have. Suddenly he released the yoke, and it jammed to the opposite side, the plane launching into a downward spiral.

And immediately sending Rudy out the open hatch.

He heard the man's shout, then a relatively ominous quiet.

And then the roar of the engine and the dying cries of the plane and the rush of the air all came back and pummeled Jack's senses at once. The kerosene-like smell of fuel and ozone, and the almost ocean-like thick air of the jungle atmosphere slammed into his nostrils.

The pilot was crawling back in the plane, Jack helping him along. As the plane tipped forward into the spiral, the man had to work a bit harder, now climbing upward. Jack helped him to his knees once in the back of the plane, tossing the man's chute over his back.

Jack got a glimpse of canopy again as he was thrown off balance. The plane bucked, hopping over a bubble of hot air.

The trees were *much* larger than they had been the last time he'd seen them.

Jack practically flung the pilot out the hatch now, holding onto the plane's wing strut as he did. Once the man was free, Jack jumped out, not even giving himself enough time to consider what he was doing.

He had skydived exactly twice before: once in the Army, when a team of PJs came for a special training session... and once at a bachelor party fifteen years ago.

Jack had *hated* it both times. The sheer terror he had felt as he had stepped close to an open door while fumbling through the air at 150 mph had caused him to nearly vomit all over the jump deck and the other passengers.

Thankfully, both times he had been tandem jumping with an instructor strapped onto his back, and both times the instructor had pushed him forward and out of the craft before he could hurl his lunch everywhere.

But there was no one strapped to him today.

JACK COULDN'T EVEN SCREAM. His body was in shock. He blinked a few times, his mouth working open and closed, but no sound came out.

All he heard was air, cannon fire into his ears as if trying to blast them off his head. And it was cold. His body felt like he had just tossed it into a frozen pond. He tried to get his arms and legs to work but couldn't help but notice they were flailing uselessly around him.

The earth was spinning around him, the horizon the seconds hand on a clock, ticking on fast forward.

His mental training kicked in then. It was not an automatic muscular response — there was no muscle memory to pull from in this situation — but he was finally able to convince his legs to stop whipping wildly. He forced his hands rigid, to his sides like tiny, mostly useless wings.

But it was enough to get him steady. Between gravity and maneuvering his body against it, he finally righted himself. Now he was falling on his belly toward the ground, arms and legs splayed out.

And he was reminded then that this was no skydiving trip. He had wasted most of the free-fall spinning around like an idiot, and now the trees were only a few hundred feet below him.

He panicked, yanking the ripcord. The parachute unfurled behind him and pulled his body upward as if a giant had grabbed his shirt and yanked him straight back toward the plane.

The impact nearly took his arm off — he had forgotten to clip the chute over his chest and belly, and his hand and arm had almost slipped completely out of the loop. His fingers grasped the shoulder strap at the last possible moment. He clenched it tightly, white-knuckling the strap as the parachute started to slow his descent.

He was still moving very quickly, the chute not intended for a low-altitude landing like this. With more space, he could come in diagonally, working with the unfurled canvas.

Now, it was more like a straight shot.

He winced as the first branches of the emergent layer of the rainforest canopy rose to meet his feet. He kicked his legs, trying to break anything that might get in the way and arrest his fall. But he knew it was going to be a *hard* fall.

He forced his arm forward, sliding the stray shoulder strap back over his shoulder while working against the reverse pull of the chute.

He flew through the canopy at speed and reached the understory layer, a ball of kinetic energy that impacted loudly with everything in its path. Branches and limbs snapped, leaves smacked against his face and arms and legs, and he pulled his hands over his eyes as he waited and braced for impact with the forest floor.

The parachute caught on something, and he lurched backward once more, this time expelling everything in his stomach. He vomited all over the ground, which he saw was still eight or nine feet below him. A few animals skittered away, and he heard birds and monkeys squawking their displeasure.

He finished heaving and craned his neck around to see what he had been snagged on. The chute had caught on a tree and was shredded, individual lines twisting and becoming a spider web as he fell.

The entire mess looked like a giant cat had unspooled a ball of yarn in and around the tree.

But he was on the ground, alive.

Well... not on the ground *yet.* Jack grabbed the knife from his belt and sliced the remaining lines of paracord. He worked inside-out, holding the blade out to his side so he wouldn't accidentally fall on it when enough of the line had been severed.

With one final cut, he braced again and closed his eyes as he was weightless once more. His feet hit the leaves below him.

...and then kept going. His legs were overextended, and he fell straight through the ground cover another five feet and landed, his left knee screaming in agony as he hit the dirt hard. He rolled to the side, already holding his left knee.

One minute into the mission and I've torn a meniscus. It wasn't the worst form of the injury — just a shock trauma, nothing major, but it would hurt like hell. He would be walking with a limp for a day or two, but it was a pain he could work through.

He lay on the ground for what seemed like an hour before urging his joints and muscles to sit up. He examined his body for damage. Besides the knee, there wasn't any trouble. Enough cuts and scrapes to drain a full-size tube of topical ointment, but he had exactly that in his pack.

My pack.

It had slipped off, and he saw it lying nearby. He let out a sigh of relief.

Your pack is your lifeline. It had been drilled into him at the Farm — a firehose of force-fed training and 'rapid experience acquisition,' as they had called it. He was Army, so he had not gone through the Farm when he had started at the Company twenty years prior, especially since he had gone into a career under the Directorate of Intelligence.

But all that had changed after a fateful cruise seven months ago; he needed a new skill set after a quick career change to the Directorate of Operations.

Jack reached up and grabbed onto a thick vine — *liana* — clinging to the side of a massive tree behind his head and pulled himself up. He brushed off his butt and his legs, worked his left knee a bit to ensure nothing was broken, then spat out a tooth from the back of his mouth that had become dislodged.

Dropping the pack down in front of him, he unzipped it and pulled out his new tool: the Taurus *Raging Judge* 513. Firing either .45 or 454 Casull rounds, it was a powerful force that would handily deal with anything hostile that got too close.

He pulled it and its belt holster out and put it on. His shirt was loose-fitting and plenty long enough to conceal the weapon at his side. It wasn't perfect, but anyone looking that closely at him would likely be enough of a concern to actually use it.

He looked back in the direction he thought Estrada had

fallen, squinting, trying to see clearly through the trees and luscious growth.

Jack Barr, Jr. was now in the Amazon rainforest, completely alone.

CHAPTER 4

JACK

THE FIRST BODY Jack came across was the pilot's.

He had seen the chute from afar as he'd stepped into an open space beneath the canopy. A small stream collected into a shallow pond at the base of this ravine, and Jack followed the trickle upward until he saw a speck of white cloth hanging high above.

It took him half an hour to climb over the rotting trees, logs, and slippery algae-covered rocks, but he saw even before he got close that the man was dead.

The pilot's parachute had gotten caught like Jack's, but rather than arresting his fall quickly, it had acted like a pendulum, changing direction and smashing the pilot full-speed — and headfirst — into a boulder.

The side of the man's skull had caved in upon impact, killing him instantly.

Jack sighed, taking a moment to allow the loss of life to center him and use it as a reminder of how fleeting that life could be.

The pilot had nothing on his person that Jack didn't

already have strapped to his back. His load-out pack contained enough gear for one man to survive two weeks in the Amazon, or longer if he got creative and used his survival training to extend it. Basics for constructing single-use shelters, MREs in case food proved difficult or impossible to catch — likely not a problem in a place like this — and weapons and equipment for trapping and fishing.

And weapons for defending himself, should he come across any of the beasts of prey the Amazon boasted.

Estrada had joked with Jack as they put the packs together back in Colombia. "The guns are for humans, Jack," Estrada had told him. "Don't bother trying to shoot the black panthers."

"I thought a few Casulls could kill a panther?"

"But you'll never see them coming. They stalk their prey. They attack from behind. One minute you're walking through the jungle, and the next —" he snapped his fingers. "No more walking."

Jack smiled but got the sense that Rudy had not been joking. The man had been in and around the jungle his entire life — growing up in the Peruvian Amazon, spending time on fishing boats and with indigenous peoples, and learning to hunt and trap. These days, public education in the region even taught kids basic jungle survival skills and gave them crash courses in flora and fauna. The jungle and its lessons had never left him.

Jack had taken numerous classes on similar subjects over the past few months, getting a rapid yet thorough education in what he might expect down here. He knew that most of the dangers they would encounter were dangerous not because of their size but in spite of it. At least seventeen snakes alone could kill a man here, and even smaller creatures could do the same damage. Many of them were nearly impossible to see with the naked eye.

Over one hundred species of poison dart frog — many smaller than a quarter, packing enough venom to kill a grown man.

Even a butterfly — the *Heliconius erato*, or Red Postman — was venomous.

And that was just the members of the *animal* kingdom that had a bone to pick with humanity. Plenty of plant life in the rainforest had evolved with their own built-in nasty defense mechanisms, and many packed enough of a punch to knock a man on his ass.

Or kill him outright.

For that reason, the most important thing they had in each of their packs was a massive first-aid kit. They were heavier than a typical ultralight field pack's kit, but they were a piece of gear Rudy told him would save their lives. "Ten extra pounds is a cheap insurance policy against an excruciating death in the jungle," Rudy had said.

Jack had already leaned heavily on the older operative. Rudy Estrada was a 30-year veteran of the CIA, mostly working low-contact assignments that required him to go deep cover for extended periods of time. Deep cover was reserved for the men and women who had decided there was no better way to spend their life than by defending the nation against international clandestine threats. They spent months undercover, their statuses unknown even to other operatives.

Estrada, like Jack, had a family. He had told Jack he didn't like to be away for months at a time, though he did it when required. His family knew he worked for the government, but he had never given anyone close to him the specific details.

Jack was modeling his career after Estrada's — he had not set out to be an operator. In fact, he still wasn't sure he *wanted* to be one. He knew now that if it involved jumping out of airplanes into hostile territory, he'd likely rather ride the desk back at Langley, as he'd done for so many years.

But the decision hadn't been entirely his. His wife of fifteen years, Kate, had urged him to look into fieldwork. After an incident on their last family vacation, Jack had surprised himself — and everyone around him — by being far more useful in the field than he'd ever thought possible. It hadn't been *fun* work, but it had awoken something in Jack.

Though the perpetrator had gotten away, Jack had helped put bad men behind bars and helped his government pinpoint the leadership of a known drug cartel and arms-smuggling operation in Venezuela.

Jack had come here to finish that work.

He had come here to find the man who had nearly killed his children.

CHAPTER 5

JACK

THE OPERATION ITSELF WAS SIMPLE: find Victor Elizondo, one of the top leaders of the *Vínculos* drug cartel, and track him along their new route. Learn the flows of the region. *Observe, record, report.*

The CIA had been keeping tabs on Victor Elizondo and the *Vínculos* cartel for years — ever since it had shown up as a veritable force in South American drugs and arms trafficking.

Jack understood the assignment perfectly well. They were there to collect HUMINT — human intelligence. It was the most reliable form of intelligence-gathering a covert operation had. Together with the SIGINT — signals intelligence from sources including computers, emails, credit card transactions, and any number of other formats — collected from the cartel, the information would provide a detailed overview of how black-market smuggling activities operated in the region.

For over a hundred years, the Amazon rainforest had been perfect cover for operations large and small to conduct illicit business. Everything from illegal logging, drug cultivation, creation, or growing, and the running of illegal contraband was easy under the thick jungle canopy and the sparsely populated area that spanned almost the entire square mileage of the continental United States.

Based in Venezuela, Victor's cartel had struck new deals with third-world countries and guerrilla armies. Each buyer was hoping to overthrow some particular government in some backwater of the globe, but the *Vínculos* didn't care — as long as their buyers paid.

Each of their customers needed weapons, as did Victor's own growing army, and there was no better way to get hands on these weapons than moving them through Victor's crew in South America.

Victor was not the head honcho but was considered second-in-command. The main cartel boss was aging but still held supreme authority over the goings-on of his cartel, asserting his influence through Victor himself. Intel had told Jack that the man was reclusive, holing up in a castle-like compound near Caracas, where he ran his empire by proxy. There were at least four men capable of running the cartel, but everyone knew Victor was the 'golden boy' who would be chosen to lead.

Sources in the intelligence community believed Victor would be the de facto leader if and when there was a coup in the cartel, or a successful assassination attempt on the boss.

And while it was not part of Jack's mission, his papers from the DI told him that an assassination would, in fact, be happening.

Jack's mission seemed simple enough. The CIA could cause unrest and disorder by taking down one of its main leaders, before Victor was ready to take the reins. Every organization of a certain size became fractured, fragmented. Factions of smaller, close-knit groups would be vying for power, trying to get their man in charge of the entire operation. Jack's boss believed that by taking out *Victor's* boss — the head of the *Vínculos* — would throw the entire region into chaos and disarray, but ultimately it would have the effect of loosening the cartel's stranglehold on South American drug and armaments shipments.

It would allow Victor to usurp the throne earlier than intended, and they could possibly catch him off guard then.

US Army intelligence had informed the CIA that they had assets in place and were prepared to both remove the current leader of the cartel in Caracas, as well as ensure the new faction that rose to power would be a puppet of the US government itself — someone who was *not* Victor Elizondo.

Since most of the guns and ammunition that were making their way through South America by way of the *Vínculos* had been manufactured in the US anyway, the thought was that the US government should at least have *some* say over where these shipments eventually went.

It was an age-old game of political maneuvering and sleight-of-hand, but none of that had anything to do with Jack.

All he had to do was find Victor.

All he *wanted* to do was find Victor.

His op parameters were to get eyes on Victor, then get a read on his cartel's new route through the Amazon. Once satisfied he knew the flows well enough, the CIA's paramilitary forces could come in and finish the job, working alongside U.S. Army intelligence and Green Berets.

But Jack had no interest in what happened *after* his mission. He wanted to be done with this entire thing in three days' time — the allotted mission timing before his extraction

— when the assassination of the cartel boss in Caracas would take place.

He would have no part in that — Victor Elizondo was his mission, and that was here in Peru.

Six months ago, he and his wife and two daughters had embarked on a seven-day cruise to Jamaica. In port, an explosion had rocked the ship and caused it to take on water, stranding it in the bay. Everyone had been evacuated.

Everyone *except* for Jack and his kids. Victor had staged the entire thing, coming aboard with a group of his cartel men to figure out who was siphoning money from his operation. He had used the boat as his place of business.

And he had used Jack's daughters and about thirty other children as leverage. He had killed innocent people and attempted to blow up a lifeboat full of kids.

It was only because of quick thinking and a good dash of luck that Jack had been able to prevent a devastating loss of life.

But that was not good enough for Jack. Victor was still out there — still terrorizing innocent people. Jack had almost failed to stop him once before.

There was a question of whether Jack wanted to spend the rest of his career doing fieldwork as an operative, but there was no question in his mind about his desire to take on this mission.

Jack wanted to find Victor Elizondo.

CHAPTER 6

WYMAN

DIANE WYMAN, chair of the House Select Permanent Committee on Intelligence, slammed the phone down onto the receiver. She kept the phone on her massive oak desk to take certain calls that needed to stay private.

Plus, she loved slamming the phone — it was a throwback to a bygone era.

Her assistant, Kenneth Ma, poked his head in. "Everything okay, ma'am?" he asked.

The permanent scowl on her face barely changed as she looked up at the young twenty-something. "I just got off the phone with Senator Nichols," she said. "He's worried once again about the new IC report."

Ma frowned. She knew it was impossible for the kid to have already read the 325-page report that had been released only this morning, but it was part of the unofficial rulebook of Washington politics to make the younger staff and assistants feel bad for spending their free time sleeping rather than stuffing their brains full of useless information.

The only reason *she* knew what the report said was that she had just gotten off the phone with one of the men who had written it.

She also knew that the report had not been *written* so much as pieced together from copy-and-pasting other pre-existing documents, with a quick two-page abstract written up by one of the countless assistants roaming the halls.

Ma was one of them, so at the very least, he would have a passing understanding of the report if he had not had time to crack it open yet.

"What does he want this time?" Ma asked, stepping further into the room as if invited. He had not been, but she only had a limited supply of vitriol, which she tried to reserve for important people.

"More money, as always. What's new?" She forced a smile, but somehow the scowl remained on her face even through it. "Don't we all... this time, his flavor-of-the-week is Albania."

"Albania?" Ma asked, stepping into the room. "I thought they were still reeling after their run-in with Kosovo last year?"

She was pleased to see that he had the new report under his arm and another stack of papers, probably a ream's worth that would take any mortal being months to read through. The expectation was that he would have it read by the end of the day. Then he would prepare his thoughts and submit them to her in writing sometime before midnight — at which point she would take them and use them as *her* thoughts, passing them up the chain until everyone involved had her published opinion on whatever it was Ma had read.

It was a grueling cycle, and it was no wonder Congress was helplessly overwhelmed. The House of Representatives and the Senate had long been a source of cannon fodder for political satirists, but sometime over the last two decades, Wyman had seen the shift in the general public's view of the legislative branch.

The media did not usually portray them in a good light, but their disdain for the legislators was unnecessary. One could walk the halls and observe any number of inefficiencies, gross oversteps, and abuses of power.

Perhaps the most telling of all was the fact that Wyman had gone into politics like they all had, naïvely: to make a positive impact on the world. She had barely a dime to her name back then and had leaned heavily on political supporters to get elected.

Now, almost 30 years later, she could retire happily at any point and have almost 200 million dollars to her name. American politics had become a very lucrative career path. She had earned a fortune just sitting in a large circular room, debating the merits of whatever thousand-page rider was on the docket that day. It was a corrupt, disgusting system.

And she loved it.

Wyman had no plans to retire — the money was just too good. As long as she kept the right constituents happy at the right time, it was, quite literally, free money.

The wet-behind-the-ears assistants like Ma all had that shine in their eyes she had had once too — the twinkle of thinking they could *actually* affect positive change and make a difference. Each one of them, Ma included, thought that *they* would be different. Thought *they* would be above the corruptions and scandalous relationships and outright bribery.

And each of them was, eventually, woefully wrong.

"I can't keep it straight," Ma said. "So are we pro-Albania or anti-Albania?"

This time Wyman's smile was genuine. "How naïve of you,"

she said. "We are neither pro- nor anti-*anything*, my dear. Albania currently needs US weapons... and we have them. Who are we to decide the fate of the free world? Who are we to have a moral high ground?"

Ma nodded, pulling the ream of paper over to his other hand to lighten the load. "So..."

"So, I need you to draft a letter to the HSPCI. A memo. I think we can push it through without much trouble, depending on how it's worded. If it's vague enough, go for it — give it to their assistants to sign."

"But we'll have to present it to the House as well?"

Ma had presented it as a question, even though it was a statement of fact. They would, of course, have to present it to the House, but that didn't mean they couldn't get a decent head start. Nichols wanted weapons in Albania, and Wyman would get weapons to Albania. She knew why he had called her, specifically. Nichols probably already *had* weapons inbound to Albania, redirecting the pieces of the supply chain he controlled — through legal or illegal channels, no one would care — and Albania would be armed within the month.

But Wyman's job was to make it appear legal or do enough handwaving so that no one would care for the next twenty years. As chair of the intelligence committee, her job was less about passing legislation for the intelligence community to abide by, and more about making their decisions palatable to the uninformed public. Thanks to the media, every decision made in Congress was scrutinized down to the last punctuation mark.

But it wasn't always scrutinized immediately. The media often got wind of something years, or even decades, after it had passed, opening an old can of worms for the delightfully igno-rant commoners to butt heads over.

The CIA had asked permission to use a slightly altered form of waterboarding as an 'enhanced interrogation tech-nique' shortly after 911. At the time, when tensions were high and everyone wanted vengeance for the terror attacks, this request was akin to asking a child if they wanted another piece of candy. Congress had worked themselves into a fury writing up the necessary legislation, and she had been dazzled when it had been presented to the house. It had passed with flying colors in both the House and Senate, and the American public rejoiced... for the five minutes it fixated on the issue.

But when the pendulum swung the other direction many years later, everyone in the judicial and executive branches had gotten new jobs, died, or retired, and everyone in the legislative branch had performed its rhetoric version of musical chairs, the media got wind once again that the CIA was involved in torture.

Lawsuits stacked up, and the press feasted on the sound-bites of fallen legislators. The CIA was blamed, of course, since they had been the ones to cook up the nefarious plot in the first place, and all the while HSPCI had licked their chops, admit-ting that the CIA was operating like a rogue agent and needed to be reined in. Their job, with the public's permission, of course, would be to ensure something like this could *never* happen again.

Until it happened again.

For some people, the game was infuriating. No one ever won except for the brokers of the deals — the politicians them-selves. They grew fatter every year, siphoning money from both sides, from the lobbyists that wanted their needs met to the budget planners who allotted 'additional funding' for whatever unforeseen projects might arise.

And Wyman had gotten ridiculously rich because of it.

"I'll have the draft over to you by this evening," Ma told her.

She felt reinvigorated after thinking it through. Just because Nichols had reneged on the previous deal and backpedaled did not mean she couldn't make the best of the situation. Nichols was still in bed with defense contractors and US-based weapons manufacturers, so she knew what incentives there were for him. With any luck, she could persuade him to grease the wheels a little and get some of those incentives to fall in her direction.

A favor for a favor, they often said.

She shook her head. "Tomorrow will be fine," she said. "Nichols isn't calling me to ask permission; he's calling as a courtesy. It's basically already done, so there's no rush. We'll present next week, so we've got a little bit of time."

Ma nodded once and left her office, and Wyman leaned back in her chair, arms behind her head, satisfied that her fingerprint was about to be on yet another lucrative deal.

CHAPTER 7

JACK

JACK POPPED his leg as he walked, stretching it and testing it. He limped awkwardly with each step. It was feeling better already, but he knew that it would harden up again tonight as soon as he stopped moving and let it rest. He wished he could get it on ice as soon as possible, but the reality was that wasn't going to happen for at least a day.

Jumping out of the plane half an hour before their scheduled landing time meant they were somewhere northeast of Iquitos, Peru. But they were in the world's densest jungle, and hiking to the city would take hours on foot.

Before he could start the haul to Iquitos, however, he needed to find his teammate. If he was still alive, Jack wanted to link up once again and continue on together. If he had died like the pilot, well... Jack would figure that out when the time came.

It would take extra time, but Jack's best opportunity to succeed here was to stay with his partner. The loss of minutes was well worth not having to camp alone in the Amazon.

He did a full circle, trying to keep his bearings. He had

been facing south when their plane had gone down. Since he had jumped out of the port side of the aircraft, it meant the river was just beyond where he and his parachute had entered the tree line.

Somewhere.

That meant Rudy would also be near this spot, not far from where the pilot had gone in.

He stopped, listening to the sounds of the jungle. When he was moving, everything seemed quiet — as if the jungle itself was a single organism, living, breathing, and existing together. He moved through it as a foreigner, clumsily stumbling along with an injured leg, making more noise than he should. But every time he stopped, let himself breathe for a few seconds, the jungle seemed to come back to life once again. Hoots and cries from monkeys high above his head swirled around and mixed with the shouts and shrieks of parrots and other aviary life.

He heard the sounds of frogs croaking, the trillions of little bugs flicking and buzzing about his head — and that was only the stuff he could hear. He knew there were infinitely more creatures around, silent and lying in wait to hunt food or become food.

He thought again of the snakes and wondered how many were looking at him. He shivered. He had never liked snakes. He didn't *hate* them and knew they had their place in the food chain. But that didn't mean he wanted to stumble across one.

The biggest fear most people had regarding the Amazon was the anaconda — the largest snake in the world. Calling the Amazon Basin home, the massive boa preferred shallows and rivers, building semi-submerged nests on the riverbanks. They could grow to lengths of up to 30 feet; pound-for-pound, the green anaconda was the largest snake on the planet. Usually not harmful to humans, humans were certainly harmful to *them* — natives and outsiders alike hunted them for fear of attack or just to put a new and more impressive trophy on their wall. Their skins were used for clothing or decoration.

But to Jack, it was a snake. A very, *very* big snake. He knew every snake got hungry, and no snake was picky about the particular flavor of meat they consumed.

He stopped and stood for a minute, taking a breath. He didn't want to sit down for fear that his leg might cramp up completely, so he listened, smelled, and looked around, trying to make sense of his surroundings. It was hot today, the thick humidity causing a haze that permeated the jungle and rose from the heavy bed of moist ferns and jungle life.

His body went rigid. He thought he heard something.

He crept forward, careful not to make a noise. It was a sound that had caused him to stop in the first place, and —

There it was again. Another noise, as if approaching from afar. He squinted, peering through a break in the trees, but saw nothing.

Jack was about to move forward when the sound moved from in front of him...

To directly behind him.

CHAPTER 8

JACK

IT WASN'T the *same* sound — he instantly realized that it was something different. A brief shake of leaves, heavy drips of dew falling to the dirt. It was something unnatural.

Jack had not found Rudy. Rudy found him. An arm reached out and yanked him backward.

"Quiet," Estrada's voice said, whispering directly into Jack's ear.

Jack allowed Estrada to pull him back into the tree. Estrada had been completely concealed as Jack had passed directly by him. The man seemed to have become the tree itself, covering his body in leaves and vines, still as the trunk he was standing in front of.

"How the hell did you —"

"You're going to get us killed," Estrada said, shushing him. "I heard you stomping around from a mile away."

"What are we hiding from?" Jack whispered.

"Those same SL assholes who shot down our plane," Estrada hissed. "Stand next to me so we can cover you with vines, at least. You still stick out like a sore thumb, but at least when they shoot at you, you won't be standing right in front of me. Maybe they'll just hit you instead."

Jack glared at the older man, but the man just flashed him a smile. Estrada was no stranger to traipsing through the woods and hiding from terrorists.

Estrada helped pull some vines over Jack's front, and Jack pressed his back up against the trunk of the tree just as the jungle to his right parted, and two men stepped out.

Both were thin, short, wearing green t-shirts and jungle camo pants. They both had dark face paint splashed across their cheeks and red bandannas tied around their necks.

Sendero Luminoso.

The men were holding assault rifles, one an AK-47 and another one Jack couldn't see well from here, as it was slung over the man's shoulder and rode on his back. But this man was wielding a machete, slicing through the thickest of the brush, leading their way through the jungle.

And they were heading directly toward them.

The two men passed within feet of Jack, and he felt he could reach out and grab one of them. He held his breath, hoping they wouldn't accidentally glance to their left. If they saw him, there would be no way Jack could get his weapon out before —

Two deafening shots rang out.

Both men in front of Jack fell, and tinnitus swirled through his head.

Estrada stepped out from his hiding spot next to Jack and rushed forward, putting another bullet into the backs of each of the two men's heads.

Jack's mouth fell open. "What the hell, Estrada? What are you doing?"

Estrada looked up at Jack, a confused expression on his face. "These guys are part of the group that shot our plane down."

Jack threw the vines off him and marched over to the two dead men and Estrada, standing near one dead man's head.

"Estrada, that isn't the mission. We're not here to *kill* anyone."

"Victor is not going to be just walking through the jungle unprotected, like these two, Jack. Did it occur to you that he will probably be traveling with a whole army as the next leader of the entire cartel?"

"Yeah, but —" Jack stammered.

"But *nothing*. They sent us into an active war zone, Barr. I know this is your first official field op, and they made it sound like it was going to be walking through a meadow picking daisies but let me tell you the truth: being successful here is all about the long game. You *must* think long-term. Even though they gave us a simple, short-term op — get eyes on and track cartel movements for a few days — *everything* goes back to a long-term plan."

Jack eyed him. "And what is that plan?"

Rudy smiled. "You think they would tell us that?"

Jack snorted. *Fair point.* He had spent an entire career as an analyst, so he understood where Rudy was coming from.

"This shit is the real deal," Rudy continued. "Special Activities Center sends guys like us out to clean up the mess after warlords duke it out. America is not interested in blowing up everything in sight. They want information, and they want leverage. *We're* here to collect that, but it's not going to be a breeze to get it."

Jack nodded.

"We don't have time to play hide-and-seek with a bunch of wannabe gangsters. The shortest distance to Victor — to finishing the op and turning in the new route so everyone at Langley can play chess with it — is a straight line. But if that straight line happens to intersect with some Shining Path punks, I'm taking them out."

Jack stood still, listening. He wasn't necessarily against killing these men. They were the literal definition of terrorists, *and* they had tried to shoot his plane down, but it still felt reckless.

"I'm just worried about the bodies," Jack said finally.

Estrada raised an eyebrow. "These guys were on patrol, likely doing a huge perimeter circle looking for us and the plane. They might have a camp less than a mile from here that heard me, but there will be no way to tell where those gunshots came from. And I can assure you, no one else is coming here."

"What if they do?" Jack asked.

"Then it's a good reason to start walking away. The sooner we do, the sooner the jungle will come to reclaim its territory."

Jack stared down at the men lying dead on the forest floor, already seeing flies and small insects buzzing nearby to inspect the fresh kill. He knew what Estrada was saying was correct — the rainforest was a brutal place to eke out an existence, and plenty of opportunistic creatures were ready to pounce on the ready-made meal Rudy had left them. He figured these guys would be eaten long before they had time to decay and disintegrate back into the soil.

Estrada turned around, then started marching back in the direction Jack had come from. "The pilot?" he asked as he passed Jack.

Jack shook his head.

"Okay. This puts us on a direct heading to Iquitos, and I don't think there are any major geologic features in our way. It'll be a little bit uphill, though — hopefully, your leg holds up."

Jack frowned. He was almost positive he had not been limping when he had walked by Rudy's hiding spot, but then again, he wasn't sure how long Estrada had been watching him.

The depth of the older man's experience and intuition was stunning, forged not just from the Farm but from an up close and personal experience with this region, a lifetime spent in and around the jungle.

Rudy didn't slow, and Jack hustled to keep up. He hoisted his pack tighter on his back, feeling as if the older operative might be even more of a lifeline out here than the gear he wore.

CHAPTER 9

JACK

THE PAIR TREKKED through the jungle for another three hours until the early signs of dusk began its descent over the rainforest. The noises of the wildlife changed, growing quieter in some ways and yet more frenzied in others, as the animals who frolicked during the day began to take cover in preparation for the nocturnal beasts that hunted at night.

Jack's pack felt heavier by the minute, so he was glad when Estrada stopped and pointed when they entered a relatively clear circle of land. "Natural opening," he said. "Good place to stop for the night."

Jack nodded and let the pack slide off his shoulder. He immediately felt relief, his sore muscles and leg aching for a break. Estrada began collecting wood for a small fire, and Jack trudged through a break in the trees toward a larger tributary. Most of these rivers were still considered too small to be mapped, and he knew there must have been 10,000 or more tiny fingers and streams that all called themselves tributaries to the mighty Amazon. The stream he found now was shallow, no more than a few feet deep at its center and perhaps a dozen feet across. Jack was surprised that this water was clear rather than the murky brown of the larger Amazon basin waterways. He pulled the canteen from his side and began to fill it, dropping an iodine tablet in.

Estrada would be boiling the water, so this step was unnecessary. Still, Jack wanted to take as many sips as possible before having to wait for the water to heat up, boil for the obligatory fifteen minutes, then cool back down to drinking temperature.

Across the river from him, he watched as a spider monkey swooped down and scooped up a handful of water, shoving it into his mouth before its tail splashed over the surface, and he disappeared into the trees beyond. Jack was impressed by how quietly the creature had descended and humbled by how quickly it had completely disappeared and become one with the forest again. It would be part of a family or group, so he was sure there were others beyond, watching him.

He got the sense once again that he wasn't alone out here. As much as he felt alone, he knew there were eyes watching him at all times.

He stood up, taking a swig of water and ignoring the sharp tinge of the iodine, then walked back to where Rudy Estrada was on his knees, working with the small collection of kindling and tender.

"Won't the fire attract more of the SL assholes?" Jack asked. He knew the answer already — of course, it would; it was part of their training not to build fires unless absolutely necessary.

But Estrada just looked at him and smiled. "Jack, those *assholes* are just men, like you and me. It is growing dark. They are as scared shitless to be out here as you and I are. They won't be doing any night patrols — they knew we weren't trying to come into their territory; we were just passing over." Rudy smiled. "And besides — we are better trained. Let them come; I would appreciate another opportunity to diminish their ranks."

Jack nodded, swallowing. A sense of trepidation had fallen over him ever since the plane crash. He pushed it away — it was obviously just the waning adrenaline after the terrifying entrance to the jungle and the subsequent discovery of the death of their pilot. In truth, he and Rudy were in a pretty good situation. The plan had been to fly into Iquitos, Peru, landing just outside of town and hoping there was no fanfare at the runway. It was a covert mission, so they needed to hike the half-mile into town from the runway without being spotted, then meet up with one of Estrada's assets. The asset would hopefully get them acquainted with a local group of drug runners working a new "flow" in the region for the cartel.

They would be undercover as drug runners — not the safest mission, but certainly the best way to travel with other low-level runners and move through the new route. They wouldn't just *observe* Victor's new plan; they would *live* it.

But the Shining Path had also moved into the region, and they were growing in strength in Iquitos, according to their intelligence. That meant Jack and Estrada could not just waltz out of the jungle just north of Iquitos and immediately blend in downtown. If anyone had happened to get a decent look at their clothing after they had jumped from the plane, they would be easily recognized. Even if not, Jack was an outsider. Their packs would immediately identify them as travelers or vagabonds, and he knew word would spread if they weren't careful.

Here, the jungle was part of life. And Iquitos was the jungle. There was no separation between city and rainforest —

the people who lived in one also lived in the other. Iquitos was a popular tourist destination, but it had a small-town feel to it, and if they caused trouble, it wouldn't go unnoticed.

"And don't forget," Rudy said. "We're going to need a small fire to keep away the larger things that might want to snack on us at night."

Jack didn't need to be repeatedly reminded of the things that might want to 'snack' on them at night. He knew full well what sorts of things awaited them in the jungle. As such, he tried to busy himself with small chores to keep his mind busy.

He pulled out his hammock and bug net, found a pair of trees about two-dozen feet away from the fire tucked back into the woods, and hung it. This was his personal hammock, not something the Company had provided. He had used it on camping trips with Kate before the kids were born, even setting it up once or twice for them to bounce around on when they were younger. Back home, using the hammock always meant using nylon straps around the trees, as damaging the trunks was considered an offense at most state parks and campgrounds.

But out here in the rainforest, carrying nylon straps and carabiners meant extra weight. Damaging the trunk of a tree with a hammock would cause the tree pain for perhaps five minutes before it grew back stronger than it had been before. The life and energy of the forest seemed palpable — as if by waiting and watching for a few minutes, he might actually see it growing and changing around him.

It really was unlike any other place he'd been. It was a shame he couldn't be here with Kate and the kids, enjoying a real camping trip. But he had a job to do. He let the pang of regret pass and the thoughts of his family dissipate — those thoughts weren't helpful in the field. They only made an operative more emotional, more vulnerable.

He needed to be like Rudy — he needed to be stoic, strong. There was time for emotional vulnerability and missing his kids, but that time was not now.

Now, he needed to stay alive.

CHAPTER 10

WYMAN

DIANE WYMAN PICKED up the hefty phone and held it up to her ear, dialing with her other hand. At 76 years old, she preferred these old phones to the dinky little cellphones everyone's heads were constantly stuck to these days.

She enjoyed slamming the receiver onto the cradle when she was pissed — and she was often pissed — but there was also something nostalgic about having an ancient-looking piece of technology on the desk. She would never admit it to anyone, but the phone also represented a piece of history. It had been given to her by her father after graduating from Georgetown. The desk itself had been her grandfather's, passed down through the generations.

She was nostalgic like anyone else, but she would never let anyone find out. She had a reputation, and she intended to uphold it.

The phone rang ten full times, but she waited anyway. There was no answering machine on the other end — no one ever listened to the messages anyway. She knew the man she was calling had a million little minions running around his offices at any given time, day or night. Eventually, someone would pick up.

She was pleasantly surprised to hear Bob Stevens on the other end.

"Well, the deputy director himself," she chuckled. "it's good to hear your voice."

"I wish I could say the same, Wyman," Stevens said. *"But I'm already wincing. How much money or pain is this going to cost me?"*

Wyman smiled, the same sly grin she used when presenting to the House, giving a speech, or really, just about any time she felt sly and in control. "Well, you know I would *never* call just to catch up."

Stevens sighed. *"What do you want then, Wyman? We're busy as hell over here."*

She looked down at her notes. Even with as sharp a wit as hers, she preferred keeping notes to help her dictate the flow of conversation, especially regarding delicate matters such as this. "I just got off the phone with one of my fellow committee members, and it's come to my attention that the situation in Albania has changed."

"I'm the Deputy Director of Operations for the CIA, Wyman. You think you've got intelligence that I don't already have?"

She skipped the opportunity to get a dig in at the man's 'intelligence' and moved on. "I'll admit you probably know *more* about the situation than I do, however, it doesn't change the fact that there is a certain... contingent of constituents who would like to affect certain policies in the area."

"Just because one lobbyist got his panties in a knot doesn't mean we all have to reverse course on foreign policy."

"No one said anything about reversing course," Wyman said. "I'm merely asking for... a slight alteration of plans."

There was a long pause.

"The request that my committee will be presenting next week is pretty easy for everyone. Just a slight change in marching orders for some of your assets."

"Slight change of... who the hell do you think you are, Wyman?" Stevens asked. She could hear his voice growing more agitated. *"I'm the Deputy Director of the CIA — you're a Congresswoman. And a pretty bad one, at that. Since when do you think you get to dictate orders to me?"*

"Since I became the committee chair, Bob," Wyman said calmly. "And I'm quite *good* as a congresswoman, as it turns out. I get what I want. But as much as I like seeing you get your panties in a knot, I'm only doing this in the interest of national security."

Bob snorted laughter. *"Tell me one thing you know about national security, Diane. Real national security. You know, the kind I get to be involved in. You're just a washed-up law school dropout who —"*

"Let's not get into name-calling, Bob," Wyman said, the strict scowl returning to her face. She stroked the massive phone mouthpiece with her free hand as she stared down at her notepad. "I'm sure I could scare up a few names to call you from your more... promiscuous days."

They had gone to school together at Georgetown for a year, But Bob then went to the Naval Academy. Afterward, he went into military service, but she had higher aspirations. It had rankled her a bit that a Navy brat like him had *still* ended up in a high-power position on the Hill, but she had known it was still a man's game here all along. That she had gotten as far as she had *without* a penis was something she considered her greatest accomplishment.

She leaned back over her elbows. "I've been told this will be financially beneficial for me. As you know, I, *of course* don't do these things for the money. And I know you don't, either. But —"

"If you're about to bribe me over a public phone, I suggest you be very careful about what you're about to say."

"I was told this phone was encrypted."

"You can't even spell *encrypted. Wyman, stop trying to play politics with me. I was a Rear Admiral; you know what that means? I actually had to fight the damned battles you clowns in your bubble got us into. And I'm still kicking, which means I won those battles. So I'd be* very *careful about picking battles you can't even understand, much less win."*

Wyman smiled, looking around at her lavish office. She, too, had won battles. And unlike Bob Stevens, she had something to show for it. She might not have a fancy Navy pension and a government salary, but at least she could leverage her experience into even more power.

And best of all, she didn't have any of the hesitations and misgivings of using that power for personal gain. These *honorable* military types often carried them like war medals.

"I respect your position and authority, *Admiral*," she said, laying the sarcasm on thick. "I'm just calling you as a... courtesy. You know how these things really work. Consider this just one friend helping out another."

He scoffed.

"It might be in the best interest of you and your organization to heed my warning," she finished.

"Congress can't directly deploy troops," Stevens said. *"As*

much as you trigger-happy zealots think you're in charge, you're just the elected puppets between the public and the boots on the ground."

"That may be true," Wyman said. "But at the end of the day, we both know who holds the real power. The press is ready for heads to roll, and the only question they're asking is which one of ours will it be this time? I'm getting out ahead of this, Bob. I suggest you do as well."

"Cut the bullshit, Wyman," Stevens snapped. *"I'm a busy man. What* exactly *is it you're trying to ask me?"*

"I need you to pull all of your assets out of South America."

Stevens just laughed.

"I'm not joking, Stevens. The request came in —"

"From whom? A lobbyist? A drinking buddy?"

"Let me rephrase that," Wyman said. "A *thinly veiled threat* came in earlier today, and I'm just trying to make sure both our asses are covered."

"Well, that's impossible. Where in South America are you worried about, specifically?"

"Peru. Colombia. Venezuela. Parts of Brazil."

"Not gonna happen, Wyman. If you understood the first thing about the political unrest going on down there, you would —"

"Stevens, I'm calling you right now *because* of the political unrest there. Those weapons *need* to get to Albania. You got intel, so you already know about the shitstorm that's beginning to brew overseas."

"Be that storm of shit as it may, it doesn't mean I can just sign off and retract marching orders for any number of assets I've got in the field."

"It absolutely *does* mean that, Stevens. You, of all people, know that."

"Wyman, we're not having this conversation. There's no way in hell I'm making the call to remove CIA assets from the entire northern half of the continent. Between the resurgence of this fun little communist terrorist group, political coups, and all sorts of trafficking bullshit, the whole place is a powder keg. What you're asking for would be the spark."

"To do nothing would be the spark, Stevens."

Stevens paused. *"This sounds less like a request and more like a threat, Wyman. Do I need to resort to issuing those as well?"*

"I may be a politician, but I'm no liar," Wyman said. "I don't make any threat I can't back up. But to answer your question, no. This is not a threat. A warning, but not from me."

CHAPTER 11

JACK

WHEN JACK FINISHED HANGING up his hammock and getting the bug net spread above it, he zipped it closed and walked back over to where Rudy was heating up a pack of MREs. "Thought it would be easier just plow through these rather than try to catch something," Estrada mumbled.

Jack nodded and accepted a fork from Estrada's mess kit. Both men had taken strenuous jungle survival courses over the past six months, sprinkled in with the rest of the training Jack had undergone. Nevertheless, their course instructor had drilled into Jack's skull that jungle survival was far easier when it felt more like camping than survival.

In other words, come prepared if you knew you were going to the jungle. Having the right gear and knowing how to use it might mean the difference between a comfortable trek through the world's largest rainforest and death.

They sat on rocks and chewed through two bags of MREs. It was a bit wasteful, but Jack knew they needed the calories, and they were less than a day's walk from Iquitos. There would be any number of small supply shops and outfitters — even grocery stores — on the outskirts of town, so as long as they stayed near the river, they would find the town easily.

"How far out you think we are?" Jack asked, trying to get some clarity.

"Four hours, max," Estrada said. He spat a piece of food onto the ground.

Jack nodded. "That's what I was thinking." He chewed a bit more. "So what's it really like?"

Estrada stopped, his eyes darting up. "What do you mean?"

Jack shrugged. "Being a spook. The Company. You've done it for a long time now. I've only seen you guys from afar, handling logistics and intel, passing it along from the safety of a desk. I've only seen the other side. So what's it really like?"

Estrada rubbed his eyes with a free hand, cleaning out some dirt and grime that had settled there. He took another few bites, chewing slowly, contemplating. "Who do you trust?"

Jack wasn't sure how to answer. "Who do I trust? What do you mean?"

"I mean, who do you trust? Blindly, no-questions-asked?"

"My wife, I guess..." Jack began. "We're on the same page about most things, and I trust her with almost —"

"*Ehh*, wrong answer," Rudy said, making the sound of a gameshow buzzer. "I'm sure you love her, but that doesn't mean you can *trust* her."

"I'm not sure I understand your line of reasoning, then. What do you mean by *trust*?"

Rudy took a long pause. "Look, Jack. This job ain't for everyone. Actually, it's for hardly anyone at all. Those of us who do best at it — the ones who get to stay alive — well, we don't trust anyone. We get orders, we do them. If you move to contractor status, you can even choose whether to accept the orders. You have to have a good gut check to say yes *or* no to a mission. But even then, you do this long enough, you realize there's *no one* out here you can really trust."

Jack frowned, but Rudy continued. "*That's* what this job is all about. You can be really good as an operative without having to trust damn near anybody, but there's always one exception."

Jack waited, knowing the punchline was coming.

"You always gotta trust yourself, Jack. That's the one who matters. You. You want to make a life at the Company, you need to know *damn* well you trust yourself. Whatever situation it is — *you*. You trust yourself, and yourself only."

Jack stared down into the flickering and darting threats of fire, hearing the pops and hissing of the wetter logs Estrada had thrown on. It wasn't exactly the answer he had expected, but he wasn't surprised, either. Rudy Estrada was an enigma, a man he knew professionally. Of his personal life, he only knew the information the older man had shared, and even then, Jack had known better than to trust the man's stories and take everything at face value. The CIA was like a massive game of deception. It wasn't that everyone was out to get everyone else, it was just that operatives lived and breathed on information — they collected it, dealt it, used it as armor.

Revealing personal information was not against the rules, but it was a faux pas. Rudy Estrada was Rudy Estrada — that's all Jack had to know. He had volunteered that he had grown up in Peru and a few other helpful tidbits useful to their mission, but Jack didn't need more information than Rudy had wanted to share.

Light rain began to fall around them, their small open section of forest was protected from the largest drops by the thick canopy sections high above their heads. Down here, rain didn't come from the sky — it simply came from the forest itself, dripping and sliding down in streams, cascading down trees and ferns and whatever else was in the way.

They finished dinner, neither man wanting to talk much more. They knew the challenges that lay ahead, and Jack sensed that both of them were running through every scenario, double-checking their library of knowledge and training against any issues that might arise. They would be getting to Iquitos tomorrow morning, which meant their conversations in English would have to be limited. The worst thing they could do was blow their cover now before the mission had even truly begun.

Still, it wasn't the scenarios and what-ifs Jack was considering when he finally turned in for the night. Instead, Jack fell into his hammock with only one question in his mind.

Do I trust myself?

CHAPTER 12

WYMAN

WYMAN WAS GROWING exhausted and wanted nothing more than to go home for the day. She had been at the office for 14 hours already. She had already missed dinner with her husband without so much as a text message informing him she would skip. Her daughter and granddaughter were visiting, waiting for her to arrive.

She would miss that, too.

But it didn't matter. She had one more phone call to make, this one the most important.

Kenneth Ma had left two hours ago, likely to go hang out with the other assistants and part-time staffers that populated these halls, enjoying the nightlife of the DC weekends. They would spend their time bitching about their bosses and boss' bosses, all while silently wishing their own time in the spotlight would come.

She had played those games before and won them all. It was why she was where she was now.

And yet, sometimes, *actual* work needed to be done. Stevens didn't sound like he was going to play ball, so she needed to take matters into her own hands. She hoisted the phone again and dialed the number jotted down on her notepad.

Unlike her call with Stevens, someone on the other end answered immediately. *"Stonefire Security, how may I direct your call?"*

"Give me the director."

Not another word was spoken, and she heard the silent, strained verses of over-compressed muzak flooding the earpiece. Considering who she was calling, it was ironic that they would choose light, airy music for their phone queue.

She reminded herself to get this person's private line. It had been years since anyone had put her on hold.

Normally she would have an assistant make a call like this, but this one was too important.

Too sensitive.

She needed to get this done without anyone else knowing. It was important to her that she keep this quiet.

The director came on the line a minute later. *"This is Reynolds."*

Wyman introduced herself, and they got the pleasantries out of the way. Yes, she had money. Yes, she knew what types of services Stonefire offered. She was no stranger to hiring mercenaries and paramilitary forces.

"All the rest is pretty simple, in that case," Reynolds finally said. *"I just need to know a little bit about the op. General theater, personnel requirements, that sort of thing."*

"Operating theater will be the region encompassing the North Amazon. Northwestern Peru, and southern Colombia and Venezuela, specifically."

Reynolds paused before coming back on the line. *"Okay, just making notes. And the target?"*

This time it was Wyman's turn to pause. She couldn't exactly say, 'eliminate all CIA assets.' Reynolds might make some assumptions from his end, but there was plausible deniability as long as she didn't give it away.

"I'm actually looking to protect someone, not... take someone out."

Reynolds chuckled. *"The difference doesn't matter to us. My men are the best around, all of them with prior military service experience. They know how to follow orders, and they're loyal to a fault. Still, they're not just a bunch of reckless rogue operators. They know right from wrong. As such, this conversation is confidential and will remain so. It's encrypted from my end, so rest assured that even if I have to decline the mission due to a conflict of interest, I won't be in a position to let any negative effects reach you."*

Wyman smiled again. It was a very eloquent way of saying, 'we're not here to be your average, low-cost hitman.'

"Very good," she said. "As it turns out, my interests are currently aligned with the leader of the drug cartel, *Vínculos*. Have you heard of them?"

"I have."

"Then you'll understand how delicate this situation is for me. I can easily see how this looks from an outsider's perspective. I don't care one way or another about the cartel, but I have reason to believe it's better if the cartel's leadership remains intact."

"So you want us to protect the boss?"

"Not the head honcho," she explained, "But the second-in-command. A man named Victor Elizondo. He's the key player in all of this. For better or worse, the leader of the cartel won't be around for much longer, anyway. Word is Elizondo will come to power after he's gone. But I've been dealt a hand with Victor's card in it, and I've recently had to double down on my bet."

"You stand to lose a lot if Victor doesn't actually take over the Vinculos," the director said.

"Precisely. This is something your men can handle?"

"With ease. It really all comes down to what sort of protection and for how long."

"I understand. We're looking for two days, but the window's closing fast. From what I've read, he's exploring a new route — somewhere — near Manaus, but he won't be there for two days and will be off the grid immediately afterward. This is a quick turnaround, but I'll pay for the privilege. Do you have assets near the area?"

"I can have teams in place by tomorrow morning. Four men to a fire team, and I've got three teams ready to go."

"One will be enough," Wyman said. "We're just trying to protect Victor from anything unexpected, but we don't want him to know."

"There will be a rush cost," the director began.

"I'll pay whatever the going rate is, including the rush fee. His protection can end in two-to-three days when my sources tell me the transition of power will be complete. At that point, Victor is on his own."

"Understood. In that case, it's one million per day. That covers the cost of men, operations, and incidentals. Any expenses incurred will also be billed to your account."

"Which I'm assuming we need to set up."

She could almost hear the Stonefire director smiling at the

other end of the call. Setting up an account meant repeat business. And though this was not the first time she had ordered private security; it was her first time working with this company. Stonefire had come highly recommended, and she knew they specialized in North and South America, understanding the politics and having teams that could look like locals.

"That's correct," Reynolds said. *"I will send you an email with an encrypted link."*

Wyman confirmed and hung up the phone, stood behind her desk, collected her coat, and then walked toward the door.

This part of the job was the fun part. She was under no illusions that the day-to-day life of a DC politician *actually* did any good for the world. But today, in a small way, she finally felt like she was doing some good.

Sure, she stood to benefit the most from it. But it felt good, nonetheless.

CHAPTER 13

JACK

THE NEXT MORNING, Jack and Rudy hiked near the Rio Itaya for four hours, finally reaching some semblance of civilization just before noon. They could hear the town before they could see it, the jungle still thick as it intersected with the main Amazon river to the north. Still, the noises shifted from that of jungle life and animals to the telltale signs of humanity and civilization.

Jack heard the roar of small motorcycles as two young men burned by them on a hidden dirt road tucked behind a bend in the river just up ahead. They reached the road a few minutes later and turned left, seeing signs pointing to Iquitos.

They had less than a kilometer to the city center. The narrow road was pockmarked with small ruts in differing stages of disrepair on both sides. As they neared the larger highway, Avenue de la Participacíon, Jack noticed they were nearing a slum on the outskirts of town. The downtown area was close, and they hiked up their packs and continued through the poor district. They were approached by a handful of beggars, but the vast majority of people went on about their daily lives without interrupting them.

They had plans to meet with two different people in the city, and the first unsuspecting guest was the very definition of a captive audience.

"We're looking for a penitentiary on the north part of town off of La Marina," Rudy said to Jack. "Run by the National Penitentiary Institute, so look for a sign." They reached the street that would take them north through the city — the bustling town on their left, the Rio Itaya on the right, heading to the Amazon. Life here in the city was vastly different than in the rainforest. Thought to Jack, it felt like a different kind of jungle. People laughed and joked with one another, older locals sitting on rickety porches overlooking the street while merchants darted around on their way to either buy or sell goods.

As they passed a small marina, a man ran up to Jack and Rudy, asking them to follow him toward a riverboat attraction. He shoved a brochure in Jack's head.

Jack smiled and nodded, claiming not to speak Spanish.

The man repeated his spiel in perfect English, with almost no Peruvian accent. Jack smiled again, impressed by the hustler's ability to commit to his act. There were probably dozens of tourists every day walking this very location, and this man had learned his craft well. Dozens of riverside tour operators like this one offered tourists exclusive river cruises for any price range.

They pushed past the merchant only to be met with two more, one selling some delicious-smelling dessert and another offering a trip to a canopy-level 'tree bridges' attraction nearby.

Jack and Rudy graciously declined each offer, and in this manner, they made their way north.

They finally reached a section of Iquitos where the jungle had been cut back, and the bustling day-to-day life of the city dwellers was behind them. The prison complex was nondescript — a single low, flat building, square-shaped, with a similarly shaped fence running the perimeter. A gate with a guard station sat near the road.

Jack followed Rudy up to the guard station, where they were greeted by an agent wearing slacks and a green shirt. There was a badge clipped to his belt, and Estrada began conversing with the man in Spanish.

Jack could understand Spanish fluently — it had been one of the main focus focal points of his six-month training and crash course in jungle survival. He had studied the language throughout school and college, so it had been more a refresher and practice to catch the nuance and inflection of the region than anything else.

Still, he let Estrada, a far more capable speaker, converse with the guard.

"We would like to talk with our friend," Estrada said.

The guard smirked. "You have a *friend* who stays here? I can recommend a better hotel."

"We won't be long; we just want to see how he's doing."

"I'm sorry, amigo, we do not accept visitors on the weekend."

Estrada glanced at Jack, who pulled out his wallet immediately. It was a decoy; he kept most of his cash strapped to a thin wallet wrapped to his inner thigh, but this was all part of the plan.

He pulled out two Peruvian bills and offered them to the guard.

The guard held out his hand but didn't remove it even after Jack placed the two bills on it.

Jack made a show of being annoyed but placed one more there.

"I can let you to the front door," the guard said. "But I must stay here at my station. Hopefully, you will also have good luck with the men at the door."

He winked at them, and Jack got the hint. *Hopefully, you have more money.*

The man let them through the locked gate, closing it behind them, and they walked to the front door of the prison office. They were heavy wooden doors and looked old, as if no one had paid much attention to them for the past 50 years. He supposed no one had — he doubted anyone inside would attempt escape. The penal system here in Peru, especially in this region, was like the Wild West. An escape attempt would not cause the guards to chase after the inmate — they would just shoot them from afar.

Their new friend left them in the care of two similarly dressed guards at the doors, both younger than the man at the front gate. They went through the rigmarole again, Rudy explaining the situation and Jack flashing bills.

Eight bills later and some more words exchanged, they were inside, seated at a metal table bolted to the floor of a windowless room. The entire place had been constructed from cinderblocks, painted over with thick whitewash, but the color had turned to a faded yellow over the years. It was a perfect replica of what Jack called 'government beige,' the nondescript color from the 1960s that painted almost every local municipal government building of every town in America.

Estrada and Jack waited in the uncomfortable chairs for fifteen more minutes. Finally, one of the guards appeared in the doorway, lugging a handcuffed beast of a man behind him. The man towered over the doorway and had to duck to enter. He sat across from Estrada, a stoic, blank expression on his face.

CHAPTER 14

JACK

RUDY WAITED for the guard to leave the room. Jack had not seen any cameras or listening devices here — that was way too fancy for an outpost prison like this — and listened as his partner began.

Estrada got right to the point. "Where is Victor Elizondo's new cartel route?"

The man's face didn't budge. "I have been here in prison for seven years. You think I know these things?"

Estrada leaned forward and smiled. "I think you do know these things. Because you're a *patrón*, amigo."

A *patrón* was a kingpin among drug runners — operating a mini cartel of their own. Usually, the smaller part-time runners operated from a single city or region. In contrast, the larger ones — like the man sitting in front of them now — operated over a much wider geographic area, akin to a dealer's supplier covering a larger area.

"I am no patrón," the man said.

Estrada flicked away a crumb of something eaten and left

on the table long before and looked the man in the eyes. "I can get five years off of your sentence."

The man's ears pricked up, but his face remained impassive. "I do not know you."

"But I know *you*," Estrada said. "Hector Bautista. And I've gotten into this room with you, which tells you I know other people, too. You ran the Reyes group in this region for thirteen years, building your own little network. You knew exactly who to pay off, exactly who to just off, and you remained alive throughout all of it. Much respect."

The man spat on the table. "And yet I am here, waiting in this hell."

"Again, I can get five years off your sentence."

"And who is this?" Bautista frowned at Jack.

"Compañero," Estrada said, not taking his eyes off the giant. "Five years, Patrón. How many more years do you have?"

"Just over five."

Rudy raised his eyebrows. "Interesting. And what could you be doing two, three months from now? Where could you be?"

"You think you will get in good with this new cartel, eh? With Victor? You think you can become like me, become a *traqueta*, running drugs and weapons across the continent? Look at me — even I was caught. You are just a bug, just like I was. A bug that gets too big gets noticed. And a bug that gets noticed gets squashed."

"Wise words, Patrón," Estrada said. "But I am not in the business of getting squashed."

"What business are you in?"

Estrada reached around and swung his pack onto his lap. He unzipped the top of it and pulled out a huge brick of pure cocaine, glistening in clear plastic. He slammed on the metal table, then leaned back as if daring the man to grab it.

The man's eyes almost popped out of his head. "You cannot bring that in here," he whispered. "You cannot be next to me with that. Do you know what will happen if —"

Jack leaned forward and put a finger to his lips, immediately silencing Bautista. "As we said, we are not in the business of becoming squashed bugs like you. We are in a very different business. One that requires we find Victor. You don't care one way or another about him. So tell us — where is the Vínculos' new route? When will it come through Iquitos, and who will run it?"

The man shook his head, then looked back at Estrada. "Five years."

"Five years."

"It does not come through Iquitos," the man said. "My boys tell me it's all new — but I laugh. There is nothing new under the sun. The route is as old as time. None of this shady jungle trek, getting picked off by Sendero Luminoso. Peruvian DINANDROs are in the woods now, running alongside us and waiting for us to stumble. I have lost three men, and I don't mean jail. They've gotten much more challenging lately, picking us off and shooting us in the back."

"So, where is the new route?"

"Victor is smart, going back to the old ways. He is using the route my father's father would have used."

Estrada frowned, then looked at Jack.

"What is the route?" Jack asked.

The man leaned forward, snickering. "It's the most obvious one of all. The one God ordained. That's the beauty of it — no one will suspect for how obvious it is."

"You're talking about —"

"Yes. The river itself. The route begins in Manaus, where everything converges. Victor is setting up a logistics depot there. Off the books — anyone local has already been paid off. I don't know what it looks like, or where it is, but I know it starts there. They sail east after that, toward the sea. No trouble, because no one is looking."

Jack recalled his and Estrada's briefing before the op, back in Colombia. There was only one more question he had for the man.

"Why are you telling us and not the DINANDROs? Surely they came and offered you a deal as well, for your valuable information?"

The man nodded, then looked at Jack and Estrada in turn. "I told them, amigos. But they only offered me three years."

THEY LEFT the penitentiary and headed back toward downtown Iquitos, again following the river on Avenue La Marina. Jack and Estrada had both been surprised to learn that Victor's new route was simple, but it made sense. When the drug and arms trafficking networks had grown large enough to invite the Peruvian DINANDROs — officers with Peru's National Anti-Drugs Department — into service, the trade had disappeared into the forest.

The Amazon Basin offered plenty of opportunity to hide and stay off the radar, so the cat-and-mouse game of tracking traffickers and illegal activity had encouraged Peru and neighboring nations to invest heavily in programs like DINANDRO. Like the US Drug Enforcement Agency, they operated a network of officers, agents, and informants throughout the region.

The river was considered too 'open' for the traffickers, so much of the cartel activity had drifted into the relative protection and safety of the woods. But now, hearing Victor's bold strategy was to use the river as the main traffic 'flow' was striking.

Something else the patrón had told them near the end of their meeting was something Jack couldn't shake. It wasn't getting to Manaus and inserting themselves as *traquetas* that would be the issue. That part was easy — Jack looked the part and spoke the language, and both of them were carrying real cocaine and real money, enough to pay off whoever might try to stand in their way.

No, the issue they would face, according to their asset, was the *newer* faction in the region. The SL tribe was out for blood. They weren't interested in drugs or weapons. They had methods for acquiring both. Bautista had told him they were out for another type of contraband: humans. The SL had been known to kidnap villagers for ransom as a way to pay the salary of its growing membership. Jack knew this to be true from what he had read about the *Sendero Luminoso*'s history. It sounded like they were taking another play out of the older group's playbook.

It seemed the SL would be much more of a hassle than they had originally thought.

Apparently, blowing our plane out of the sky and trying to hunt us down in the jungle isn't enough.

They walked together side-by-side, looking like Peruvian soldiers enjoying the town while off-duty, but it had been drilled into Jack from his army days that he needed to keep his guard up in hostile territory.

Every face he passed, he scanned. Were they watching him? If so, what were they interested in? Did they think he was a foreigner who might have money? Or a tourist, who would *definitely* have money? He tried to read the questions on their faces, finding most of them innocent and just curious. Even though Iquitos hosted a population of nearly 300,000, it still felt like a small town. Most people would know everyone else, and even though there was a decent transient population day in and day out, Jack didn't want to invite extra scrutiny.

They crossed through a patch of costumed street performers and a throng of casual observers. One man dressed in bright, flowing colors juggled flaming torches, and a small crowd cheered. A row of food carts sat on the edge of the street.

"Time to find your other asset," Jack muttered, his voice low enough that only Rudy could hear.

Rudy gave a quick shake of his head.

Jack glanced over. "Why? What's up?"

Rudy didn't respond; he just turned around and began walking into a small shop. The smell of coffee and pastries hit Jack's nose as he followed Rudy inside.

Estrada walked to the back of the room, and Jack followed suit, looking at each person inside. A mother and daughter were seated at one table, a man reading a newspaper looking out the front window, a barista behind the counter who waved and smiled as they walked past.

It was quite the jarring juxtaposition — a modern coffee shop in a bustling city, and yet six hours ago, Jack had awoken in the middle of the Amazon rainforest in a damp hammock, not a soul in sight.

Rudy sat down in a chair in the corner, immediately picking up another newspaper on the table. He folded it over so that it formed a small square and was easier to wield. It covered his mouth, and he spoke quietly. "Two guys, across the street. Men, my age."

Jack kept his eyes on Rudy, following the paper as Rudy

waved it around in front of his face, between Jack's spot and the front window. Estrada pointed down to something on the paper but opened it up so that Jack could easily glance from just above it and see the two men standing across the street.

Staring at him.

They were tucked into an alley, both wearing the clothes of street performers. One was dressed as a pirate, and one a parrot.

"You think they made us?" Jack asked.

Estrada shook his head. "Not made, but they're definitely keeping an eye on us. I saw them outside the penitentiary as well."

"I did, too," Jack said. "But they were real performers, right? The pirate was actually doing backflips."

Jack knew how stupid it sounded as soon as the words left his mouth. He, of all people, should know. The CIA recruited people from any number of careers — the military, of course, and other clandestine organizations. But it needed assets worldwide who they could call on to keep an eye out for the intelligence community at large. They needed to blend in, to be indistinguishable from locals. For that reason, they often employed men, women, even college-aged students — from any number of career fields.

Not every undercover contractor working for the Company was a spook, either. Sometimes informants went about their daily lives for years without getting a call but would suddenly be told to be at a certain place at a certain time to keep an eye on someone new to town.

Jack had not suspected these guys across the street were originally part of the intelligence community, and he wasn't convinced of it now. That Rudy had picked them out and that they were still conspicuously spying on them told Jack they weren't well-trained.

They were *Vínculos* or Shining Path — informants for one of the organizations. Just a couple of local boys working the same hustle they had for decades, knowing that they could make an extra buck or two by passing along information. Two newcomers, looking more like soldiers than locals, would be plenty of reason for these two guys to be suspicious.

"What's the play?" Jack asked quietly.

"Shut up and follow my lead. That's always the play."

"Should we split up?" Jack asked.

"If you want to die," Rudy said, smiling.

Jack stood up a few minutes later, once again following Estrada. The barista frowned at Jack as they left but didn't ask any questions. For all she knew, they were just a couple having a little marital spat and wanted a little privacy.

Jack saw the two performers across the street, still eyeing them as they left. Neither was on the phone, which Jack took to mean they weren't quite ready to call in anything to their bosses.

Or Rudy was wrong, Jack thought. *Maybe these guys really are just curious.*

Estrada took a hard left once again, continuing toward the downtown district.

The man did not so much as glance over his shoulder — it didn't matter. They had been spotted already, and Jack knew if the pirate and parrot were really working for a hostile group, he and Rudy needed to get out of sight — quickly.

But they also had a mission — they still needed to find Estrada's confidential informant; someone could help them get ingrained into the cartel as a *traqueta* or low-level smuggler.

They crossed the street a few blocks later, moving through an alleyway, and then left again toward a square. There were more street vendors around a central park, a government building on the opposite side. The square was structured like most of the small Spanish towns in Central and South America — a government building at the center, a Spanish mission-style church or hotel saddling the opposite side of the square.

He glanced around quickly to see if they still had a tail, and nearly missed Rudy turning to the right.

Directly toward a tourist attraction.

CHAPTER 16

JACK

RUDY HEADED TOWARD AN OLD MANSION. Though the word 'mansion' appeared on the large sign in front of the house, it hardly fit the definition. It was small by today's standards, and certainly tiny compared to some suburban homes back in the States.

Rudy Estrada aimed toward the house at the square's edge, Jack following closely behind. He saw now that it wasn't just an old house — it was a museum. The sign in front called it *Mansión de Goma*, built during the second rubber boom in the World War II era.

When Europeans discovered uses for the substance from the rubber tree in the 1800s, a period of extraction and industrialization began in 1879. Heightened production caused a second boom during WWII when wealthy rubber barons built mansions like this.

A group of tourists was already preparing to enter the museum, but Estrada casually sidestepped them and walked through the wide-open doors into a well-appointed foyer. Jack followed, ignoring a question from the museum guide who had gathered the people outside.

It was as good a place to hide as any, Jack figured. He wasn't sure if the two street performers would pass on information that they had seen outsiders and identified them as persons of interest, needing to be watched, or if the men would try something themselves and follow them inside.

Estrada walked straight toward the stairs at the back of the mansion, a new coat of paint sparkling on all the walls. It seemed the place had been freshly renovated and likely had been kept up well over the many decades since it had been built. Jack heard voices from another tour group somewhere deeper into the main level, perhaps from an out-of-sight kitchen or parlor.

But he didn't want to waste time looking around. He walked straight up the stairs and found Estrada about to enter a room to the right of the landing.

Once inside, Estrada shut the door. Jack saw they were in an old hexagonal-shaped office, the decorations all late 30s and 40s. It looked like the office of a British Navy captain, as if they had walked onto the captain's quarters of a naval ship.

Dark wood wainscoting stretched halfway up the walls, met with nautical-themed wallpaper that ran the rest of the way to the ceiling. The wainscoting sat behind matching wood bookcases on four of the walls.

"You've been here before?" Jack asked.

Estrada shook his head. "No, but this will tell us what those guys are doing. If they're trying to follow us and keep an eye out, they'll park it outside. And if they're just going to pass on the information to someone else in whatever group they're with, we'll be able to see them walk away."

Estrada walked over to a window behind the old oak desk on the far wall and peered out.

"They're not outside anymore," Estrada said.

Jack started toward the window himself but stopped when he noticed another window directly to his right. It didn't look outside but back into the mansion and down the stairs. Curtains hung over the small square porthole-style window, but he saw that its position would allow him to keep an eye on the stairs and part of the foyer down below.

He pulled one of the curtains back an inch, peering out.

Within seconds, he saw the two ridiculously costumed men entering the museum. The pirate began jogging up the stairs, and Jack saw a glinting flash of metal in his right hand.

A knife.

"That's because they're here," Jack said. "I guess their orders *weren't* to just keep an eye on us."

"Guess not," Estrada said.

Jack stayed where he was but allowed the curtain to close once more. He pulled off his pack and set it on the floor next to him. Situated next to the door, the men outside would have to open it inward toward him, which would conceal his position for a moment.

Estrada ran across the room and joined Jack against the wall on the opposite side of the doorway.

Opposite each other on either side of the closed office door, they waited. He heard the footsteps, the creaking of the old house as the men stomped around, looking in every room for the two of them. They were clearly not professionals — one of them should have stayed at the top of the stairs to prevent Jack and Estrada from simply sneaking back down and out.

But Jack and Rudy weren't going to be sneaking anywhere.

Jack remembered Estrada's actions back in the jungle, as well as his words later. These people — whoever they were, whether cartel or SL — had identified Jack and Estrada as outsiders, foreigners. They were making assumptions about who they were, but it was clear what their intentions were.

Jack was committed now. They weren't going to run away. Sure, they would leave a wake of bodies behind them, but Jack was not about to let these guys get back to their boss and tell them exactly what the two CIA officers looked like.

He and Estrada did not need to discuss terms of engagement, nor did they need to discuss a plan. Guns would be too loud, and there was no time to retrieve combat knives from their packs. This would need to be as quiet a meeting as possible unless they wanted to attract local police to the mansion.

It didn't matter. Jack was ready. He and Rudy had practiced together, trained together in hand-to-hand combat, as well as how to fight with knives, guns, and anything else at hand. Estrada, obviously, was far better at these things than Jack, but Jack was in better shape, younger, and could hold his own. He lacked field experience, but he made up for that with a proper mindset and physical fitness.

Barely 42 years old, Jack was not worried about fighting one of these guys.

But he *was* worried about that knife. Knives were clumsy, unpredictable. Their wounds may not kill immediately, but they caused a lot of damage. A stab wound would absolutely slow them down.

Plus, his leg was still a bit tender. Moving helped, but the longer Jack stood still, the more it was going to tense up.

The door burst open suddenly, and both men rushed in at

once. They had apparently decided that the only place left for the two foreigners to hide was the only room they hadn't yet checked.

Estrada began his attack on the first man — the pirate — in an instant, swinging his heavy pack around and clotheslining him with it.

Estrada brought the man down to the ground by executing a simple jujitsu takedown move, his favorite style of hand-to-hand combat and one he had practiced extensively. But Jack saw Estrada's back now, clearly exposed.

The second man, the parrot, also noticed. He was also wielding a knife, a thin switchblade. He rushed toward Rudy.

Jack swung his foot around and kicked the man's shins with the top of his feet, sending him flying *over* Estrada and his partner, landing headfirst in front of the old desk.

While Estrada grappled with his pirate, Jack ran around him and kicked the parrot in the side once more. He then dropped an elbow, aiming for the man's throat, but the man squirmed to the side and brought his switchblade around in an awkward backhand maneuver.

The knife sailed inches away from Jack's cheek as he recovered. The attacker got to his feet, flicking the knife from one hand to the other in a perfectly amateurish motion that told Jack he had seen some action movies but had never seen *real* action.

Nevertheless, the knife was a huge threat. It was light enough and sharp enough to be dangerous in any number of ways — the man could throw it at him, could twist around and stab him to parry Jack's attack, or he could simply get lucky and stick it into something Jack would rather keep *un*stuck.

Jack lunged forward, waiting for the man to strike in response.

Predictably, he did. The man's knife hand came down, but Jack pulled his arm back just in time. He used his left hand to chop the man's wrist, hoping to dislodge the knife and send it clattering to the floor. Instead, the man held on tightly, ducking his feathered costumed head and spinning around, showing Jack his back for a moment as he created more space.

Jack followed along, knowing the man was baiting him. He was planning to turn around and surprise Jack. He guessed the man would twirl around to his right, as that direction was *against* the movement he was still completing.

He was right. The man had been hoping to take Jack by surprise, expecting Jack to attack his *left* side. Instead, the parrot-man came around with his knife held in a closed grip.

Jack was ready. He caught the knife between his hands and squeezed, digging his fingers into the man's flexor tendons on his wrist.

The man snarled and let out a cry of pain but still did not let go of the knife. Jack kneed him in the groin, sending him backward toward the bookcases. He smacked against one, hitting it hard and dislodging a few books.

And still, he held the knife.

Jack was now standing next to the desk near where Estrada had been looking out the window. Jack looked over and saw something hanging from a mount near the window, something he had missed before. It was a prized historic item, something not meant for action any longer, but he didn't care.

Desperate times.

He grabbed the sheath at its middle and yanked the entire display off the wall.

CHAPTER 17

JACK

THE BACKING PLATE fell from the mount and clattered to the floor loudly, and Jack pulled the blade from the sheath.

He could hear his attacker rushing him while his back was turned. For that reason, Jack concealed his movements as much as possible, waiting until the footfalls were only a few steps away. He knew the man's reach would make it close, but to compensate, he ducked backward and fell to a crouching position.

He pulled the sword out of its sheath and held the saber pointed upward.

The man simply ran through it.

Jack held the blade steady, letting it stab completely through the parrot costume and the body inside. The man's momentum carried him all the way to the hilt. Jack held steady, feeling the sickening squelch as the razor-sharp blade pierced flesh and bone. Blood immediately poured over the hilt and onto his hands and wrists.

The knife finally fell to the floor. The man blinked a few times in shock, let out a guttural sound, then fell to the side.

Jack let go of the blade as both man and steel fell to the wooden floor.

He had just killed a life-sized parrot next to a man dressed as a pirate, inside what felt like a naval warship.

This day really is getting weird.

There was no humor in the sentiment, however. These two men had been trying to kill or incapacitate Jack and Estrada, likely having no idea that the two men were operatives but wanting to protect their cause anyway.

Based on their intel, men like this were everywhere around Iquitos. It was the largest city in the region, now controlled by SL and the Vínculos cartel, and each was vying for power and dominance. Neither took kindly to strangers, especially strangers trying to peel back the layers of power that existed here.

It was a shame these two men had to die for a cause they believed in, but Jack would not lose any sleep over it. Their cause was something Jack wanted to wipe from the face of the earth.

Estrada, having successfully incapacitated his own pirate-costumed man, stood and brushed his hands off on his pants.

"And here I thought you were a pacifist," Estrada mumbled.

"Should we clean this up?" Jack asked.

"And where should we put them? There is no time."

Jack couldn't argue with his assessment, so they left the room full of blood and torn costumes just as a woman with frazzled hair met them outside the doorway.

She was short, wearing a shirt with the rubber mansion's name on the pocket, and Jack recognized her as the curator who had yelled at them outside.

And she looked extremely angry.

She leaned over, trying to see inside the office, but Estrada pulled the door closed after Jack exited.

She spat off a string of sentences in Spanish, faster than Jack could understand.

Estrada smiled nonchalantly. "We had a disagreement. But it is resolved now."

She raised her voice but slowed her words enough so that Jack could understand. "You did not pay! This is a *museum*! A historic monument!"

The tour group was now making their way up the stairs, but they had slowed to watch the altercation.

Estrada pulled out his own wallet and peeled off a few banknotes. He handed them over to the woman, whose mouth dropped. Apparently, this was far more than the entrance fee to the museum.

Estrada did not mention that it would also need to help cover the cleanup she would find inside.

He turned to Jack and nodded.

Time to go.

CHAPTER 18

JACK

A MINUTE LATER, they were back outside. Jack made a snap decision to wave down one of the taxis he had seen rumbling through the streets. A young driver smiled and waved through the open passenger window as he pulled up alongside Jack and Estrada.

Jack heard a scream from inside the museum and winced. He leaned down and shoved a wad of cash in front of the man's face. "Can we borrow your car?" he asked in Spanish.

The man's eyes widened as he saw the amount of money being offered but stammered a response. "I — I drive you wherever you need to go."

"Not good enough, amigo. Look, I'm not trying to steal it. We just need to borrow it. I'll take it around the block a few times, then bring it back by the end of the day. I'll park it right here. You have my word."

The young man was about to argue again when Estrada pulled open the door the driver-side door. Jack hadn't even seen him move around the vehicle, and the young man looked shocked as well. He wasn't wearing a seatbelt, and Estrada yanked him from the car.

"Hey!" The taxi driver shouted an obscenity in Spanish.

"My friend asked nicely," Estrada said. He eyed the young man. Even from the other side of the vehicle, Jack felt the intensity.

The kid stammered a bit more but then nodded. Estrada was in the driver's seat before Jack had even realized what had happened. Jack made a face as if to say sorry to the young man. He walked near Jack, and Jack slid the wad of cash into his hand. He got in the passenger seat, and Estrada was pulling away from the curb even before he had closed the door.

"So, you got us a car," Estrada said matter-of-factly.

"Actually, *you* got us a car," Jack answered. "And you could have saved me a bunch of money if you would have just done that in the first place."

Estrada shrugged. "If you would have told me you wanted a car, I would have."

"I just think it's easier to stay out of sight in a car. Plus, we can talk."

Estrada scoffed, pulling his sunglasses up from the clasp on his shirt and putting them on. "You want to talk?"

Jack smirked. "I mean, I just sensed that you might be feeling a bit emotionally isolated," he said. "I know you love to talk."

Rudy snorted in laughter.

"Anyway," Jack continued. "Those guys back there — they weren't the first men we've killed today. We're starting to stack up quite the body count, Estrada."

Estrada didn't say anything, chewing on his cheek as he drove the car slowly around the square.

"The mission isn't to single-handedly take out all of the bad guys we find down here," Jack said. "We're just making ourselves bigger targets each time. We're going to get ourselves killed."

Estrada finally turned away from the square and eyed Jack from behind his sunglasses. "Tell me, Jack, what would have happened if we didn't fight them in that room up there?"

Jack didn't answer.

"Exactly. *They* would have killed *us*. Without a doubt, no questions asked. This isn't America, where these men are worried about repercussions from the police or the government. We are in their world, and even though we look like we fit in with the general population, we don't. And they know it. They may not know who we are or what we're up to, but they'll kill us just because we don't belong. Because we're not from here."

"You *are* from here," Jack said.

"According to my *legend*, sure," Estrada said.

Jack frowned. Surely the company wouldn't withhold information like this from its own operative? Surely the story he had read about Estrada's past — what IC personnel called their 'legend' — wasn't *entirely* fabricated? Jack thought Rudy had grown up in Peru, moving eventually to Colombia and then the United States for college.

It didn't matter, really. It was just a reminder to Jack that he couldn't take any information at face value. Even from his partner.

"What did they tell you about me?" Jack asked. "You know my legend?"

Estrada shrugged again. "Who cares? They told me you were capable. From what I saw up there, I'm starting to believe it. You have to trust yourself, though, remember. Don't trust me; don't trust what you've been told by the CIA. Trust *yourself*."

Jack grabbed the handhold above the window and looked out. The road off the square they were on now was abuzz with life, and he could see the old rubber mansion museum in the mirror. There was a small crowd gathering outside. Some he recognized as the tourists who had been on the curated guide through the house, and they were once again gathered outside on the front steps.

It would only be a matter of time before the police arrived, and perhaps even more members of the SL or cartel, trying to figure out which of them had knocked off the other. They would assume it was a turf battle between the two hostile groups, which helped Jack and Rudy's cause.

But they couldn't afford to continue attracting attention.

"If we can't trust each other, we can't complete the mission," Jack said under his breath.

Jack felt frustrated, but he couldn't exactly pinpoint why. Estrada seemed flippant, as if he didn't really want to be here. Jack couldn't blame him for that — it wasn't like they were on vacation, traipsing around Peru to see the sights. They were working, and this work was hard.

But he had not sensed any of this in Estrada while they had trained together. He had not guessed that Estrada's attitude would be so nonchalant, so laissez-faire regarding the pile of bodies they were leaving behind.

"Are you worried that causing this much attention going is to make us?"

"Both sides will think we are against them," Estrada said. "SL suspects cartel work. Cartel thinks SL is getting antsy.

Neither of them has any idea that the CIA has operatives in Peru, and certainly not actively tracking them down."

"Victor knows —"

"Victor is a cartel boss. He knows almost everything we know, because his job is to assume the worst and plan for it. But he's not going to tell his new recruits, his low-level grunts, that there are intelligence assets watching their every move, will he? He would have to be stupid, trying to cause unrest in his own men."

Jack nodded. "Yeah, that tracks. Still, I feel like this whole thing is very precarious. Like —"

Estrada cut him off. "Like our intel was no good? Like the CIA just sent us down here on some half-assed mission to figure shit out on our own? Look, Jack, you've been around the Company since your mid-20s. You understand how it works from the intel side. You know half of the intelligence is shit, and the other half just smells like it. You guys back in Langley might as well throw spaghetti at the wall and see what sticks, then hand out assignments based on that. Or use the horoscope to decide where in the world to send assets."

"It's not that bad," Jack said. "I mean, we really try to make things as accurate and useful as possible."

"I understand that, and I believe that. But the *reality* is never simple. The intel we get — as you now know — is too basic to be of any help in the field. 'Track Victor and find his new route?' Great, we know what it is. It's the Amazon itself."

"We can't just go back to Langley with that."

Estrada laughed, smacking his palm against the steering will as he drove. "Of *course* we can't go back with that, Jack. *That's* why we leave a few bodies around, sprinkle some guns or whatever else it is that's going to tell the DI stooges what's what, and they'll write it up as some fancy operation they can then send up the chain to Congress. They'll rubber-stamp everything, do the handwaving and song and dance, and our little line in the budget will grow just a little bit."

"It's not about the mission, is it?" Jack asked.

Estrada shook his head. "It's *never* about the mission, Jack. 'The Company' is called the Company for a reason. It's a business. And business is booming. No one will ever talk about it openly, but that's why we exist. Every bad guy we kill means one less bad guy available to terrorize our home country. And when every country in the world seems to secretly hate yours, it makes things a little more complicated."

Jack smiled. "But when we're in Peru and guys are rushing us and pulling knives behind our backs…"

"It makes it easier to know who the bad guys are."

Jack sat with this as Estrada drove through the less busy streets farther away from downtown Iquitos. They met up with the river once more, driving north.

"Trust yourself, Jack," Estrada said once more. "You don't need the Company to tell you who the bad guys are."

CHAPTER 19

JACK

"SO, who is this asset we're supposed to find?" Jack asked.

Estrada smirked at Jack. "An asset."

"Thanks."

Estrada laughed. "Someone I used to know a long time ago. They came back into my life a few years ago, and I have been working them a bit, plying them for information. The Company doesn't even know the details; they just know I've got an asset in place."

"Who's the asset, Rudy?"

Rudy smiled. "Quite the spook detective, aren't you? I'm not withholding information from you because of trust issues, contrary to what you may think. It's because of habit. I don't usually work with anyone else in the field, and the few times that I did..."

Jack sensed the man was growing nostalgic, thinking about some situation years ago. He had been told that Estrada had a partner once long ago, but that it had ended only a year later. He was not given the details as to what had happened nor where in the world it had gone down.

He wasn't technically Rudy's 'partner,' either — at least not officially. Rudy's handler had instructed him to show Jack the ropes. Rudy knew the region; Jack knew the target. It was a good match to get Jack up to speed without anyone expecting a long-term partnership.

CIA operatives were not like cops — they didn't drive around in cruisers looking for trouble, a partner and dispatch to rely on if things got hairy. Most of their time in the field was spent in isolation, of acting and living and being completely alone, all the time. In rare situations like this, where a senior operator was asked to train a newer, younger one, it wasn't seen as a partnership — it was just training. Sure, the mission was real, the stakes were high, and everyone wanted to come home alive. But Jack did not expect to maintain much contact with Estrada down the road, after returning home in a few days.

In fact, because of the nature of the undercover operation, even their extraction points would be different. Estrada would remain in-country for another week, blending in with the locals and making his way toward Cuzco. Jack would leave from another airstrip deeper in the rainforest, posing as a riverboat operator flying home to Lima to see his family. From there, he would board a commercial flight and be on his way back home to his wife and kids, bouncing through four different airports along the way.

All of this was stored only in Jack's head — the particulars of the mission were not written down anywhere, and he had memorized them shortly after hearing them from his boss, Rudy's handler.

As Jack was still very much in the training phase of becoming a field operator, he was a case officer in title alone. He had not been assigned his own handler yet, working instead under Estrada's for this mission. If successful, he would be shuffled around the Company and given a handler who worked with his personality profile well.

They bounced over a few potholes in the road and Estrada suddenly opened up, talking more about himself than Jack had ever heard. "Most of my legend is true," he said. "Not my name, of course. But that's pretty much because I started out doing deep-cover assignments in Syria and Kosovo, and I was interacting a lot with the locals and US forces on the ground. I had to have a name, so I picked Rudy." He shrugged. "It was my grandfather's."

Jack listened intently.

"My mom really was from here — I grew up not in Iquitos, but close enough. The *Shining Path* was a real problem back then, even though they operated farther north. I thought it was weird that they came back — they don't seem to have a leader who's interested in making a name for themselves this time. The first iteration of the group was a Maoist regime, with Guzmán at the helm. Now... no one. Seems odd."

Jack listened, watching the roads as they drove through Iquitos. "I couldn't believe they actually came back into power, at least some similar version of it. But whatever. I was tapped to work for the Company after college. I never thought I would end up a spook. I assumed they were all just spies, backstabbers. Double agents and all that James Bond shit. I didn't know what it was really like, what I could really do."

"Military?"

Estrada nodded. "Army. Wanted to go to Ranger School, but they called me up to the Farm before that."

Jack listened on, captivated by the man's past and willingness to share openly. Or at least captivated by the man's acting skills. He still could not be sure Rudy Estrada *was* Rudy Estrada — he already knew Rudy was not his real first name. The man was an enigma, but Jack should not have been surprised about that. For 20 years, he had dealt with operatives from afar. He knew their stories, at least on paper, their legends. He had even interacted with the handlers who helped create them. The men and women that made up the paramilitary force of the CIA were the ones who did the real work and got none of the glory.

Men like Estrada, who had been operating undercover in hostile territory for almost four decades.

If he had chosen the life of a professional mercenary, the man driving them around might actually *be* a legend. Since he had chosen the Company — or it had chosen him — any and all of his accomplishments would be forever hidden from the world. No matter what goals and desires an operator had, Jack knew one thing was certain: none of them did it for the attention and honor. None of them would be more than a star on the wall at HQ when they passed away.

And while it seemed as though the world didn't care about these forgotten souls, men like Jack cared.

With any luck, Jack might one day be able to fill the shoes of someone like Estrada.

"Where do we find this asset of yours?" Jack asked. He knew the plan had been to get to Estrada's asset immediately after leaving the prison, but he also knew — and Estrada had just verified — that operational plans and mission parameters were just a list of bullet points. Real dates and times like extractions and insertions were the important bits, as well as the larger goals and deliverables of the mission.

It didn't matter exactly when they met up with Estrada's

asset, only that they did. They had the packages — the drugs and enough cash to prove they were runners, but they were missing one crucial piece of the equation: somebody on the inside willing to vouch for them.

Their asset would help with that, getting Jack and Estrada inserted into the Vínculos drug and arms flow.

"Owns a liquor store on the other side of town," Estrada said. "Pretty much the only one around."

Jack looked to his left and right, as they passed through a narrow avenue, two-story buildings on both sides with balconies hanging over their heads. A general store they passed displayed dozens of signs advertising different types of local beer and malt liquor. "Only one around?"

Estrada smiled. "Well, the only one quite like it on that side of town. You don't just come in for liquor when you're looking for what they're selling."

"Drugs? Guns?"

Rudy nodded. "We'll ask for 'help finding something we lost three days ago.' That's the code. But pretty much anything you might want. Stuff that isn't always illegal, but also not something you want people squawking about. Small town like this, especially where it is, you get lots of ears and eyeballs bent toward you when you go looking for AK-47s."

"So it's either talk to your asset or talk to the cartel," Jack said.

"Exactly. Some people just want to go hunt with a cool gun. Shouldn't be anything wrong with that."

Jack filed this information away. He knew Rudy would be able to drive him right to the guy's doorstep when he finally felt comfortable, but Jack liked knowing the plan. He understood the reasoning, but he hated being kept in the dark as to the specifics. "Are we just trying to get some distance between us and what happened back at the museum?" he asked.

Estrada had taken an offramp that wound back down toward the Amazon and bent around to follow it, and Jack recognized the name of a street they passed as one about three kilometers north of Iquitos. It didn't seem like Estrada had any plans of stopping anytime soon.

"That and making sure we didn't somehow pick up another tail," Estrada said.

"Not by the looks of it," Jack answered, looking in both mirrors.

"Not by the looks of it. But I've looked in the wrong places before."

CHAPTER 20

JACK

AS RUDY DROVE toward the Amazon and its surrounding forest, heading north of town, Jack thought about the two costumed watchers they had killed. Were they Victor's men? Part of the Vínculos cartel? Or were they Shining Path? Jack had been briefed extensively on the Shining Path group and their cult-like influence that had suddenly sprung up in the region. The nuisance was more than just a thorn in their side. The Shining Path was in their way. They reportedly had a stronghold over parts of Peru, and as they had four decades ago, they had taken over entire villages and forced locals and native populations to swear fealty to them.

Jack felt confident the two men they had eliminated belonged to Shining Path and not the cartel. The cartel's interest would be in making sure no one interrupted their trade, and Jack and Rudy had done no such thing — yet. Sendero Luminoso, on the other hand, would be interested in just making sure no one encroached on their territory.

He knew SL was weary of outsiders — it went against their very reason for existence — and they would be even more nervous about the growing presence of cartel in the region. He had heard reports of small skirmishes between SL and Peruvian law enforcement, but the intel wasn't verified. So far, the SL's presence in the region had been a surprise to everyone back home.

He wondered if Shining Path would continue to give them even more trouble as they moved through the region. They would have to be on the lookout now, but they had dispatched the two men before they could get the word out to their superiors.

Hopefully.

They had not found any sort of communication device on either man. It could be that the men had called it in while back at the coffee shop when they had seen them across the street, but doubted these men were well-trained, and the lack of a cellphone on their person spoke volumes. They had fought well, almost getting the jump on Jack, but these clearly weren't operatives or agents from a Peruvian special forces or counterintelligence team.

They had to be low-level grunts; cult followers only interested in making sure their land was protected.

Whoever they were, the pair would not be giving them any more trouble.

But Jack was still worried. The body count was continuing to rise. The bodies they'd left in the jungle likely would never be found, but it didn't matter — the soldiers would not be reporting back to their command, and eventually someone would grow suspicious. Their plane had also been brought down directly over Shining Path territory, a very obvious and visible infiltration. There would be a search out for whoever was in the plane, and the fact that two of the Shining Path warriors did not make it back to camp that same night, coupled with the two dead bodies that would cause a fuss in Iquitos, likely meant the hunt was on.

The noose had been tightened, and Jack felt anxiety building. He began to feel impossibly outnumbered and outgunned. Sure, he and Rudy might be better trained, but there were only two of them.

And though they had researched, read, and been briefed on both factions, why the Shining Path had reappeared *now* of all times was anyone's guess. And besides that fact, there were still two different factions here. Two different armies vying for control, for power.

Neither group would be pleased to find out that Jack and Rudy were here, working against their interests. They were outsiders, and eventually, if cornered, both groups would be able to figure out they were Americans, working and operating undercover.

It wasn't a dire situation yet, but it had certainly grown more tense. Jack gripped the handle above his head in the taxi again as Rudy bounced over a few potholes on a dirt road leading out of Iquitos. He wanted to talk through it, wanted to get answers.

He also wanted to get a reading on how Rudy was feeling. The older man was far more experienced, had been in the field for years, and had worked countless ops like this one. He had not hesitated to leave the bodies in the jungle and the mansion, but Jack wondered if that was a façade.

Murder affected people. It had been part of his training, not from the past six months but from the past 20 years — the CIA was an intelligence organization. *Tertia Optio,* or the fabled 'Third Option' for the President of the United States.

Their entire world was espionage, intelligence and counterintelligence.

Their ultimate objective was *direct action:* removing specific players from the playing field.

It was dirty work. Wet work. Assassination was no easy matter, even on paper. The entire existence of the CIA was to allow the government and military plausible deniability in case things went south.

While this operation was not intended to be 'direct action' against Victor and his Vínculos, it was always an option. Always a possible component of the mission.

Jack had told everyone — including himself — that he was ready for such a job. That he was capable of wet work, to take matters into his own hands, that he could do the job necessary.

Now, he had done that job — directly and indirectly, and the results of that were lying dead on the floor in the mansion and in the forest.

This game was not for the faint of heart, but it was just that — a game. A game played by kings and dictators, played by powerful men and women that far outranked him and always would. They fought with words and money, but when the dust settled, Jack and Rudy were the people that had to carry out their orders.

Jack thought he had steeled himself enough before they had left Colombia, but since they had flown into this region — since the plane had been shot out of the sky — he was feeling less and less prepared.

He needed to trust his own instincts, just as Rudy had said.

He needed to trust himself.

JACK

"GOOD IDEA GRABBING A CAR," Rudy said suddenly. "Much easier to move without being tailed if we can go faster than whoever's tailing us."

They passed a small truck going in the opposite direction, but Jack hadn't seen any other cars following behind them since they left town. He took it as a good omen.

Rudy continued. "I'm thinking we get out away from town a bit, camp in the jungle again tonight, keep our ear to the ground. We were seen back in town, so the best place for us to be for the next half-day or so is in the middle of nowhere."

Jack didn't disagree, but he wondered about their time-frame. "What about getting to Victor in time? Finding your asset so we can get into the flow as *traquetas*?"

Estrada shook his head. "We were just handed the best luck we're going to get all weekend," Estrada said. "Our buddy back at the penitentiary said the route is the river itself, which is always the fastest way to get around. Certainly the fastest way to the Atlantic."

"Certainly the fastest if you're trying to smuggle drugs or guns," Jack quipped.

Rudy nodded. "We've got more time than I initially thought. We shouldn't squander it, but it's more important we don't let anyone else track us down. We need to stay out of sight so we can get back into town tomorrow morning. We'll meet up with my asset and figure out how to get us into the flow."

Jack nodded silently as he looked out the window. The road was dirt, cut into the jungle itself, and the rainforest had already begun reclaiming its territory. Luscious vines and trees hung out over the sides of the road, the brown strip disappearing forty yards in the distance as the small hills and valleys of the relatively flat forest floor converged and created the horizon. They drove like this for another fifteen minutes, then Estrada pulled the taxi to the side of the road. "Let's hike back toward town a bit; then, we can cut back into the woods."

It was a good call. By backtracking another fifteen minutes or so on foot, anyone coming from the city trying to find them would see the taxi and assume that's where the men had entered the woods to camp. But it also meant Jack and Estrada would hear their vehicle long before they turned back in this direction.

They hefted their packs from the backseat and threw them over their shoulders. They began walking over the same small hills they had just traversed, this time on foot. Jack's leg stung a bit, but if there was a tear in the meniscus, it was small enough not to be a burden. He had exerted himself plenty back at the mansion, and his leg had held up so far.

Jack felt bad for the young man they had stolen the taxi from, but he had paid him more than a month's salary. Hopefully, the car would show up missing and eventually be found outside the city.

They turned southeast, then headed through the narrow strip of the jungle toward the river.

There they waited an hour, quietly taking in the jungle sounds. Both men were left to their own thoughts, Jack's mind wandering back to his family. He didn't know if this would be a sustainable enterprise for a family man. His two daughters were getting older, now eleven and eight, and being in the field even for a single weekend felt like years. While they were rare, there were ops that could last months.

These missions came with a heavy cost — he had a lot to think about.

Almost exactly an hour after arriving at the spot on the river, they saw a riverboat passing by, a single fisherman piloting it.

It was long and low to the water, basically a canoe with a small outboard motor.

Rudy waved the man over with a wad of bills in his hand, and Jack saw the man's eyes widen at the prospect of making some easy money.

Rudy haggled with the fisherman for a few minutes, and then they shook hands. Jack was impressed by the price Rudy had offered. The fisherman seemed even more impressed.

He offered them his premium seats — two horizontal slats near the front of the boat, even sliding the dripping-wet net off the second slab and onto the floor of the boat. The man asked if they spoke English, and Jack and Rudy shook their heads.

When they had first begun building the story of why each of them was here, they had been instructed to fabricate more than one. Talking to a suspected cartel member or leader would require them to act like they, too, were cartel members. Small-time runners working their way up in the organization, trying to impress the higher-ranking cartel leaders.

But they needed other covers as well, ones that would fit neatly into the story of their cartel existence but neither confirming nor denying it. It was the story they both immediately leaned into when the fishermen asked if they spoke English.

No, of course they didn't, they told him. They were Peruvian locals who had grown up on the river, fishing it and working. They were just passing through this particular area to get downriver.

The fisherman didn't ask any follow-up questions. Apparently, the money said enough to get them downriver without questions.

Rudy sat in the seat in front of Jack, facing him, not bothering to watch the river up ahead. Unsurprisingly, he wanted to watch what would be the closest threat to them — the riverboat operator himself.

Jack took up the mantle of paying attention to the river and waterway as they moved, but there were no other lifeforms even visible from here. The jungle flora danced around as they moved, but any creatures gave them a wide berth as they sailed downstream.

For a moment, the trip was peaceful. Jack wished this were nothing more than an idle day trip down the Amazon and not a dangerous jaunt into the heart of enemy territory.

CHAPTER 22

JACK

THEY LEFT the boat fifteen minutes later and hiked east, keeping track of their coordinates with a compass and paper map. Getting lost in the jungle was a death sentence, no matter how prepared one was. Eventually, gear would break, food would run dry, and catching and trapping animals would be the only way to stay alive.

And the jungle would fight back. Something poisonous, something predatory, something microscopic even. All of it could kill them if they weren't careful.

They made camp, and Rudy made another small fire, this one half the size of the one before. While they could have made a raging bonfire on the forest floor and the dense jungle would have hidden it from anyone more than ten feet away, it was wise to keep smoke to a minimum. The best way to signal their location out here was straight up — exactly where the smoke would go.

Once again, Jack hung his hammock between two decent-sized trees and came back to find Estrada chowing down on another MRE, this one taken from Jack's pack.

It wasn't a personal slight — both packs were largely the same, interchangeable in almost every way.

"I saw the picture," Estrada said.

Interchangeable except for that.

Taped to the inside of Jack's pack, facing inward so it would not be easily seen, was a picture of Jack's wife and kids.

"Stupid move," Estrada said.

"Why?" Jack asked. "I wasn't planning on leaving my pack anywhere. And besides, no one knows who they —"

"We're on the cusp of having facial recognition technology that can identify a person from a satellite image."

"Okay, point taken," Jack said. He leaned forward and ripped the photograph out from the inside of his pack.

"Now what are you going to do with it?" Estrada asked, smirking. Jack could tell the man was enjoying this. No one had told him *not* to hide the picture inside a pack he was basically wearing all day. He knew better than to stuff it in his wallet or tuck it under the brim of his, but he figured a thumbnail-sized photograph hidden away inside his bag wouldn't have negative repercussions.

"You can't put it on your person," Estrada said. "If you get killed, they're going to strip you. They'll want to know what secrets you are hiding."

Jack shrugged. "What should I do with it, then?"

Estrada poked the fire with a stick, not answering. Suddenly Jack realized what he was implying.

"I can't, I..."

"Jack, do you want this? Or do you want *this*?" He took the flaming stick out and stuffed the tip of it near the photograph in Jack's hand.

"It's my family, I —"

"And you still *have* a family. If you're careful and don't do stupid things like this, you always will. I'm not asking if you want to keep your *family*, Jack. I'm asking if you want to keep a stupid piece of *paper*."

Jack crumpled the photograph in his right hand, squeezed it, then released it over the fire. It immediately began to melt, the chemicals turning the flames green and blue for a moment before the carbonized remains became ashes.

"Sorry," Jack said. "It's just... it was something I saw someone do in the Army. We always had our rucksacks with us, and we would get everyone in trouble if we left them somewhere. I figured I'd have it with me..."

Estrada nodded knowingly. "This ain't the Army, Barr. You're not going to have to run laps or do extra push-ups if you get caught out here. Out here, you die. You make a mistake, you die."

By now, Estrada had hammered the point home a thousand different ways, and Jack was starting to feel annoyed by the whole thing.

But Rudy had one more piece of advice for him: "Jack, this is information you *will* need. Got it?"

Jack frowned but nodded. He accepted the rest of the pack of MREs, spooning out the rice with the same dirty spoon he had eaten from the night before. He had lied to himself about this operation — he had told himself it was going to be relatively easy — just camping in the rainforest with a senior operative, learning the ways of the CIA like he was Luke Skywalker with his own personal Yoda.

But reality was far different. *Everything* out here was trying to kill him, including, it seemed, himself.

He wasn't even sure if he wanted this lifestyle in the long

run, but how could he ever find out, if he couldn't even get out of his own way?

He noticed Rudy eyeing him suspiciously as he drained the bag of Spanish rice into his mouth. He crumpled the package, knowing immediately what Rudy was thinking.

Trust yourself, Jack. Trust no one else.

CHAPTER 23

JACK

SLEEP WAS hard to come by. Whether it was the killings, the narrow escape from death itself, or the brightness of the moonlight that managed to find its way through the trees and thick canopy of the forest itself, Jack didn't know.

Jack lay in his hammock, hands behind his head, staring upward at the jagged lines of the bug screen and net above his head. He practiced a solo debrief, a method of running through the day's events as if he were speaking with a handler or commanding officer. What could he have done differently that would have netted a better result? There had been failures today — any operative needing to resort to hand-to-hand combat or close-quarters fighting had failed some aspect of the mission. They were down here for reconnaissance, to watch Victor and keep an ear to the ground. They were supposed to stay undercover, supposed to move quietly, without bringing much attention to themselves. By working together, Rudy and Jack could actually be less visible than a single man traveling around Iquitos and the surrounding region alone.

Or so he had thought. The two costumed attackers seemed

to have known their exact position, seemed to have been waiting for them. How had they known where to look? Why had their plane been shot out of the sky by SL forces? Were they just curious, or did they know the pilot was ferrying two CIA operatives?

In places like this, the walls had ears. Every building in Iquitos was listening, taking notes.

Even the jungle had ears. Jack shuddered as a cool breeze found its way through the clearing and chilled the humidity's stickiness on his body. He rolled to the side, hoping to catch at least a few hours of sleep. He had to pee but felt it could wait until morning. He wanted to try to take advantage of the relative quiet of this portion of jungle.

Tomorrow, they would head back into Iquitos, working carefully to stay in the shadows, moving toward Rudy's asset. It would be their last shot at getting in touch with someone who could help them traverse the country as sanctioned cartel associates. Jack did not know the details, but Rudy thought they would have a good chance at getting in tight with a small group of *traquetas* on the way to Manaus, and that his asset would set it up.

Without the asset's help, they were as good as dead. They might be able to try to hitch a ride on a fishing boat, lay low until they reached Manaus, but what then? They were carrying Vínculos drugs in their packs, drugs that *only* could have originated from the supplier itself. And every one of the Vínculos suppliers was a known entity — which meant every one of their carriers would need to be a known entity.

There was always the chance they could move unnoticed, could get the drugs to where they needed to be, or simply hold onto them altogether, opting to try to just get eyes on Victor without getting too close. But their best option still would be to work with a few small-time runners who had taken up a certain flow in the region.

They would bring the drugs to Manaus, to the drop zone, which was the warehouse where Victor himself would be. Their intel suggested that without drugs — without acting like *traquetas* — there would be no access to the drop zone. No way to fight their way in.

At least not a way to live to tell about it.

So in the morning he and Rudy would sneak back into town, find his asset and their instructions, then move to wherever they need to be in order to pick up the next leg of the journey.

It wasn't easy for Jack to operate without knowing the details of a plan, but none of this work was easy. Even back at his desk job the work had been challenging; the puzzles and pieces of information he had to put together to make something constructively useful to the Company was sometimes mind-boggling. He loved the way someone at the Company had put it long ago: *people who don't want to be caught don't want to be caught.*

Victor, of course, did not want to be caught. From what he knew about the man, Victor Elizondo was not a glory-seeking terrorist but a calculating, ruthless operative himself. The man preferred to stay hidden in the shadows, much like the CIA operators themselves.

It was only because of a command directly from the leader of the Vínculos that Victor had been in the Caribbean seven months ago, when he and Jack had first met.

Jack shuddered again as the memories of that event returned. He remembered the fear and devastation as he had watched a lifeboat — one he thought was filled with children — explode in the bay, all by Victor's hand. Every step of the way, Victor had been calculating, scheming, running the show. He had been one step ahead of port authority, of the Jamaican SWAT team, and the US government. The CIA had sent a man undercover to find Victor. He had happened to be on the same cruise Jack and his family had been on.

It had not ended well for the *other* CIA operative on board.

But in two days, Victor's boss would be dead, and Victor himself would be poised to take the Vínculos throne. He did not know that Jack was here, tracking him and waiting for the perfect moment. Victor may not die by Jack's hand on this op, but the intelligence he and Rudy would gather would get them closer to taking out Jack's tormentor once and for all.

Victor would die soon — Jack was certain. His job was to grease the wheels, to gather the correct intel and pass it up the chain so that the assassins could move into position and finish the job.

Jack had been good at his previous job, and he had no reason to suspect he wouldn't be good at his new one.

As long as I trust myself.

He shifted once more, finally feeling comfortable enough to shut his eyes and catch some sleep. He breathed out a sigh of relief — the nightmare he had lived the last six months, picturing Victor's face, his smirk as he told Jack he was going to kill him and his girls — all of it flashed through Jack's mind every night.

To the rest of the world, actions here were just normal drug-related war. It was business. Impersonal.

But to Jack, this was *very* personal.

CHAPTER 24

JACK

EVENTUALLY, Jack had to get up to pee. Despite all the training he had been through over the past twenty years and the accelerated, intensive CIA-specific training he had done in the past six months, nothing could change nature.

Forty-two years old had taught him he would have to pee at least once per night, and there was nothing he could do to prevent it.

Frustrated, he rolled to the side, landing on the Taurus that had slid down the hammock. He stuck it into the holster, standing up. His feet found the soft ground, and he heard the sound of some rodent-sized animals scurrying away. He ignored the noises, shifting the holster into a better position. It was not the best way to sleep — fully clothed, prepared for battle — but it was certainly the safest.

Jack yawned and stretched, surprised at how bright it was. It was just past midnight, and the moon was high above his head, still leaking through the thick canopy. He saw shadows dancing around, either from the waving leaves and trees or animals he had disturbed. He set his target on a tree ten feet away from the hammock.

Jack relieved himself, listening to his surroundings. He heard a rustling behind him, turned to look but couldn't see anything. The heavy shadows danced closer to the ground now. It was unnerving. He finished, clicked his belt closed again, and turned back to his sleeping area.

He heard a different sound then, movement from about thirty feet away. Over by Rudy's camp.

They had spread out around the centralized open space, opting for a small amount of privacy but mostly separating themselves from one another in case either of them had to make an emergency run for it.

This wasn't the Boy Scouts; the 'buddy system' was *not* in effect. They weren't out here for fun. The mission required stealth, covert action at all times. There was no reason to let anyone else know they were working together.

Jack paused before heading back to his hammock, listening hard. He thought he heard Rudy snore, a low guttural sound, and he walked a few steps closer. He placed his feet over a thick matting of leaves that covered the sounds of his footfalls. He waited there again, hiding behind the bulk of a large bush, allowing his senses to pick up anything foreign.

He definitely heard footsteps now, someone shuffling around quickly. Perhaps Rudy had to pee at the same time?

Suddenly Jack heard a yelp. A man's voice.

Jack took off toward the campsite, swerving around a low trunk and jumping over a fallen branch as he stayed wide around the clearing. He wanted to stay hidden as much as possible in case someone was attacking Rudy. He charged through the jungle, knowing the sounds of his approach would easily be heard over the general blanket of forest noise. Crickets and insects had stopped chirping as if watching the scene unfold.

He raced around, seeing the edge of Rudy's light-colored hammock and bug net swaying in the night. It was moving gently with the breeze — and the thin shape of it meant no one was inside.

Rudy had left his hammock, then he had shouted.

Where the hell is he?

Jack waited, tried to listen again. He heard no more noise, no sounds of human movement.

And then the crack of a single gunshot.

Jack bolted again, clearing the last few yards and landing in Rudy's camp. He nearly tripped over Rudy's bag, which was no longer affixed to the side of the tree next to his hammock. The man had taken it down for some reason. What was he trying to get out of it at midnight? He noticed that the top of it had been unzipped, left open. Jack looked at it for a split second, cataloging this new information, but he was more interested in finding his partner.

He saw the man's legs poking out from behind a tree about a dozen steps away.

He slowed to a jog. The man's upper body was still hidden behind another fern, and Jack flew around it and came to a stop right at Rudy's boots.

He looked down, the moonlight helping to illuminate the scene.

And he wished that what weren't the case.

Rudy was dead.

His partner had a fresh hole between his eyes, directly in the center of his forehead. Execution-style.

Rudy was seated, propped up against a large trunk and leaning back against it, his mouth open slightly. His neck and torso were covered in blood that was still pouring out, gurgling between his lips and down his chin.

The gruesome sight shocked Jack to his core, but his instincts kicked in. He ran forward, grabbing Rudy's wrist for a pulse, knowing he was going through the motions. The man was dead, though it had happened only seconds ago.

In his other hand, Jack held the Taurus. He lifted it quickly as he rose again to his feet. There was no more helping Rudy — now it was about his own survival. They were still here, whoever had done this. Were they searching for him, now? Perhaps they had circled around the other side of the clearing just as Jack had done on the south side, hoping to find Jack's hammock.

He placed his back against the tree, aware that his left foot was nearly touching his dead partner's shoulder. He watched the jungle around him, watched the shadows. Some of these shadows must have been men, must have been killers.

They had snuck into their camp, pulled Rudy from his bed, and dragged him across the jungle floor.

Jack didn't see any signs of movement that looked human, nor did anyone jump out to attack him. He waited there for a full two minutes, listening, watching.

There were no assassins hidden behind the trees; no one came out to shove a knife into his neck. Finally, after what seemed like an eternity, he dropped the gun to his side, still gripping it tightly. He turned again to his partner, now ready to examine exactly what had happened here.

The execution-style killing had drilled a hole through his

partner's head, so most of the blood from that wound was pouring out the back of his skull.

Jack looked around, trying to figure out what he was missing about this whole thing. The man's hammock and gear were still here, as his killers likely had fled into the forest before Jack could catch them.

The gear.

Jack hustled back to Rudy's bag, frantically searching through it to see what they had taken. What was missing might give him a clue about what these people had been after.

He lifted objects out — weaponry, ammunition. Rain poncho, a lightweight stove, a mess kit. The same first-aid kit he had in his own bag, all duplicates of things he carried in his pack. The heavy brick of cocaine.

Jack checked the internal pouches where the men carried the wads of cash, finding everything accounted for.

It took a minute, but he finally stood up, satisfied that everything was in place except for the hammock, which was still strung between two trees.

Whoever had killed Rudy had not bothered to go through his things. They weren't here for stuff, for equipment.

They hadn't been here for drugs, either. Did that mean they were Shining Path? Did that mean they weren't cartel or just a roving gang of murderers? The latter was an unlikely case, but it wasn't impossible.

But if it had been a gang or solo murderer, they would have gone for the gear — anything they could sell later — and certainly would have seen the brick of bright-white powder wrapped tightly. They would have known immediately what it was and would have taken it. It was worth a fortune here, as was the money itself.

So it hadn't been cartel or petty thieves or criminals.

That meant it *had* to be Shining Path — it had to be part of the same group hounding them since they landed.

It had been Shining Path all along, the ones who had shot down their plane to the ones who had chased them through Iquitos, and now this.

If *Sendero Luminoso* had a bone to pick with anyone, it would be against him and his CIA partner. Of course they would be out for blood; of course they would have hunted the two men who had already killed four of theirs.

This was no act of random violence. This was a vendetta.

Shining Path had killed Rudy, which told Jack something else:

They were going to come for him, too.

CHAPTER 25

JACK

THE SHADOWS NEVER STOPPED. Their intensity grew with each passing hour. Jack was beyond terrified; it wasn't that death itself was the enemy; it was that he was not in charge of when it would arrive.

He knew he had been putting himself in a dangerous situation by accepting this op. Hostile forces were fighting one another for control over this region; he knew that going in and pretending he was one of them was a dangerous game.

But this was something else — something he could never have expected. Not only had they been spotted, their cover almost made, but they had also left a trail of blood every step of the way.

And that trail was now leading directly back to them. Jack and Rudy were no longer undercover, unable to move without being seen.

Because they *had* been seen. They had been tracked, followed, until their guard was down and they were at their most vulnerable. They had been sleeping for hours before the attack had happened, and even then — Jack couldn't make sense of it. Why had they chosen to execute Rudy? Why had they only targeted the older operative and not Jack himself? Surely they knew Rudy was not operating solo. It would have been evident from anyone tracking them, even for anyone stumbling upon their location on accident.

Though they had not revealed anything about their overall strategy, it would have been clear to anyone listening in that there were two men here — not just one.

Whoever had killed Rudy had wanted *him* dead, and not Jack. They had targeted Rudy specifically.

Although that meant Jack was still alive, it did not sit well with him. He couldn't make heads or tails of their motives, and he wasn't about to chalk it up to accidental luck. In his line of work, luck didn't exist.

That said, he wouldn't wait for lightning to strike twice. He grabbed Rudy's supplies, leaving Rudy in situ, having no better option now. This wasn't the Marines. Everything, including the environment itself, was hostile, and any extra weight would slow him down too much.

Jack was now working alone, operating without his partner. Without his mentor. And the 'extra time' Rudy had referred to earlier had just evaporated.

Jack dragged Rudy's pack over and laid it next to his. It was half-past midnight, and Jack had the constant sensation that someone was looking in on his movements, watching him, studying him.

It didn't have to be a Shining Path member or the cartel itself. Plenty of other predatory creatures here would love a midnight snack, but if Jack kept moving, the chance of that happening diminished.

He was tired, but this was no place to camp. He dumped

out the contents of Rudy's pack and sifted through them. He discarded the mess kit, stove, and extra canisters of butane fuel. He had these already, and the canisters would only add extra weight he couldn't afford. He took all of Rudy's weapons — two grenades and two pistols, a .45 caliber and a shorter 9mm. He needed all the ammunition he could get he could carry as well, so he added a box of .45 rounds that Rudy had been carrying.

Rudy had been sleeping with his combat knife on his belt, but Jack had pulled this from him back at the murder scene. He placed it into the holster on his belt, next to his combat knife. He would need to reorganize, maybe move one of the knives somewhere else in case he lost his belt, and he made a mental note to look for a drop-leg holster or something more concealed back in Iquitos tomorrow morning. Perhaps Rudy's asset would be able to help him find something.

He tossed Rudy's hammock aside, keeping only sleeping accoutrements for himself. He wasn't planning any dates; so be it if he lost his pack. The rest of this trip was not going to take place exclusively in the jungle, so he opted to take a single first-aid kit instead of two, although he grabbed a few extra bottles of medication and an extra roll of gauze, just in case.

Finally satisfied and hefting his pack to see that it was not prohibitively heavy, he hoisted it over a shoulder and stood. His shirt was soaked through with sweat and humidity, but he barely felt it. There was only one thing on his mind: getting away from this scene. He needed to head west again, toward Iquitos. Somewhere along the way, he would sleep for two more hours, maybe three. It all depended on how quickly he could move. He would wait until the break of dawn, which was the time when the fishermen would begin their early morning excursions, so he was optimistic he could find a cheap ride back toward town then.

With any luck, he might be able to get back to the taxi he and Rudy had ditched on the side of the road unless the local police happened upon it overnight.

The crickets and insects sounds had returned now, as well as the sounds of frogs singing lullabies.

When before it had soothed him, relaxed him even, now it just seemed like noise. It seemed like each one of these creatures, no matter how small, was pushing him away, trying to convince him to leave.

This isn't where you belong, they said. *This isn't where you belong, and you know it.*

He didn't feel particularly sad about Rudy's loss, yet; he didn't feel *anything* yet. He would have time to grieve later. Right now, he was more frustrated than anything. The greatest asset he had in the field was Rudy, and he was now gone. Sure, Jack was capable and had been briefed as well as Rudy, but Rudy had grown up in the area. Rudy knew the ins and outs of both the Shining Path and cartel, and spoke better Spanish than Jack.

Rudy knew the asset.

Oh well, he told himself. *This is it. This is all I've got now.*

He threw the other strap of the pack over his shoulder and took one final look around. He saw his partner's legs again, his body hidden behind the tree. He saw the spot where Rudy had...

Wait.

Why had Rudy dragged his pack out? What was the purpose of that?

Jack stopped, staring. He took in the scene a final time,

trying to force his mind to piece it all together for him. *Did the murderer drag the pack over?*

No, he shook his head. That wouldn't make sense — they would have had no use for the pack if they weren't even here to steal from Rudy.

He walked toward the spot where the dirt and matted leaves lay. He looked down at it.

Trust yourself, Jack.

And then, *this is information you* will *need.* He remembered Rudy's last words to him.

Was he trying to tell me something?

Jack ran over to where he had laid Rudy's pack before emptying its contents and ripping it open. He felt around the inside, working his hands over the fabric near the zipper instead of just focusing on the main storage area. He brushed the interior fabric with the palm of his hand, moving over the spot where he had taped the picture inside his pack.

There was nothing there.

He moved his hand to the opposite side of the bag, then repeated the process. He felt the slightest change in texture, a seam.

He frowned. He didn't remember his pack having a pocket inside. He pulled the flap open more, trying to get a better view. It had no weight to it, whatever it was. A small rectangle slightly darker than the rest of the fabric.

He pulled his knife, then tore a section of fabric away. He could see where Rudy — or someone — had made an extra pocket, inserted whatever was inside, then sewn it shut.

Jack ripped open the hidden pocket and felt inside. Paper, smooth to the touch.

What the hell?

He couldn't believe it. Rudy *had* been sending him a message. He had been trying to tell him something all along.

Why not just... tell me? Jack couldn't figure out Rudy's ultimate goal, but he pulled the picture out nonetheless. He turned it over in his hands, squinting in the moonlight to force his eyes to focus.

It was a girl — a woman. Perhaps a few years older than Jack, and she was beautiful. Long, dark hair. Full lips, and eyes that seemed alive even in only two dimensions.

Is this your wife, Rudy? Had Rudy been mocking Jack before when he'd found his own picture hidden inside? Sure, the sewn pocket was a much better hiding spot, but what was the meaning of the charade before?

And why, then? Why had Rudy only mentioned the picture to him at the campfire?

Jack's fear had not subsided, but his mission had just gotten more complicated. What was happening out here? This was not just about finding the Vínculos and Victor's new route to the Atlantic.

This was about something else. Something Jack was only just discovering.

JACK

MORNING CAME FAR SOONER and far rougher than Jack would have liked. He had not found great trees to set up a hammock once again, and he didn't want to get too cozy, so he had simply rolled out the hammock and a couple of t-shirts over the forest floor and laid on top of that. He had set his watch to wake him in two hours but wished he had just kept moving. The sleep only made him groggy and sore.

He had stumbled out of the forest a few miles north of where he and Rudy had camped previously and was able to wave down a fisherman relatively quickly. A bit of haggling later, he arrived near the road leading into Iquitos. Rather than jumping off and hoping the taxi was still in place a half-mile up the road, Jack asked if the river fisherman could drop him off in port.

Once his feet were back on the firm ground of the city, he planned his course of action. He still needed to scope out the area to see if a shop might supply him with the ability to carry more than one weapon on his person rather than in his pack. But he also wanted to get to Rudy's asset as soon as possible.

He hailed another taxi and had the gentleman driving take him to the south side of town. Rudy had described where the asset worked in the liquor store, so he picked a random place on the map nearby and told the cabbie to head in that direction.

He saw the target building from across the street, a block away. He had the taxi driver drop him off there, then he disappeared into a general store for a moment. He picked up a sports drink and a protein bar, leaving a single bill on the counter for the attendant, and walked back outside.

His trained eye saw no signs of anyone spying on his actions, unlike the day before at the café. He had had his guard down then, but no longer. Jack was not taking any chances. He waited another five minutes, walking up and down the street on both sides, finally arriving at the small liquor store. Satisfied he was truly alone, Jack opened the door and heard the bell connected to the top of it ring.

He waited in the darkly lit interior for a few seconds before someone called out in Spanish.

He answered. "I'm hoping to find something I lost three days ago."

A woman's voice replied with a similarly cryptic phrase. "Lost time is the only thing we can't get back."

It was code intended to let each party know they were who they thought they were, but Jack had no idea if he was hearing the correct message or something... else.

His feet were already moving, deciding for him. He walked down the narrow rows of shelves toward the back counter.

He had been surprised to hear a woman's voice but realized Rudy had never told him whether the asset was male or female.

She appeared, pushing open a creaky door that led deeper into the small one-story building.

Jack almost gasped. He swallowed, doing his best to hide his shock. He recognized her. It wasn't just *anyone* Jack was looking at — he was looking at the woman from the photograph.

The one from Rudy's pack, hidden within the secret pocket. He knew, undoubtedly, that the picture had been of Rudy's asset. This woman. She was a bit older now, but her striking features were the same. Dark hair and eyes, skin that seemed to glow. She was beautiful, and even more so in the soft light inside the shop.

She frowned back at him as he walked toward her. He stood by the counter for a moment while she walked by him, shut and locked the front door, then flipped the sign on the window to 'closed.'

Finally, she spoke candidly. "You're alone?" she asked.

"You expected someone else?"

She waited, but he wasn't going to give anything beyond that simple answer. When dealing in information, it was a delicate game of give-and-take.

"You're his partner?" she asked.

Jack spoke evenly, keeping the Spanish simple and not verbose. "Just trying to get to Manaus, to link up with the flow."

She contemplated this for a moment as if choosing her words carefully. "The flows are strong this year; I hear the cartel is doing swift business up north."

"Up where the Sendero Luminoso is operating," Jack said. "You've heard something?"

She shook her head quickly. "Nothing new. They're... getting a little greedier lately. You're not the only one who wanted to get in on the action. Shining Path might not care about the drug routes, but they certainly know there's money to be made from them. There's also money to be made in preventing the others from running them."

Jack chewed his lip. This was not new information, but it felt affirming to hear it from someone who lived and breathed information like this every day.

"Can you get me on a route?" he asked.

She paused. "I don't know the route, but I can get you with a team. There are no fools here, however. They will make sure *you* know the route as well, that you're not some newcomer looking for a free handout."

"I know the route," Jack said. "I just need the cover."

"You don't; they come after me."

Jack nodded.

"You can meet them in an hour."

Jack raised an eyebrow. "I thought we had all day?" he said. "I thought they weren't leaving until nightfall."

She shrugged nonchalantly. "You thought wrong. Be at the end of Calle Leticia at the top of the hour. For someone like you, you should know them when you see them."

"In case I don't recognize them?"

She sighed. "It will be a group of three men. All around the same size and build, but they'll stand out from everyone else."

"How so?"

She smiled. "Because they'll be dressed like cops."

CHAPTER 27

JACK

IMMEDIATELY AFTER LEAVING the liquor store, Jack took a circuitous route back to the general store he had stopped in. He had intended to buy a burner phone all along but didn't want to carry the device while he spoke with Rudy's asset. Things like that often made informants and assets skittish, and he didn't want to deal with having to explain his real motive.

As it turned out, his real motive was simple: he needed to check in, to report Rudy's death. Besides changing the mission parameters, it was the decent thing to do.

He waited for the phone to turn on while standing under an overhang next to the store. Passersby barely glanced at him, and he saw four other tourists or locals across the street, also yammering away on phones. He dialed the number from memory, waited for the connection.

"Eagle Seven."

"Nightcrawler two," Jack replied quickly.

"Secure?"

"Not from my end."

There was a sigh. *"Should be from mine. Where is One?"*

"He's not going to be making any more calls."

There was a long pause, but Jack didn't fill the space with words. He assumed Rudy's handler would take the news hard; it would feel like a personal failure to the man.

"I'm sorry to hear that, Two. You okay?"

"I'm still operating, yeah. Just got word of my meetup location for Phase 2. I'll be radio silent after about an hour."

"You think this is a good idea?"

Jack frowned. "Can you clarify the meaning of good?"

There was a slight chuckle. *"Two, you're fresh. Capable, and you've got twenty years under your belt. But... not this kind of experience, not out in the field."*

"My capabilities never came into question before," Jack snapped.

"Of course not. My apologies. However, One's loss does throw a little more complication into the mix. My job isn't just to make sure you accomplish your mission. It's to bring you back home."

"I'll be fine. Things are progressing smoothly now, and I plan to keep them that way. I'll have eyes-on in less than a day, and once I get to the exfiltration point, I'll upload a full report. We should be able to move forward with the larger plans as soon as I'm wheels-up."

There was another pause. *"Listen, Two. There are also some... complications on my end. The Deputy Director has been pressing on me and some of the other handlers who have ops down there."*

Jack frowned. "Pressing on? Since when?"

Another sigh. *"Since two days ago, really, and this morning, too. I've been pulling all-nighters the last two days, trying to keep him from going ballistic."*

"Why the uproar? Why now? We've had assets in the region

for years, and we've all known that Shining Path is trying to shake some trees, see what falls out. We know the cartel's been pushing Peru pretty heavily as well."

"Yeah, we knew it was a tinderbox ready to explode. That's not the issue. It's more... political."

Jack rolled his eyes as he listened, now pacing up and down the street as he talked. "My job isn't political. My job is anything *but* political. I was given orders to watch Victor, to learn his new route, and pass it up the chain. I still fully intend to do that. Once Victor's boss is taken out, we'll be in a perfect position to focus our attention on Victor himself and —"

"I don't know if the cartel boss will *be taken out, Two,"* the handler said. *"Things are changing here, quickly. Changing every minute, it seems. The Deputy Director personally told me to start bringing assets out of the region."*

"Assets like me?"

"Yes, Jack. He wants to make sure that whatever happens down there happens 'organically' — his word, not mine. Without our unique fingerprint on it."

Jack squeezed the phone tighter. "Our *fingerprint* is lying in the jungle against a tree, with a bullet hole in his forehead. Our *fingerprint* took out four Shining Path assholes and —"

"You took out four terrorists, Two?" The man said, incredulous. *"Your orders were* not *to intercept; they were to observe. You get feet on the ground and immediately start blasting away bad guys? What the hell is wrong with you?"*

This wasn't how Jack had hoped to share the news that they had already made some noise down here, but he wasn't about to be chastised for it, either. "Hey," he said, his voice icy. "You hear anything about that plane crash? That single prop that went down northeast of Iquitos?"

The pause was longer this time. *"Shit, I didn't put two-and-two together. That was you guys?"*

"I'm here, and I'm finishing the job. Report it however you want, but you and I both know this cartel needs to be brought to its knees. Victor needs to *go*. You can change plans all you want back in DC, do the elbow rubs and back pats, but I'm down here now, so I'm going to get it done."

"Jack, this could easily backfire on you. It could backfire on me. Best option is to start heading to exfil. Lay low for a day, then come home. Let's figure it out from there. Whatever the suits want on the Hill, they're still figuring it out. They'll decide soon enough, and I'm sure we'll be able to make a move by the end of the month. For now, just —"

"This is bad form, man. Don't forget I did this for *twenty years* on the other side. Changing shit up on the fly? That's not something we do."

"It's absolutely *something we do, Two. You've been insulated from it for two decades, but this is the MO. You think I like it? You think I don't want every single one of those cartel assholes to burn? I do. But we need to make sure we're not starting a war in the process, especially one in that territory. I need you to come home without causing more trouble."*

Jack white-knuckled the phone now, gritting his teeth. He waited, pausing a beat. "Hey, Seven?"

"Yes?"

"Nightcrawler One had a picture in his pack. I found it last night."

"A picture of what?"

"It was a picture of the asset I just got done talking to."

CHAPTER 28

VICTOR

VICTOR ELIZONDO ANSWERED the call on the first ring. His voice was clipped, abrupt. "Hello?"

He was busy; there were plans to be made and plans to execute. He didn't have time for interruptions, but a call from this line meant something important had happened. It was one of his many spies, this one a man in Iquitos.

"Sir, I believe we have found someone of interest."

"Of interest? Were you attacked?"

"Not attacked, sir, but someone suspect."

Victor frowned. "So what? Is that something that sounds abnormal to you?"

It was a rhetorical question — it should not be something out of the ordinary. He had good men, however, so he suspected there was a good reason for this man calling him now.

"No, sir. It's just that with the deaths of the two Shining Path watchers yesterday, everyone's on high alert here in town. With the new route —"

"There is nothing to worry about in that regard. We have

plenty of men to defend our boats and plenty of capable runners. This is why we moved our route from the jungle."

The smaller dealers and runners needed the support of the Vínculos to get the shipments where they needed to go without intervention from authorities. He had set up a warehouse in Manaus for this purpose, planning to defend it with dozens of handpicked cartel men. He had to pay off a number of police officers and DINANDRO staff in the region, as well, but it was worth it. The sheer volume they could run using the Amazon itself would bring in far more than what it would cost to defend the route.

And as long as the runners made it to Manaus, the cartel itself could take over from there. They had an army of men ready and waiting for that very thing.

"I had a boy walk by," the man said. *"A kid, to try to hear his conversation."*

Victor smiled; this was a wise move. "And?"

"And he was conversing in English, sir. Using codenames instead of actual names."

"Send me a picture. Can you do that without him seeing?"

"Of course, sir. Give me a few seconds."

Victor waited as he heard the shuffling of getting into position, trying to stay out of sight but also capture a picture of this 'person of interest.'

A minute passed, and finally the man's voice returned. *"Should be coming now, sir."*

Victor waited again, but this time the picture appeared on his phone within seconds.

He pulled it away from his ear and clicked on the image, then pinched to zoom in on the man on the phone. The picture was crisp, but the quality of the man's face was not perfect. Part of his hand obstructed the view. He wore sunglasses, obscuring his eyes.

Victor cocked his head to the side. "This is a person of interest, indeed," he mumbled. He pulled the phone back up to his ear.

"What's that, sir?"

"I said, yes, this man I would like to watch. *Very* closely."

He would recognize this man's face anywhere. It had been about six months since he had seen him last, but he had had a feeling then that it wouldn't be the last time they met.

About six months since Victor had nearly killed him.

Hello, Mr. Barr.

"This man works for the CIA," he told his watcher. "His name is Jackson Barr, Jr. I am surprised to see him down here now, but something tells me he is here looking for me."

"Sir? The CIA has an op against you?"

"They are just gathering intelligence. It doesn't surprise me they are poking around in my business."

"I see. How would you like me to proceed?"

Victor thought for a moment, then spoke. "I would like for you to eliminate this man. I'm moving another squad under your control. Do you understand?"

The man he was speaking with was military-trained and was no stranger to taking a life. He wasn't the best soldier Victor had, but what he lacked in intelligence, he made up for in brutality.

"Copy that, sir. I will inform you when it is done."

Victor hung up the phone and began pacing the room, an old habit. *Jack Barr is here, once again meddling in my affairs.*

This time, Jack could not play him for a fool. He could not

pretend he was not with the CIA, could not pretend he was ignorant about everything going on.

No, Jack, you have come into my backyard now. You are playing a game you cannot win; on a field you don't even understand.

He stopped pacing, realizing there was nothing more to worry about. Jack Barr, Jr. would die soon, and Victor could simply move on with the rest of his plans.

JACK WAS MADE.

He hung up the phone and shoved it into his pocket. He could discard it another time, in a trash bin on his way out of town.

And he *did* need to get out of town. He had been spotted.

The man he was concerned about stood a block away, at a corner just past the liquor store where he had met with Rudy's asset. It had seemed only slightly suspicious at the time, but he had watched as the man lifted a phone and snapped a picture of him.

Of course, Jack couldn't be sure what the man was actually doing, but he had watched in his peripheral vision as the man lifted the phone up, aimed the back of it directly at him, then lowered it. There was no explanation for it other than that the man had snapped a photo.

Jack was not about to take the chance that the man was trying to wave his phone around to get a better signal.

After ending his call, and without looking back at the man watching him, Jack turned in the opposite direction and began walking down the street, heading south. He was in a subdivision of Iquitos, which mixed homes with small commercial establishments, usually in the form of two-story buildings: homes on the top floor and stores accessible from the street on the bottom floor.

He needed to hustle, to get into position once again so he could meet up with the three targets. He didn't want to miss whoever would be helping him down the river, and he had less than an hour to get there.

The trouble was, he didn't want to head directly there. Signaling the direction he was traveling to the man who had snapped a photo of him — and likely had sent it to his superiors — meant he was signaling his direction to the cartel and Shining Path.

Jack examined his mental map of the city, trying to figure out a relatively circuitous route that would take him to the meet-up location without making a direct line. He needed to shake this and any other tail it might turn into. He focused through the far edge of his sunglasses, where the tiny reflection there showed him an out-of-focus, yet usable, view behind him. Every car that passed caught the sunlight in a particular way that allowed him to keep watch on his six for a few seconds at a time.

The man followed, staying on the other side of the street but making quick progress. He thought the man was closing the distance, but he didn't dare glance over his shoulder to find out for sure.

At the next intersection, Jack waited for traffic and watched the man approach on the opposite side of the street. He had his phone up to his ear once more. To his credit, he never made eye contact with Jack. It was possible this man was nobody, but Jack wasn't going to risk it.

He crossed the road and picked up his pace just a bit, trying to move at a reasonable speed so as not to attract undue attention from any locals, and traversed this block and waited at the corner of Guardia Civil and Quiñones. Horns honked — a common occurrence in this area of the world as soon as the stoplight turned green — and once again, he paused as he waited for traffic to slide by. Cars and carts passed, and Jack saw to his left a vehicle barreling down the slight hill toward the busy intersection. He began his way across the street, timing it so he could pass before the speeding car reached the three-way intersection.

He kept the car in his peripheral vision and was about three-quarters of the way across the street when he noticed it had shifted out of its lane and changed course.

It was heading straight for him, and it was speeding up.

Jack continued along the street, feeling his heart rate rise. He reached the curb and hopped up onto it, immediately feeling relieved.

He flicked his eyes to the left, only then realizing his mistake.

The car was *also* on the sidewalk, and he heard shouts from a street vendor and passersby standing nearby as the car raced past them, inches from their stands and booths.

The car was on the same pathway as Jack now, still speeding toward him, so Jack ran full speed toward the entrance of the building situated on the street corner. It would be close, but he forced his leg to ignore the dull ache from his previous injury, then dove forward the last five feet.

He heard the vehicle's engine whining against the strain as

its driver applied still more gas, trying to run him down. There was a passenger inside as well, leaning out the side window. The car swerved to the left, catching the corner beam of the building that held up the front awning.

Jack landed. He hit the ground hands-first but fell into a forward roll and popped back upright inside the building's entrance as the car bounced outside just behind him, now facing in the opposite direction. He glanced over his shoulder and saw that its front-left tire had been almost sheared clean off, taking the cosmetic bumper with it.

And still the driver pursued him, pulling the car around in a tight arc to face it toward the building's entrance. It hobbled, but it was still rolling.

And still moving fast enough to kill him.

Jack started running back out onto the street while the driver overcorrected for the unwieldy vehicle's movements. Shouts and screams rang out, and Jack noticed a few people already holding out cell phones to record video of the devastation. Jack figured his face would be streaming online in a few minutes, but he had no interest in sticking around for an encore performance.

He turned left and followed the street, seeing the end of the building the car had run into just ahead. Jack saw a slight recess there, a cavity between it and the next building over. He hoped it was the entrance to an alleyway, or at least a recess deep enough that the pursuing car couldn't get its front end into it.

He reached it thirty paces later, pulling his Raging Judge out of its holster with his right hand as he threw his left hand over the frame of the building's corner. He used his left arm as a rudder, sailing his body to the left and around into the alleyway.

It was as he had hoped. The alleyway was far too narrow for a vehicle of any sort, and he turned into it and ran, hurtling a few trash cans and recycling bins behind him, to dissuade any foot traffic from following him in. He looked ahead as he ran, seeing a busy road. This alleyway seemed connected to the same street he had been on previously.

The car screeched to a halt, doors opening. He didn't look back — he knew he could outrun anyone trying to chase him down, so it wasn't the men behind him that worried him.

It was what lay in front of him. How many more men had that person called? How many more goons would be homing in on his location now?

If the man had, in fact, taken a picture of him, the cartel — or the *Shining Path*, whoever the man had been working for — would know his face now. There was no more hiding in plain sight, no more cover using his real face.

And if it were the cartel, Victor would recognize him immediately.

In his pack, he had thin, horn-rimmed glasses and a ball cap that had some long, scruffy blonde hair attached to the sides of it. It would work about as well as the inane costumes the two *Shining Path* men had been wearing the day before, but it might work to get these guys off his tail for the time being.

He didn't need a perfect, infallible disguise — he just needed to get out of town.

HEAVENS

HEAVENS LOOKED at the other three men in his squad. "Joseph, Szymon, you two are on point. Alameda, you're with me. We split up, try to get eyes-on, comms-up. I want a tail on these guys within the hour."

"Copy," Alameda said. Szymon and Joseph nodded, but Joseph raised his eyebrows slightly.

"What's up?" Heavens anticipated the question.

Joseph cleared his throat. "These guys are American assets, yeah?" he asked.

Heavens nodded. "The op is *just* recon, got it? Reynolds called this one in yesterday. Guess he needs someone to babysit them for a couple more days."

"It's not a hit, though?"

"Not a hit," Heavens repeated. "We just need eyes-on, make sure they don't get into any trouble. We're just here to make sure the assets are safe and accounted for — and that they stay that way."

Heavens had given each man a bullet-point brief covering all of this, but he appreciated the questions. Questions — and answers — meant clarity. These men were professionals, military trained and experienced, and had run missions with him in and around South America for over a year. Stonefire was a well-regarded paramilitary and security company based out of Boston, with operatives and soldiers in almost every corner of the globe. Most of their operations were simple security- and recon-based, like this one. Protect something or someone, provide an additional layer of security for some rich businessperson, or take on the protection and security systems of a company itself.

Stonefire had amassed a reputation in the private mercenary industry as the one to call for reputable, above-board security and operations.

Reynolds ran teams of two to four, but sometimes up to ten, depending on the mission and responsibility. Heavens had been with this exact squad for a little over a year, and he trusted and respected each of his men and their capabilities. Joseph was a Marine, his other two men, like him, ex-Army. They were good at what they did, no matter what they were required to do.

While this was no party, it shouldn't be a tough op, either. The weather would be nice, the location was great, and the pay was exceptional.

Plus, they had no reason to suspect the American operatives were doing anything but recon, collecting HUMINT, so the assets shouldn't come under fire. He knew the men could handle themselves if they did have to use any of the arsenal of weaponry they'd brought along, but it shouldn't come to that.

Reynolds had given Heavens the overview: someone with enough money and enough power to know how to wield it back in DC wanted the CIA out of the area for the time being.

The CIA, however, was not going to budge. They answered to the Director of National Intelligence, as well as the President. Receiving stand-down orders from anyone but those two, following the proper chain-of-command, would fall on deaf ears.

Heavens didn't understand the politics around why he was here now, but he didn't need to. It was an op, like all the others.

And this one was easier than most. Find the American assets, follow them around, report back.

Make sure no one tried to screw with that.

Due to the nature of the op, he had been filled in a bit on the precarious situation of the region. Reynolds had not flat-out explained it, but since he was here to protect CIA assets, he had been given a few other important details.

There was a cartel operating in the region, and the second-in-command was running it. He was expected to be in the area soon, and while there was no overt action in Heavens' purview, he had to suspect that the Americans were here to watch the maneuverings of this particular cartel boss.

It was a game of cat-and-mouse, but with multiple cats and multiple mice. The CIA wanted to be the ones pulling the strings, so they wouldn't take kindly to someone on the Hill telling them to stand down.

Moreover, there was talk about another hostile third party in the region: the old Communist group *Shining Path*, or *Sendero Luminoso.* Heavens had no idea how these goons fit into the equation, but he had been told to watch his back and keep his eyes open.

Heavens looked over at his men seated across from him. They were flying in the back of a cargo plane, landing on an airstrip just south of Iquitos. A four-person ATV large enough to carry the squad and their gear would bring them close to town, where they would immediately begin their operation.

"Loadout is the same as always — M4 carbine, sidearm of your choosing. Rules of engagement apply; we won't be seen or heard. If we do our jobs right, no one knows we're here."

"Cover?"

Heavens shook his head. "No, no time to set all that up. We're going in as soldiers but not picking a fight. Military presence down here isn't uncommon right now, and there's no reason to suspect we should catch flak from anyone if we're just minding our own. We'll stay in the shadows, well away from the target, and leapfrog quadrants around him in order to stay alongside."

"Got it."

"Great," Heavens said. "Let's get a move on. We've got a spy to eye."

CHAPTER 31

JACK

JACK GOT his first good look at the man pursuing him in the car when he turned back and proceeded up the street on the other side. A construction scaffolding had been erected along the side of one building currently getting a makeover to its façade, and Jack doubled back to hide behind the plywood front of the bottom of the scaffolding.

If he had to guess, the men following him were locals or native to the region. Dark skin, dark hair, easily fitting in on the streets of Iquitos.

He could not know for certain, but he guessed these were cartel men, people working for Victor. Victor would have many spies in the region, especially now, and the way these two operated so far seemed more professional than the watchers for the *Shining Path* they had come across the day before.

While the car chase was reckless, Jack had to admit it *almost* had been effective.

And it was quick — the man on the phone had gotten them here almost immediately. That spoke volumes about Victor's organization and preparedness.

Were these the men who had killed Rudy in his sleep?

Once again, Jack wondered about his *own* preparedness — was he in over his head?

Jack doubled back to try to get a look at his pursuers, but also to attempt to use the maze-like streets of this corner of Iquitos against them. At some point, he would have to stop running, so he would need a better plan than just guiding his pursuers through the streets. While he had never been here, he had studied layouts and maps of Iquitos and Manaus at length, and he felt he knew the towns better than any recent transplant would.

But he couldn't run forever. Victor had many men operating here as well, so it would only be a matter of time before he had them arranged in such a way as to be a trap that would be impossible for Jack to escape from.

The street he was on now ran perpendicular to the main highway he had traversed before with Rudy. Eventually, this road would veer to the northwest and drop them off at the same back road that had led them out of town their first day in Iquitos.

And turning to the right would take him directly to where he was supposed to go to meet up with the team that would help him down the river.

Jack was not currently being followed. He didn't recognize anyone around him, but he had lost the men who had chased him with the car.

The streets were calmer now, locals and tourists once again going about their daily activities. The glances he had been getting from innocent bystanders as he ran had stopped.

Still, he was not out of the woods yet. He knew the man who had marked him with the cell phone was out here somewhere. Very likely he had called in more reinforcements than just the two in the small car. Already, the search would be on. He was going to need to disappear.

He needed to get somewhere with more human activity, a place where he could blend in and get lost in a crowd. With a population of just under 400,000, Iquitos was not the kind of city where he could find a large crowd around every corner, but there were still options.

He knew of one such option, looking up at the street signs as he viewed the map of Iquitos in his mind. He was only three blocks away. He could get there in fewer than five minutes at his current pace, perhaps seven if he slowed to a brisk walk.

Jack reached the end of the scaffolding and stopped, knowing his cover would soon be gone.

Two men stood at the end of this block, one of them pointing at him.

Shit.

One man said something to the other, then held up his cell phone. Jack immediately recognized the man as the same one who had marked him before.

Dammit, he thought. *Guess I'm not going to be walking after all.*

Jack changed his course of action. He needed to get around this building to its other side, where he could follow that street down two more blocks. But if he turned around once again and ran through the scaffolding, and turned right at the end of the line, he would have to chance a close encounter with these two men in front of him.

Unless...

Jack turned around but didn't retrace his steps. Instead, he walked back through the scaffolding halfway, then looked up.

The structure had a plywood ceiling above his head, but he had noticed during his jog through the scaffolding that a section had been cut open, allowing access to the second floor of the building.

He first tossed his pack upwards and onto the second-story scaffolding, then Jack jumped straight up, grabbing the edge of the plywood floor. He pulled himself onto the plywood, rolled over, landed on his back on the second floor of the scaffolding, then turned and saw exactly what he had been hoping to find.

An entrance.

Or, rather, a missing wall on the front of the building itself. He stepped over a pile of masonry tools and bricks and entered the old building.

It looked to have been built around the same time as the mansion he and Rudy had visited, but this place looked more industrial. Even stripped, Jack could see that the interior brick walls had always been dirty and grimy, and old mechanical tools and lifts still hung from the ceiling of the space.

It was empty now, no workers in sight, and a quick look around told him that the building was completely unoccupied — the entire place was getting refurbished, not just the front wall.

Jack started off through the building's second floor. On the far side of the block-wide space, he saw windows with daylight streaming through them. That was the street he was aiming for, and he had just found a convenient shortcut.

Shouts reached his ears from down below, and Jack was surprised that the men had made it across the street and to his previous location so quickly. No matter — he was already on the move. He couldn't run full-out, since there were more human-sized holes in this second floor still waiting to be patched, and he couldn't trust his steps. There were tools everywhere — cords to trip on, saws on stands, buckets, and bags of smaller handheld tools scattered around. No surface was free of some sort of construction equipment.

He reached the halfway point of the second floor just as the first man's head appeared through the same hole he had entered from.

Two shots cracked through the air. Jack ducked mid-stride, then rolled forward and crawled behind a concrete beam running vertically through the building. Another shot smacked into the front of the concrete post and Jack pulled himself back even farther around it, cutting off the angle.

He slid his pack off his shoulder and down to the floor, simultaneously reaching around to retrieve his Taurus. His free hand worked over the pack's zipper, searching inside for the object he needed.

For a moment, he worried that he would have to break cover to look inside the pack, but his fingers brushed against the cold metal, and he grasped the item and pulled it out.

CHAPTER 32

HEAVENS

THEY GOT eyes-on a little after 0900, about three hours after they had landed and driven to the outskirts of town. After rechecking loadouts and making sure the mission was set, Heavens and Alameda took up a position spread out over about 200 yards that spanned three city blocks. Joseph and Szymon were across from them, separated by about a mile, at the north end of the quadrant. All comms were up and working, and Heavens listened to the chatter of his men as they waited.

Alameda reported seeing a man carrying a pack, wearing sunglasses. They waited while Alameda and Heavens kept an eye on this guy, watching him go up and then back down a block, finally stepping into a liquor store.

"Bit early for a drink, don't you think?" Alameda said in his ear.

Heavens smiled. They paused another few minutes before the man appeared once more on the street. Interestingly, Heavens spotted another man across from their mark talking on a cell phone, holding it up and doing what could only be snapping a picture of the guy.

"That's our mark," he said quietly. "And he's been noticed by the cartel. All units on me."

"There's only one guy, though," Szymon said.

"Doesn't matter. Where there's one CIA dude, there are two CIA dudes. These guys are whip-smart, well-trained. The other asset will be close by, probably already out of sight watching *us* watch his partner. Either way, we're just providing recon, so we'll follow the one we've got."

"Affirmative."

He knew it would take some time for the other two men to close their sides of the box surrounding the American, and he didn't want to lose sight of him in the meantime, so he had Alameda run parallel to the guy, staying ahead of him as much as possible, while he followed far behind both the man and the guy who had been taking pictures.

They had followed the asset in a circuitous route around these blocks, and Heavens had been surprised to see the man eventually start to sprint away. He saw a car nearly take him out, then watched as the man doubled back, jumped into a building currently under construction, and then as four other men, dressed like locals, followed him up. The two pairs of men entered, separated by a two-minute gap. Heavens watched all this while Alameda reported from the other side of the building, which he had worked around the last two minutes. *"Target is still inside,"* Alameda said.

Heavens confirmed, then told the others to stand by. "I've got north and south covered. Joseph and Szymon, find a position on the east and west side of this city block. He's got to leave sometime, no matter what happens up there."

"Actually, sir, I've got movement."

Suddenly there was an explosion, and a hole was blasted into the side of the old building.

It was Alameda again, and Heavens waited for his report.

There was a shout. *"We've got him! Guy just jumped out a second-story window."* There was a pause. *"In pursuit now!"*

"Looks like he's got two hostiles behind him."

"Copy that, Alameda," Heavens said. "Mission stays the same — *do not* engage any of them. Try to run a tail parallel to the lead guy, if possible, so he doesn't know we're here."

"Already on it, sir."

Heavens looked down at a map he had stored on his phone, trying to figure out where the man would go next.

Seeing the layout of the city like this gave him the ability to think like an operative. This was no tourist; he wasn't looking for something to do. This man would hide, likely try to find someplace busy enough he could blend in with the crowd.

And in a city as relatively small as Iquitos, that would not be easy to do.

He looked at the map, measured the direction the man had been traveling, then smiled.

"All units, I think I know where he's going. Joseph, Szymon, set up on the corners to the southeast. Alameda, stay on him. I'll pull up the rear. I'm pretty sure we can funnel him down in between both of you, but remember — we're not here to engage, even though we're pretty sure who the bad guys are. Stay out of sight and let them pass."

Three sets of *'copy that'* sounded through his earpiece.

While Heavens' orders may have been to not engage the target, there was another group after him that did *not* have the same orders. Heavens wasn't the sort of guy to ignore orders, but he couldn't easily just stand around and watch bad people kill good ones.

This CIA guy had gotten himself into a pickle. He wouldn't intervene beyond keeping a close eye on him, but if the men after him began killing innocent bystanders, that's where Heavens drew the line.

He heard Joseph's voice next. *"Shots fired!"*

No one spoke, all four men waiting to see how this played out. The target had entered the market, a great place to go to hide in plain sight.

He had guessed correctly. It was the exact place Heavens would have chosen.

The operative had apparently been made, and the two locals still chasing after him were one of the same pairs of men Heavens had seen entering the construction building. The first two men who had gone in after him had never reappeared.

Heavens was impressed by the guy's ability to keep moving, even in the face of death. These CIA types, while trained in a broad array of fields, often froze up around death or in the middle of an intense battle.

Heavens was not squeamish about death. He had killed before and would again — it was the nature of his job. But not everyone was like him; not everyone could stomach it.

This man seemed to be able to stomach it just fine, or at least he could successfully compartmentalize it. He was more like Heavens, more like his men.

He did what had to be done.

It made Heavens like him, just a little bit. He had assumed they would be babysitting an asset, someone trained but not battle-tested, the type of person too smart for their own good to think that they'd ever have to get their hands dirty.

This guy seemed different. Reckless, but in a calculated way.

He seemed like he held a grudge, like he was on a mission that went deeper than just keeping an eye on some local thugs.

Heavens' focus immediately turned to screams and shouts as they reached his ears. They fell through his comms and from the air in front of him as he watched people in the market — locals and tourists alike — ducking for cover. The person chasing the asset was now shooting at him. It was a small-caliber pistol by the sound of it, and because of the noise and din of the normal market chaos, he was sure most people hadn't even heard the gunshot but were just reacting to the screams they heard.

He stepped into the market from the south side, knowing Alameda would be flanking his position at the other end of the block. Szymon and Joseph would rotate around and post up to the side of the asset's position now, waiting for him to emerge. No matter which side the CIA man decided to turn, one of Heavens' men would see him.

He only hoped that one of these idiot locals wouldn't try to shoot him first.

CHAPTER 33

JACK

BOTH OF JACK'S pursuers were on the second floor with him. He heard their footsteps, their quiet whispers discussing how to flank their prey.

They chose wisely, opting to take a wide route around the edges of the building. That way they wouldn't have to watch their backs, but also so they could approach Jack's position behind the concrete pier from two directions.

But their footsteps weren't completely silent, and they gave away their movements. Jack was able to discern their positions as they moved around him.

One of them tripped over some construction equipment, cursing as he fell. Jack focused his attention on the other guy, as this man would be coming from Jack's left and would reach him before the second man could get into position.

The man chasing him from this side would make his way around the perimeter of the second floor, staying against the front wall of the building where the scaffolding was, but eventually he would turn and head up directly toward Jack along the side. Jack needed to time everything correctly — and even then it would be a long shot.

As if reading his mind, the man stopped moving — or otherwise started moving silently — and suddenly, Jack had no sensory information as to the exact whereabouts of his pursuers.

Jack picked up the hand grenade he had pulled from the bag and pulled the pin, tossing it away. He held the explosive's latch closed in his fist, waiting a few more seconds to time it correctly.

Finally satisfied this would be the best chance he had, Jack released the handle, counted out two long seconds, then tossed the grenade side-arm along the wall.

The orb clanged against the sheet metal on the exposed wall and then bounced along the plywood floor, landing directly in the corner of the room about five feet from the walls on either side. He watched the table saw over in the corner, with more plywood and lumber leaned against its front, offering a perfect place for someone to hide behind.

He had marked the location when he had run through earlier and decided that this would be the place his first pursuer would choose to post up. This would be where the man would try to pin Jack down while waiting for his partner to flank from the other side.

The explosion came a second later, blasting the saw and pieces of wood outward in every direction. Debris and concrete dust flew as well, creating a cloud of debris that made it impossible to see anything. There was also a scream — surprise and no small amount of pain.

Jack wanted to wait for the dust to clear, to see if the man was down for the count, but he had another priority now.

If it hadn't been a direct hit, the grenade blast would at least give the first man enough to think about for the next few seconds — meanwhile, Jack needed to take out the second man. He rolled sideways, daring a brief exposure, hoping the second man had been startled and was looking back toward his partner. He came up to his knees, getting his bearings immediately, noticing the second man hiding behind another post on the opposite side of the room.

However, this man had been hiding from Jack at an angle that would have hidden him from Jack's *previous* position.

Now, Jack had a clear view of the attacker's side.

The man realized this at the same time, but it was too late. Jack fired three rounds, one hitting the man in his side and another in his foot. He grunted in pain, falling forward. Jack was running now; he hurdled a pile of bricks in his path and brought the Taurus up again, this time straight-on with his target.

Impossible to miss.

He fired again and this time the man fell backward, dead. He slid in front of the man's feet, using the cover behind this post to hide from the first pursuer. He waited there for a moment, catching his breath.

The debris from the explosion had mostly stopped. He didn't hear any other noise, any sounds of someone crawling away from the explosion, nor did he hear the sounds of scuffling feet as they tried to get into position once more.

He dared a look around the post, squinting through the dim light across the room. The opposite corner of the space had been decimated — a new hole had opened on that side of the building. The wood floor around the grenade blast had been ruptured, and he saw extension cords and tools falling over its edge to the first floor below.

And next to all of this, he saw the silhouette of a man lying on his back. His arms were splayed out to the sides, palms up.

He rose, started walking over to the first man.

As he moved, he heard more shouts from down below, from back outside. Either pedestrians wondering what had happened, what had blown up...

Or more people coming after Jack. More of Victor's men. More *Shining Path*.

He snuck forward a few more feet, half expecting the man to jump up and surprise him.

Suddenly a crashing sound came from just outside the building's front, the same place he and the two pursuers had entered from.

He heard orders barked quickly in Spanish — '*he's in there, go*' — and Jack decided to change direction again. The first man may not have been dead, but he certainly wasn't up and fighting, either. That would have to be good enough for now — Jack was about to have new pursuers on his tail.

He threw his Taurus back into his belt and ran to the first hiding spot, scooping up his pack and zipping it closed, then slinging it over his shoulder. He continued running, aiming out toward the back wall where the windows brightened the interior. There was a door there leading out to a second-floor patio or deck, and he knew it would be his best bet at getting down to the street below.

He shifted the pack on his back and made a beeline for the doorway.

CHAPTER 34

JACK

THE MARKET WAS a perfect place to hide. He didn't look like a local or a tourist, but there were plenty of both in the marketplace, and no one was paying him any attention. Jack approached the market from the northwest side, coming into the city-block-wide maze of shops and open-air stands from that corner.

Immediately he was bombarded with sensory overload, hit with throngs of people shouting and talking and laughing, smells of cooking and raw food, and a rainbow of color in every direction.

Streamers called attention to dozens of booths, each busy with tourists and locals alike, shopping for meals for their time in Iquitos or knickknacks and souvenirs to take home.

He slowed down, no longer needing to run but wanting to move quickly to get further lost in the beautiful cacophony. He still needed to be across town, and the clock was ticking.

Getting lost didn't take much effort. He stepped farther into the plaza and toward a long, low table set against the wall to his left. It was covered with fresh fish, many freshwater varieties, but also some saltwater species laying on ice, obviously having been flown in from one of the coasts. Jack smelled both the scent of raw fish as well as the even more intense aroma of fish frying in a pan. He saw where it was coming from, a large wok on a stove near the end of the line, an adolescent teen shaking it back and forth vigorously as smoke rose above it.

Three or four people were standing in front of the wok, shouting and pointing at whatever was inside. It was like Wall Street, but instead of stocks, people shouted food orders and tried to gain the attention of the young cook. The cook would nod and continue working, continue moving the wok back and forth on the hot flame, only stopping to dump a steaming pile of food into a paper serving bowl.

Jack smiled at an older woman as he passed. She raised her eyebrows in a silent question, her hand full of woven crafts. He shook his head and continued through, deeper into the market. He made a target of hitting the statue rising from the center of the square, but still made a serpentine route through the space. He turned back when he reached the statue, his eyes scanning the crowd for anything out of the ordinary.

His senses immediately went on high alert, his subconscious trying to clue him in on something.

He narrowed his focus to the area directly in front of him where he had entered the market square.

There.

A man was standing there, staring directly at him.

He was holding a pistol.

Jack started forward, still not running but now walking much faster than he had, moving diagonally toward the man and also back toward the back northern wall of the square. He put three vendor carts between him and the would-be attacker, but the man had moved to the side and was now lining up a shot.

Surely he's not going to fire at me from here. He'll hit someone else —

The man fired two quick shots that ripped through the air and popped over his head.

He heard one round ping into the side of one of the metal carts; another whizzed by over his head. The pistol was small, and the man was far enough away for it to be a difficult shot for anyone, but it would still pop a hole in him. He had no interest in bleeding out on the ground in Iquitos.

How the man held himself told Jack this man thought himself a crack shot, a hero. Jack assumed this was another local cartel member, someone not professionally trained.

Shouts rose from the people directly around him. Screams hammered at his ears as people dashed away. He saw two children run across his path, away from the shooter.

Jack ducked his head, keeping it low in a futile attempt to hide behind one of the vendor carts. He crouch-walked in this way toward the opposite wall, soon finding another fish vendor directly in his path.

The vendor was still shouting prices over the heads of the people around, another crowd gathered in front of him. No one here had even heard the shots, though there were still some shouts of confusion to his left.

He needed to distance himself from the shooter so the man wouldn't try a wild potshot again. He turned hard right and began running now, pushing a group of larger men out of his way. He swerved to the left, then ducked back to the right in front of a cart selling strange herbs and medicinal-looking concoctions.

He read the hand-painted sign in Spanish, then got a thought.

This vendor booth had been constructed from three tables in a 'U' shape, and he saw plastic boxes stacked behind it, forming the back of it. The woman smiled at him from behind the front table, and he smiled back, nodding quickly. He wanted to show her he was not interested in what she had to sell or striking up a conversation, even though he was *very* interested in one particular thing.

His eyes scanned the booth for a moment longer before he saw it and turned back to the left again once he was a few feet away from the table. The woman's attention was now on a group of tourists who had sidled up to the front of the table, each light-skinned and wearing a fanny pack, chattering in German.

Perfect.

He would usually never consider stealing from locals, but in this case he was in a hurry. He didn't want to even waste time to pull his pack off his shoulder and dig around for some bills, and he didn't currently have any in his pants pockets.

He came around the booth, aiming for the back-left table where he had seen the small sign. Just then, above the old woman's head, he saw his attacker approaching from the north again.

But this time, he was not alone. Two other men made their way toward the center attacker, each also working diagonally toward Jack.

None of them seemed interested in anything in the market. None of them seemed interested in shopping at all.

Well, this day just got worse.

He felt the Taurus behind his back, knowing it was good

for a last resort but not wanting to cause even more commotion in the square or paint himself as an even larger target. So far, no one knew he had been the man his attacker was shooting at, and he wanted to keep it that way. All he needed was a group of angry and threatened locals pressing in around him, holding him hostage until the attackers could get close enough to finish the job.

No, he would do without the Raging Judge unless he had no other choice. He released his grip on it and sidled up to the table just as the woman looked down to accept money from the tourists she had been talking with.

Now or never, Jack, he told himself.

Jack saw what he was after, then scooped up three bottles and deposited them in his front pocket and turned away from the table as quickly as he'd approached.

But it was too late. The tourists must have seen something, as one of them began speaking rapidly, and the woman turned around and started shouting and pointing at Jack. "Thief!" she shouted. "This man stole from me!"

Jack immediately felt the tension rise around him as he felt all eyes in the market piercing his back. This was certainly not the outcome he had desired.

Just as he feared, the group of larger men he had pushed through earlier was standing nearby, and they all began converging on him, prepared to treat him like a petty thief that needed to be stopped.

They worked around him, making a half-circle so he couldn't escape.

He wanted to turn back, to look at the attackers and see how close they were to his six, but he didn't want to risk getting tackled by one of these locals either. *A rock and a hard place.*

Except the rock was a gun, and the hard place was a bunch of locals who wanted to hurt him.

He swallowed, feeling his new find — the tiny bottles — weighing down his left side. They formed a bump on the side of his pants that stuck out clearly, and it was easy to see that Jack had, in fact, stolen something and shoved it in his pocket.

Was it worth it?

He had no use for the items now, but he had nabbed them in case the opportunity arose.

The last thing he wanted to do was pull his gun on these men and threaten their lives. They were innocent and did not deserve to die fighting a man they didn't know.

But they were still in his way, and Jack had to do something.

CHAPTER 35

VICTOR

VICTOR LOOKED DOWN at his phone once more. It had been vibrating incessantly today, and he had already silenced it for the better half of the morning so he could focus on work. But he was waiting on this call and was happy to see it had finally come. He pulled it up to his ear and answered it quickly.

"Olivia, you have an update?"

His sister's voice came over the line. *"Yes, brother. He is dead."*

Victor closed his eyes and let out a sigh. This was good news, but they still had the pressing issue of the *other* CIA man out there. "And the other? He is leaving a trail of bodies everywhere he goes."

There was a short pause before the reply. *"Yes, brother. I am working on it."*

"That is not what I want to hear. I want him brought to me, where I can see him face-to-face. We must know what he knows — what the CIA thinks of our new route. I will kill him myself after."

"Patience, Victor," Olivia said. *"He is on the run, scared.*

He no longer has his partner with him, and while he seems to be well-trained, he is not making any friends. He will grow tired, weak. The jungle is a rough place for outsiders, as you well know. Give me time, but I will bring him to you."

Victor smiled but felt the strain of a headache behind his eyes. He knew he could count on his sister. She was as hard as he was and always had been. That she was one of the most powerful members of his cartel was one of the best-kept secrets they shared.

No one suspected her. Hardly anyone even knew she existed.

And Victor had worked hard and paid lots of money to keep it that way. His sister was the best operator he had, but because she was family, he rarely let her dictate the terms of operations and missions. She was very good at what she did, but often got in over her head. She liked taking things into her own hands, and Victor was afraid that she would eventually meet her match.

She had operated on a whim about a year ago, deciding to execute the man responsible for stealing from him while working for the Jamaican Port Authority by putting a bullet between his eyes. He had been helpless, locked in a jail cell awaiting trial.

That trial would have ended with the man rotting in prison, but Victor could have used his knowledge and the information he had extracted from the cartel to further his plans.

He had been upset at Olivia's rash actions, but he understood them. She was a soldier through and through, fiercely loyal to Victor. To her family.

But she was even more loyal to the cartel, as she had proven today.

He would never be able to live with himself if she took matters into her own hands again and got herself killed, so he tried to keep her at arm's length, using her for intelligence-gathering and logistics support. She was a gift, a perfect silent partner for Victor's authority, but he did not want to waste this secret — he had to keep her away from the action.

I have a plan," she said. *"Our men are tracking his every move. He is good, but we have more eyes on him than he even knows. He is trying to find you, Victor, so as long as we keep the funnel pointed in your direction —"*

"I will be ready," Victor said, gripping the phone tighter. "It is about time I see my old friend face-to-face once more. He wants to find me, so he will."

She confirmed.

"But Olivia — If you happen to kill him before that, so be it. I want to know what he knows, but my mission is far too important to be sidetracked by this vendetta. Do not waste lives trying to keep him alive. He is but a pawn."

"Of course, brother," Olivia said. *"I will keep you updated. See you soon."*

Victor thanked her once more, then hung up the phone. There was much to do before tomorrow when he would fly to Manaus. His men had done their job well, scaring Jack Barr and preparing the way for the cartel to take over the entire region. Barr was good but naïve; he was too young to understand the dynamics and powers at play. It wasn't just the cartel playing this game — Barr's government had skin in the game.

Victor would kill Barr soon. But if possible, he wanted the CIA man to get closer to him first. For now, their interests were aligned. Barr and Victor, strangely enough, both wanted the same thing.

The leader of the Vínculos — Victor's boss — would die tomorrow, of that Victor was sure. He sensed the CIA wanted the same thing, which must be why they had sent Jack down here in the first place. They wanted to know when the cartel's power structure shifted and changed hands. They wanted to know for sure that Victor was moving onto the throne.

He looked outside the small house he had rented. His assistant was returning, driving a black sedan through the front gate.

Good, he thought. *We need to discuss plans.* There were flights to book, preparations to be made. Tomorrow would be a busy day.

Tomorrow he would take over a cartel.

CHAPTER 36

JACK

JACK RAISED his arms slowly above his head. He stood there, waiting for the half-circle of six locals to do whatever it was they were about to do.

He needed them to hurry — whatever was about to happen, he wanted them to make the first move so he could parry the attack or dodge it and run away. He couldn't afford to stand here, to let the three attackers from behind get close to him. Their pistols were weak, and they were untrained, but even they wouldn't miss from a dozen steps away.

One of the men in front of him spoke first. "Thief?" the man asked. "You stole from her?"

Jack shook his head, gritted his teeth. "I just needed to borrow something. I'm — I'm in a hurry, just passing through."

Two men to his left started toward him. He had known they weren't going to like his response — and six men against one only made them feel more powerful, more prepared to protect their turf and their fellow local shop owner.

"Trust me, you don't want to do that," Jack said, shaking

his head. His arms were still up, but he pulled his hands behind his head, slipping a thumb under the shoulder strap of his pack.

He stared straight ahead at the man speaking to him, but his peripheral vision focused on the two approaching from his left. He knew he had only seconds to act before the other three men behind him would be in a position to take an easy shot at the back of his head.

He forced the issue. He crouched down, sliding his hand fully under the strap and then wriggling out of it, simultaneously moving his right hand to the strap on that side, holding it and letting it fall as he crouched. The whole movement created momentum, and he stood up and into the man approaching from his far left. He swung as hard as he could, arm extended, his heavy pack making sick contact with the side of the man's face. It was enough force to send him flying, even leaving his feet.

Jack pulled the pack back around and aimed at the second man, but this guy was ready. The man ducked out of the way, and Jack almost found himself off-balance. He slid the pack back over his shoulders and kicked out a foot as the man dodged to his right. This impact found a home on the man's shin, and he howled in pain. Jack ran to the side, aiming for the brick wall of the building behind and next to the fish stand. He ran two steps up the side of the building and then sprang off of it, aiming at one of the men who had previously been standing in front of him. He landed on top of this man, tackling him to the ground while the other three simply watched in stunned surprise.

They hadn't expected parkour and acrobatic moves.

Jack was no gymnast, but he was in great shape and knew

how to use his body to gain momentum. Still, the injured leg hurt, and he almost went down.

He swung his right elbow around and connected with a man's temple, knocking him out instantly. He would have a major headache later, but he wouldn't be dead. Finally, he picked himself up off the ground while sliding the Taurus out of his back and holding it out so the others could see.

He didn't need to fire it to threaten these guys. They already knew he wouldn't go down easy, to let them also see that he was better trained than they might have thought.

A shot from another pistol whizzed by his head. He turned to the right and noticed the same man who had attacked him before now on the other side of the line of carts, only twenty feet away.

More shouts echoed around him as passersby realized the first attack they had heard had in fact been shots fired, and Jack had been the culprit.

The three men still standing, including the one who had been talking to him, now backed away with their arms up, mimicking Jack's motions.

He spoke quickly in Spanish. "I told you; I don't want to hurt you. I mean no harm. These men are after me, and I needed to borrow something from her."

As he spoke, he moved to the side, keeping the Taurus pointed at the three locals, but his eyes focused on the three attackers still making their way over to him from the other side of the cart.

The man who had been speaking nodded at him, and Jack didn't wait for any more of an invitation than that. He bolted away, sprinting as fast as he could through a new break that had formed in the crowd. He needed to make it to the edge of the market, to the road leading down to the port.

This time no one blocked his way. It was as if the entire market had stopped what it was doing, the myriad noises and movements becoming one, each of them watching Jack's actions and deciding for themselves that he was the good guy.

They parted to let him pass, then coagulated again into a throbbing mass, blocking the attackers who were still trying to push their way through.

Jack ran harder now, his narrow escape giving him the adrenaline boost he needed to reach the edge of the market square. He got there in seconds, immediately turning left.

...at which point he slammed straight into a man wearing all black, holding an assault rifle.

CHAPTER 37

HEAVENS

HEAVENS LIFTED THE PHONE. He began speaking immediately to his boss, not wanting to waste a second. "Reynolds, Heavens. We've got activity. Just had shots fired in the marketplace in downtown Iquitos."

He waited for the reply. There was a one-second delay already, since his phone was connected via satellite to the servers that would digitize and eventually direct the call to Reynolds' office in DC.

"Understood. I'm assuming our targets have been playing leapfrog with the locals?"

"Affirmative, sir. Our men have just been providing recon, surveilling the situation. Seems the CIA guy has made himself a few friends since he's been down here. We don't see the other guy, though. Only one asset. My understanding was that he had a partner."

There was a long sigh. Heavens could almost see his boss grabbing the bridge of his nose, pulling his glasses down and squeezing, a common tic he used when stressed. *"Yeah, he* should *have a partner. If they're not together, that means there's probably a body somewhere. Not your concern, however. We need to keep our eyes on the prize. Especially now."*

"Sir?"

"There have been... maneuverings. Lots of rich assholes throwing money around. For some reason, seems like Congress can't decide which way they want it — half of them seem to think we should be in bed with the Vinculos cartel, and half of them seem to think they're the enemy."

Heavens nodded as his boss spoke. Neither he nor the owner and lead of Stonefire cared much for these sorts of political hand-wavings — all they wanted was money from a completed job — but it did make things rather complicated when situations changed overnight. "I'm assuming someone has countermanded our previous orders?"

There was a chuckle. *"'Countermanded' is a kind way to put it,"* Reynolds said. *"Rumor has it, there have been some pretty disgusting threats made. That's a typical Tuesday for those assholes on the Hill. But yeah, it sort of changes things a bit. We need to be careful where we step."*

Heavens waited. Finally, he asked the dreaded question. "What are you saying, sir? Mission parameters regarding the asset changed, as well?"

"Correct. Recon isn't the primary objective, Heavens. Not anymore. I'm being told we need to totally prevent any *American intelligence operations in the region, using force, if necessary."*

Heavens frowned. "Sir, that's the sort of order the Army should be getting, not us. I'm four guys."

"Yeah, and I'm pretty sure Army Intelligence has already gotten those orders. As has CIA and Navy Intelligence and whoever else has assets in the region. This whole thing will blow up in our faces tomorrow when this cartel boss is offed,

and those cold windbags back home are afraid all their fingers in the pie will leave fingerprints on it. They don't want to have anything to do with this, so they change their mind about their involvement. Easier plausible deniability, I guess."

Heavens sighed. "But we're left holding the bag. We're the ones who get to fight their war?"

"Pretty much," Reynolds said. "Same mission, new objective. I need you to take him out. Both, if the other one pops up."

"Just to be clear, you're asking me and my men to take out an *American* asset?"

It wasn't that Reynolds had never asked something difficult of Heavens — he had certainly eliminated American citizens before — but it was still a heavy burden to bear, especially when the American in question was no terrorist. He wasn't one of the bad guys.

"If you're able to scare him away from following the Vínculos cartel, so be it. We just need him away from the mission field for a couple of days. Taking him out gets the job done cleanly, but if you want to risk getting close, so be it."

Heavens paused. "You don't *want* him dead."

"Hell, Heavens, I don't want any Americans dead. But..."

"Still, you're asking us to eliminate an American... on what grounds? Some penny pincher in Congress thinks this will push their bill forward?"

Reynolds' voice shifted, dropping. *"I'm not asking; I'm telling. I'm sending another squad down as well; they should be there in half a day. You will be in charge of both teams, and I'll double the pay."*

Heavens raised an eyebrow. "Damn, somebody really does want these guys dead."

"Somebody wants the ultimate plausible deniability, Heavens. Dead men tell no tales."

"So I've heard. But you're basically admitting that they got to you, too."

The pause this time was even longer. *"They have me by the short hairs, Heavens."*

"How so?" Heavens knew his boss was a smart man, someone who protected himself. But he was no match for the greedy lawyers and backstabbing professional blackmailers who populated DC. If there was any dirt — or leverage of any kind — to be found on Reynolds, someone had certainly found it.

And it sounded like they were trying to exploit it.

"I can't say, obviously. But... I'll lose everything. It's not worth it, Heavens. Just take him out, be done with it. Heavens, if this fails, it'll blow back on you, too —"

"Is that a threat, Reynolds? You going to find something to hold over my head, too?"

Heavens felt this whole thing spiraling quickly out of control. He didn't have a ton of money socked away somewhere; he didn't have a massive nest egg someone could use to threaten him.

But he had family, friends. There were people who could harm him by threatening people he cared for.

"Rules of engagement, sir?"

"You're not playing defense anymore, Heavens. Take out the target and hop on the next flight home. Collateral damage should be avoided, but not at all costs. We just need these guys out of the picture, and I need it to happen fast. My other phone is ringing off the hook, and I'd love to give them good news before the end of the day."

"Copy that, sir." Heavens ended the call and stuck the

phone back into his pocket. He rubbed his temples with a free hand. They had the proper loadout — they were ready for a mission like this.

But was *he* ready? Nothing about this op added up. It seemed hasty, tossed together. Everything he had heard so far explaining the 'why' of the mission just seemed like a bunch of toddlers arguing over a toy.

His job was simple now, and that's what unnerved him. The simple jobs were always the most complex, in a matter of speaking. Somebody wanted somebody dead, and they called him to do it.

Heavens' job wasn't to ask questions. He had made a career — a very lucrative one — *not* asking questions. He followed orders, did the dirty jobs no one else wanted to do, and he got paid well.

Now, Reynolds was offering to double their pay if they accomplished this latest task. Heavens had already committed to the job, and he knew that sometimes jobs' objectives changed. Reynolds wouldn't have to entice him by doubling his pay in order to keep Heavens on task.

Which told Heavens that his boss was desperate.

JACK BACKPEDALED and tried to get around him. The man said something into his ear, but Jack didn't stick around long enough to hear it, only that it had been in English.

Running into the commando seemed to surprise both of them, which was good — if the guy *hadn't* been surprised, Jack would have been dead. He hadn't been aiming the rifle at Jack, nor had he tried to fight Jack when they bumped into each other.

Who the hell was that guy?

The man had seemed as surprised to see him as Jack was.

Jack pushed away the new questions and opted to ignore them for now, aiming once more in the direction of the port a few blocks away, which should be just ahead and around a bend in the road.

Before he could get too far from the marketplace square, he saw a sign to his right that caught his attention. It was another tourist attraction, one he had heard of and read a little about but had not considered visiting. He wasn't here for sightseeing, but this particular place might now be useful to him. First, it was a place to hide from the people still chasing him. Second, it should offer a way to get to the port and his meetup location faster than by just following the streets around.

There were still at least three cartel men after him, plus any number of Shining Path watchers and soldiers in the area who surely knew he was here.

Not to mention whoever these mercenaries were that Jack had slammed into. Jack couldn't begin to understand who the newcomer was, but he knew the man would not have been working alone. He had watched him speak into his comm, talking to someone he was working with somewhere.

And Jack had to assume the man was talking about *him*.

That means another group trying to intercept me here.

He needed to disappear, quickly. There was no way he could simply walk to the port and meet up with his three cartel buddies now, not immediately after everyone in town saw his face. He needed to disappear for as long as possible, until just before his scheduled departure time, and the sign he had just seen offered a place to do just that.

Jack made it to the tourist spot depicted on the sign fifteen minutes later, jogging the entire way. He had not seen anyone else trying to attack him, nor had he seen any of the mercenary's buddies, and he needed to regain some energy. Sprinting through the streets, the building under construction, and then the marketplace would take its toll sooner or later. Besides that, his leg was still slightly sore, and running would only hurt it more.

As it was, he needed to get some space and use some of the painkillers from his pack. He couldn't do more for his knee; a few pills would be the best care he could receive at this point.

Perhaps when he got onboard the Manaus-bound riverboat, he could take some time to rest and recuperate.

He passed the front entrance to the tourist attraction without delay and walked down to where the canopy tour welcoming station lay, just in front of a sprawling section of rainforest.

This wasn't the only tour of its kind nearby, but it was the largest and most popular. Still, few people were standing around, and nothing in the way of security. Breaking into a place like this was impossible, because there was nothing to break into but the jungle itself. A small, rectangular asphalt parking lot sat to his right, while a turnstile-fed entrance to the canopy walkways was just in front of him.

As he was walking slightly downhill, he could see the canopy walkways from here. A few sloped upward, passing over a low section of forest, while others he could see in the distance, arranged from one looming tree to another, extending out into the distance.

He knew from his research that the space between Iquitos and the port area he was trying to reach was almost completely covered by this very attraction. The canopy tour rope bridges would form a faster — if not direct — path through the trees, hopefully dropping him right onto the doorstep of the river-boat and its police officer-attired contacts Rudy's asset had informed him of.

He approached the main walkway and saw a line where a group of visitors waited behind a turnstile and a young employee collecting tickets, but he had no interest in playing tourist right now. He needed to get onto the canopy tour's land and disappear, and he needed to do it quickly.

Jack waited for the young woman wearing a badge to start

talking with the tourists at the entrance of the first of the rope bridges, and he made a large loop around this visitor building to sneak around the back. He thought he saw the three men from the market behind him, already gaining ground, but they weren't looking in his direction.

It was a chilling observation. They didn't know to look for him here, so how had they gotten here so fast?

Unless his assumptions about how many watchers the cartel had were woefully out-of-touch.

He decided not to press his luck. He needed to assume, from now on, that *everyone* here — tourist and local alike — knew exactly who he was and what he looked like, and that it was only a matter of time before someone spotted him and called it in to their superior.

The chase was very much still on. As if on cue, his knee acted up again and urged him to slow.

He ignored the pain. Jack found a fence running alongside the back of the building where the tourists and visitors had been waiting, and he jumped this and ran straight into the thick jungle. Though this land was protected and owned by the state, with permits issued to the tourism company, it was impossible to completely close off, as doing so would prevent the natural ecosystem from flourishing.

The jungle was not something that could be owned — or tamed.

Jack found a platform, about thirty feet directly above him, built of logs and metal banding and no small amount of massive turnbuckles and bolts, with thick, wound ropes attached on two sides. He followed the ropes down and saw where they hit the ground, finding another platform there.

He climbed over the rope gate, entered this platform, then

started up the rope bridge to the platform that marked the beginning of the course.

This canopy tour company had built numerous platforms in this region, all connected by rope bridges. Tourists could pay to spend a day traversing the bridges and ladders, swinging high out over the Peruvian rainforest. Most of these platforms were mounted to one another by rope bridges but enforced with metal turnbuckles and clamps for safety.

But not all of them. A few of the platforms — closed off to the public, were considered historic, maintained in situ as they had been left by the tribes that had built them. The bridges leading to these platforms were made of twisted rope created from jungle plants and tree bark, and the platforms themselves were nothing but logs and sticks fitted into angles and notches in tree trunks, then fastened to the tree with more rope.

Jack aimed for the left side, where a sign pointed the way to 'natural bridges,' and jumped over the low fence rail blocking the way.

Assuming the old natural rope bridges were still intact, Jack figured this direction would get him to the port in less than fifteen minutes. Far faster than by just following the city blocks around this forested area.

He was halfway up the first angled rope bridge, nearing the platform about fifteen feet off the ground, when he heard more shouting behind him. "There he is!"

Immediately, shots started ringing out, but flew wide. While his pursuers were within earshot, they were nowhere near close enough to get a decent shot lined up.

The jungle swallowed the gunshot sounds, but the men were close. He looked back and saw the first of them climbing up to the rope bridge. Thankfully, the jostling and shaking of the rope floor forced the pursuer to hold the rope rails with two hands — ensuring his gun was not in one of them.

But the other two were working their way through the jungle as well, moving underneath the platform he was aiming for and trying to get into a position where they could fire up at him.

He needed to move faster. He needed to reach the platform.

And he pulled out the Taurus from his back, because he needed to do something else, too.

He needed to kill again.

CHAPTER 39

JACK

JACK'S SHORTCUT may have been a bad decision. He thought that by skating through the trees, traveling over the forest floor, he could skip navigating the thick ferns and luscious fauna down below, as well as travel over the heads of anyone still trying to pursue him.

It should have been faster.

But while it was faster, it made him a sitting duck.

His mind raced as he tried to compartmentalize and organize what he knew of the factions now chasing after him. He knew that engaging any Shining Path soldiers would only end in calling *more* attention to himself, and then there was the overt threat of the cartel members themselves, like the three from back at the market who were now chasing him through the trees.

Still, if it were just these two factions to worry about, Jack could stop and start taking potshots at the three men chasing after him; he knew he was a better shot, and he had the upper hand. He could easily turn back now and take out the one climbing the bridge behind him.

But the two on the ground would then have a clean shot of him, and they had disappeared deeper into the jungle, likely getting in position to start shooting at him from below.

But there was still the *third* faction — the new group — that he had literally bumped into. Clearly mercenaries, clearly soldiers for hire. Their gear and tech were top-of-the-line, so he had to assume they were better trained than he was, better prepared to kill.

And yet... the man he had bumped into had *not* killed him, nor had he even tried. Had he just gotten lucky? Scared the guy?

No, that didn't make sense, either. He had bumped into a man who ostensibly had been watching the market, ostensibly been watching *Jack*. He should have known Jack was coming in that direction.

If the guy had wanted to kill Jack, Jack would be long dead by now.

So, what did that mean? Where did that put these men in terms of Jack's progress through Iquitos? What were they here for, if not to join in the fight to take down the rogue CIA agent making things difficult in the Peruvian rainforest?

As he tried to place each particular faction in its own space in his brain, he prioritized them as well. The obvious immediate threat was the one climbing up the tree behind him. The two heading for the space beneath his platform had disappeared farther into the woods, likely trying to get in front of him.

Jack had no doubt they would pop up soon, they weren't just going to wait around for Jack to come back down. They would get in position, try to snipe him as he ran across the rope bridges, or simply wait at the bottom of whatever tower he ended up coming down.

But they had left their third attacker to fend for himself. The guy behind him now was moving as slowly as Jack had been, so Jack felt he might have a slight edge over him now.

It was almost humorous; Jack had a crippling fear of heights. Because of the rope railings and reasonable heights, the platforms and rope bridges had not caused him any issue. But the platforms would only get taller, only get farther from the forest floor down below.

He remembered the cruise ship — the tension in his hands and wrists as he clung to the top of the rock-climbing wall on deck.

And that had been *before* he had inadvertently crossed paths with the cartel.

So, ironically, while the last six months had been like drinking from a firehose in technical knowledge and training, his boss and handler had made sure to spend plenty of time helping him through his biggest fear: heights.

He had not only completed eight different ropes courses in record time, but he had also done them on the advanced mode — jumping from the tops of vertical logs, 75 feet in the air. He had hopped around up there like they were lily pads, trying to ignore the anxiety of feeling completely out of control if he were to fall.

So while he was not completely cured of his phobia, he now felt capable of traveling quickly over an otherwise terrifying set of creaking, weathered rope bridges, higher and higher above the jungle floor.

And there was no harness now, either. To fall from these

heights would be certain death, no matter how soft the forest floor tried to make his landing.

Even now, he heard the strained groans and felt the gentle swaying as his weight fought against the old ropes, worn and beaten over decades of use in the harsh jungle.

But there was no other choice. If he stopped now to take out the man behind him, his two partners would have an easy shot at his back.

And if he stopped to take *them* out, the man climbing behind him would catch up. He needed to keep going forward, keep pressing on. He would stop and fight, but it was too early yet.

He closed his eyes and swallowed, pushing the anxiety away. Not the anxiety caused by his fear of heights, but from the fear of getting shot in the back.

Or the foot. Or the side. Or the head.

CHAPTER 40

JACK

JACK WAS HALFWAY across the rope bridge when the men down below began firing again.

He ducked, not sure at first where they were coming from, then realized why it was hard to tell.

The three men pursuing him had been coordinating their efforts all along. The two men who had disappeared into the forest had doubled back, each flanking one side of this rope bridge he was on. They waited until the man chasing Jack up the ladder had reached the top of the platform and traversed the first of the rope bridges.

Now, all three started firing at the same time. It was a challenging shot for all three men, but one of the bullets nicked the side of the bridge, right where his hand had been, fraying the pieces of old rope there into twine.

Jack did not trust the strength of the bridge to carry his and the pack's weight, especially if any more shots hit the ropes holding it up.

Maybe taking the old route was a bad idea after all.

He leaped forward, trying to scale the rest of the rope

bridge in front of him to get to the next platform. He reached it in another four seconds, then rolled past the gigantic trunk of the tree it had been built around. Three rounds smacked into the side of the tree where his head had been only a moment before.

The two men on the ground could not get a shot upward now as the wooden platform extended around the tree five feet in every direction, but Jack was pinned against its trunk. If he crept forward to look for them, he would offer his head as a clear target.

He realized that the three shots had landed close to where he had been from a shallow angle — meaning they hadn't been fired by the men down below. He turned around, Taurus in hand, and fired three shots at the man still pursuing over the rope bridge. The smart play would have been for the man to wait back on the previous platform, to use its steadiness to aim and get into a more successful position from which to fire on Jack.

But he had not made the smart move. He was eager to be the one to take down the prize.

For his eagerness, he was rewarded with a bullet to the chest.

Jack's second shot sailed wide, but the third hit the man in his right leg. He was already going down from the hit to the chest, and Jack saw that he was wearing no body armor. A round stain of blood was already forming on his chest, and he saw it beginning to spit from the corners of his mouth and nose as well.

He was as good as dead, but he still had a gun in his hand.

Jack checked his magazine, knowing by the weight of the gun he still had plenty of rounds left but wanting a precise count. Ammunition was precious, and he wasn't sure he would be able to reload and re-outfit himself anytime soon.

Satisfied he had a couple of rounds to spare, he fired two more into the man on the rope bridge.

There was more firing from behind and below him now as the two men on the ground tried their best to aim upward and hit him through the platform.

He felt the *thwap* of the bullets slapping against the underside of the platform, but none punched through. Their small rounds would not stand a chance against the thick wooden beams and planks that held together the platform Jack was standing on.

However, he would not have the luxury of staying on this platform forever.

He needed to reach a point where he could fire back at them without getting shot. He had the higher ground, as well as the better shot, so this would have been no issue.

But there were two of them and only one of him, and they had smartly decided to split up, covering Jack from both sides.

He had one more grenade but didn't want to waste it in the hopes of only taking out one man. Besides, out here in the thick jungle, the explosion would be tempered by the trees and leaves themselves, not having any hard walls to bounce shrapnel off of.

He heard shouts from another direction now, surprised. All of the tourists and visitors on the canopy tour bridges were focused back near the main building, and they had been taken to a route of bridges that had been modernized, likely for safety reasons. As such, he had not seen anyone else out on the rope bridges around him. Besides, he assumed that after the men had started firing at him, the employees would have pulled everyone inside and called the authorities.

He had no idea who was shouting now — what new arrivals to the scene had shown up — but a few seconds later, he got his answer.

More gunshots sang through the trees, only this time they were from an assault rifle.

He wiggled his ears, turning his head to take in the noise. It sounded an awful lot like an M4 carbine. The rounds smacked into the tree above Jack's head once more, and he instinctively rolled to the side, shifting his position around the tree again.

The mercenaries.

Whoever they were, they were now trying to kill him as well. Jack knew by the sound of the shots and the direction they had come from that the men were farther away than the cartel guys pursuing him, but that did not make him feel any better about the situation. Their guns were also far more powerful, with much farther range, and they were better trained.

Whomever he had run into outside the open-air marketplace had followed him here — and he had brought friends.

He wasn't interested in staying put on this platform, but now he had even more reason to move.

Jack needed a new plan, one that didn't involve running across rope bridges and exposing himself to the army down below, or cowering on a platform, waiting for someone to move into a position where they could get a clean shot.

And all he was armed with was his gun. As trusty as the *Raging Judge* felt in his hand, he had only one. He still had the items he had taken from the table in the market stuffed into his pocket — the small vials of powder — but these were useless to him now, with this much distance between him and each of the attackers.

And how many enemies were here, anyway? He knew there were two remaining cartel men down below, not to mention any number of reinforcements that would be on the way once they found out Jack was alive and accounted for, but there were also the mercenaries.

He shook his head, trying to make sense of all of it. Trying to figure out his next best move.

He knew what it was in an instant.

The forest around him was different here — the space between this platform and the direction of the port sloped away from him. The homogenous rainforest had morphed into a ripe jungle valley, starting just below him.

Jack knew what he had to do, but that didn't mean he liked it. Heights were not his thing, no matter how much training he had just gone through. Sitting up here on the platform, now over thirty feet above the ground, did not help, either.

But he had no choice. There was only one way out that the men below wouldn't expect. First, he needed a tool besides the gun. He peeled the pack off his back and swung it around. Unzipping it, he watched the forest around him, content in the temporary silence. He didn't have a lot of time, but their maneuverings down below would offer him a bit of reprieve to prepare for the next phase.

He found Rudy's combat knife and bit it, holding it between his teeth as he swung the pack back over his shoulder. Then he rolled over the edge of the platform and held onto it with a hand. His eyes adjusted quickly, providing him the sensory data he needed to spot the first of the attackers close by.

They didn't see him — yet.

He held onto the bridge with a single hand, still swinging, while he fired three rounds from the Taurus. One of them hit its mark, clipping the man in the shoulder. He went down, but Jack fired two more rounds into the bushes the man had been hiding behind.

Good enough for government work, he mumbled.

He slid the Taurus back into its holster, taking a brief moment to get his bearings. His arm burned with the exertion, holding him and his pack with just a finger grip on the planks. Once his Taurus was away, he used his other hand to steady his balance, then brought his left hand up to retrieve the knife again.

He really hated what he was about to do, but it had to be done.

Jack hefted the thick blade up to the first of the three ropes that held the old bridge to the platform. He hated desecrating ancient tribal work, but he had no other choice.

CHAPTER 41

JACK

WHILE JACK HAD BEEN EXAMINING the space around the platform he was on, he had noticed something unique about this section of canopy bridges. This rope bridge was anchored in three spots instead of two. Rather than two trees holding a bridge between them, this bridge stretched from one tree to another but had a length of coiled rope stretching to a third tree, about fifty feet away from the middle of the platform.

The triangle was skinny and elongated, the two distant trees close together across the expanse of deep valley down below. The opposite cliff was about a hundred feet away, a bit higher than the ground on this side.

He was no physicist — and he certainly didn't have time to think it through. But he figured this meant that severing the ropes would mean the bridge would not simply fall straight from one side to the other, but rather pulled diagonally.

He was right.

But that meant he was now swinging freely, gripping one of the sturdy ropes he had just cut through, and the bridge itself was falling into the valley. His heart caught in his throat as he fell straight down, dropping a hundred feet alongside the edge of the cliff in seconds. He squeezed the rope with both hands, his Taurus behind his back and Rudy's knife between his teeth. His eyes bugged out of his head. Had he calculated wrong? Was he going to hit the treetops in the valley below before he started swinging toward the opposite side?

The bottom of the arc came quickly, tensing the rope and almost yanking Jack's grip from it. It would have been the end of him too, considering there was still another twenty-five feet to fall before he hit the valley canopy.

The knife clattered out of his mouth with the impact, falling away to the forest floor. He held tight to the rope, the momentum shifting, now swinging freely over the valley floor. His biceps and wrists bulged with the exertion, the forces pulling him straight forward and whipping him slightly to the side as the third anchor point pulled back.

He swung like a monkey, a crazed Tarzan holding on for dear life. The entire rope swing, now free from their tightly wound mounts on the platform behind him, unwound and fell apart as he flew. Frayed sections of sinew fell away.

Still he held on.

Jack reached the apex of the arc and began swinging back up over the opposite wall of the narrow valley, hoping against all hope that the ropes would hold just a little longer.

Three seconds. Three more seconds.

It was an interminable amount of time for him to wait, but still he held.

There was no aiming, no changing his trajectory. He would be deposited on the hill wherever his makeshift swing decided to place him. He winced, hoping that it would be a relatively soft landing.

It wasn't.

Jack landed on *very* solid ground.

He had let go of the destroyed bridge near the end of its upward swing, then tumbled end over end, his leg bashing against a rock which caused him to turn sideways and start a barrel roll down the shallow downward slope on the other side of the valley.

It felt as though he rolled down for an hour. Finally coming to a stop, he lay in a daze, the squawking jungle birds and unseen animals unhappy with the newcomer's noisy arrival.

But Jack was unhappy as well, about something very different.

He had landed on a rock, then bounced over a small bush, breaking most of its branches in the process.

And one of these branches had been shoved straight through his side.

He groaned in agony as he slid his hand down the backside of his body. Immediately, it came away slick with blood. He was leaning on his left side, the stick protruding from his right.

He closed his eyes, wincing in pain, squeezing back tears.

It felt even worse than being stabbed, as this thumb-sized, six-inch-long stick was far dirtier and more jagged than a sharpened blade.

And it had caused even more pain because of that.

He whimpered quietly, already hearing the shouts and vocal signals from the two teams pursuing him on the other side of the valley. There was still gunfire, and Jack assumed they had met up. *Clearly they're not working together*, he thought.

He glanced around. He had taken the 'direct' route and ruined the bridge in the process. The teams wouldn't be able to cross the valley easily, but another bridge spanned the distance about 500 feet to the west. They would all have to move and converge on that spot, or pull back and go all the way around, hoping to catch him on the other side.

This was Jack's opportunity to get away and get down to the port. If he could persuade the three men waiting for him there to leave quickly enough, he might even be able to get there and exit the scene without being spotted. But Jack was not going to make it in time if he was bleeding out on the jungle floor.

Maybe I will *just die here.*

An injury like this could be potentially life-threatening, but he had enough first-aid training and the equipment in his pack to treat himself.

He slowly reached over his shoulder and slid the pack off of it again, letting the weight of it and gravity cause it to roll to his front side, but that ended up making him stretch, causing even more tearing where the stick had gone in. Still, it was better than hitting the stick with the pack directly.

He needed to remove the stick, clean up the laceration as well as he could, then treat it with something antiseptic and wrap it in gauze.

No small feat for a guy stuck to the rainforest floor, chased by enemy troops.

He fumbled around the pack once more, pulling the first-aid kit out. He pulled the zipper with his teeth, opening the bag and letting its contents fall out onto the jungle floor. *Doesn't matter*, he thought. *I need to move quickly.*

He was going for speed, not care.

He picked up a roll of gauze and a sterilized antiseptic cleaning wipe. There was a small bottle of isopropyl alcohol as well in the pile, and he pulled these three things aside. He would need them later, but not yet. First, he needed to get the stick out and stanch the blood flow, so he could at least keep moving. Once onboard the riverboat, he could perform a full and thorough cleaning. Then stitches and a strong painkiller, and hopefully the people he was trying to meet up with would have some sort of drinkable alcohol to *really* numb the pain.

But for now, he needed something that would dry quickly and allow him to at least move toward his destination. He chose a spray-on adhesive and another antiseptic wipe to hold back the blood for a moment. It would be tough work, not passing out from pain while holding the inch-wide hole closed long enough to spray the super-strong adhesive over it. It was rated for wounds of this magnitude but intended only to be a temporary fix. Eventually, the blood would soften the hold and seep through, opening the wound again.

And it was certainly not meant for a guy to be running downhill, chased by gun-wielding cartel men.

The stick had to come out first, though. He found another branch nearby, pulled on it, and broke it free. He shoved this into his mouth, biting down as he had with the knife. It wasn't much of an anesthesia, but it was the best he had.

With the antiseptic pad in one hand, he reached back with his right hand and gripped the stick. Already, the pain was unbelievable. He had barely touched it, and he knew he would have to twist it to wrench it free.

Judging by the pain and where he could feel it inside his body, he guessed it had gone in about three full inches, perhaps four. He closed his eyes, bit down as hard as he could on the stick in his mouth, and twisted quickly, yanking the stick out with enough force to give it momentum but hopefully not enough to cause additional damage.

He screamed through his teeth, and then passed out.

He awoke a few seconds later, blood pouring out of the open wound. His eyes widened, then rolled around. He was already growing dizzy, but he forced his mind to stay focused.

Get the wound clean. Get the bandage on.

And get down the hill.

JACK AWOKE COVERED IN BLOOD. More blood than he thought possible. Apparently he had passed out again, this time for a longer period.

Shit.

The stick had fallen out of his mouth, but his right hand held the bloody stub of the other one. The wound was gaping, flushing blood over his pants and torso. He wailed in pain as he brought the antiseptic wipe around to push over the blood flow. He knew he had lost a significant amount of blood, but he must not have been out for too long.

He no longer heard the shouts of the men pursuing him, so there was that. Whether it was good or bad news remained to be seen — they may have given up the chase, or they might be already working their way around, hoping to cut him off at the pass. Jack was satisfied that none of them knew where he was ultimately trying to go, so at least he could move toward his destination without much interference.

Or so he hoped. For all he knew, he wouldn't be moving at all.

The bandage pulled away a bit of coagulated blood, and the open wound began gushing more. Jack pinched the skin closed, ignoring the sharp pain as his dirty fingers worked around the skin, and he did his best to hold it shut against his slippery fingers.

He applied the adhesive bandage generously — in that there was nothing clean left of it when he was finished. He just sort of slopped it all over the hole, hoping it would hold long enough to get gauze around it. One bandage was not going to cut it.

He had been laying on his left elbow, and that hand was almost completely useless now, long since having fallen asleep. He shook it free, then shifted a bit, now lying flat on his back. He saw the rock in the bush he had bounced over about twelve feet up the hill. It would be very clear to anyone tracking that a large object had moved in this direction, and he knew the pool of blood on the forest floor and leaves surrounding him would be like a beacon.

He needed to move, at least get away from here. A few monkeys had stopped whatever it was they were doing to peer in on him, eyeing him suspiciously. They weren't a threat, but they represented the constant threat the jungle itself posed. Somewhere, something was looking at him. Waiting to see if he was an easy meal or not.

He groaned and pulled himself up to a sitting position, testing to see if the adhesive bandage and gauze had stanched the blood flow. A bit seeped out, and he used the now-wet roll of gauze to dab it away. Then he unrolled the gauze again, tore off a foot-long section of blood-soaked material with his teeth, and began wrapping his entire torso with it. He placed a cleaning pad on top of the adhesive bandage. The two chemicals would not cause the adhesive to loosen, but there was a chance the cleaning compound would make its way down into the cut and provide extra protection from anything trying to get in.

It was basic battlefield medicine. Clean, treat, seal. If you couldn't do the first two, at least stop the blood flow and get to safety. It was the sort of thing that wouldn't hold up anywhere near a doctor's office or hospital, but he wasn't anywhere near one to begin with.

After the gauze, he applied some tape from the first-aid kit over the hole, sealing it shut. It was going to be nasty business taking this all off and pulling against the dried blood, but that was a future Jack problem. Right now, he needed to get out of the forest in order to stay alive.

He shuffled all the leaves and dirt away, and the remaining first-aid items into the small kit, zipped it closed and tossed it back into his pack, then pushed against the pack itself to come to his knees.

The pain was there, certainly, but less so than it had been before. He grabbed a small pack of sealed medication — acetaminophen — and popped the two pills into his mouth, swallowing them dry. He steeled himself, taking a few mouthfuls of air and pumping them back out, then pressed against the pack and tried to stand. He fell once, then again, but finally forced his legs to comply and tore upward with a force he was sure would rip the bandage and tape completely off of his side.

Surprisingly, it held well, and though the pain was excruciating, he was now upright.

He almost screamed trying to get the pack on but slid it slowly enough over his shoulder that the weight transferred to his back easily enough.

All that was left to do was start walking.

He did, slowly at first, every step causing him agony. Eventually, his body seemed to understand that Jack was not in an argumentative mood. He was going to move, whether his body liked it or not. He checked his compass on his belt, aimed the right direction, and continued on.

Best guess was he would get there in about fifteen minutes under normal conditions.

These conditions were decidedly *not* normal, and he had to admit it was going to take probably twice that long to stumble all the way to the port.

He really hoped the guys would wait for him.

CHAPTER 43

JACK

THE THREE POLICE officers were clearly ready to go. He saw them from a distance, from within the jungle. Jack had already made them wait an extra ten minutes, but he saw two of them now, tossing the mooring off of the pier, one of them pushing the two-story boat off the dock. Another man stood on the second-floor deck, peering out into the jungle.

Jack tried to shout, the words escaping him. "Wait — help!"

The pack was impossibly heavy now, and his side was leaking again. He was weak, the lack of blood and energy taking its toll. He wanted to toss the pack, to let it roll down this last hill toward the water, but he knew that to part with it was to part with his only lifeline.

He almost felt the heavy brick of cocaine inside, his ticket aboard the boat.

He waved, using his left hand so he wouldn't inadvertently stretch his right side and the gaping wound there. He felt blood trickling down over his belly, knew that the seeping was continuing as his blood thinned with the exertion.

I'm going to make it. I have *to make it.*

He thought of Rudy. How he had sacrificed everything to set this up.

He thought of Kate, how she had urged him into the CIA's Directorate of Operations. To become a CIA field officer.

He thought of his kids. The whole reason he was here now — protecting them, keeping them safe.

I'm going to make it.

Rudy's asset had been right — as they came into view, Jack saw that these men were dressed as police officers. He didn't know if they were crooked cops, paid off by the cartel, or if they were in disguise themselves. It didn't matter to Jack; he just needed to get there.

He fell, then slid on his butt and feet down the hill. About halfway down, still waving frantically, he saw the man on the upper deck begin to shout. The man snapped his fingers, then pointed at Jack, still yelling.

The man who had pushed the boat off the dock had jumped on again, but raced again to the edge, leaning over the railing and looking up the hill.

Jack waived more frantically now, tried to tell them to wait.

The boat slid farther out, but another few seconds passed, and he heard its motor start, the third policeman now driving. He piloted the boat backward toward shore, and Jack felt a wave of relief pass over him.

Finally, he thought. *Finally, I can relax. Just get... to the... boat.*

He pulled himself back to his feet once more, shifting to let the pack settle on his back against the pain of his side, then he walked, one foot in front of the other toward his destination.

He was having a hard time keeping his eyes open. He really

hoped one of these men would be capable of cleaning and dressing a wound, because he wasn't sure he was going to be able to stay present enough to do it himself.

One of the men finally rushed over to him. He saw the police officer examining him, saw his eyes dancing over him, trying to make sense of what he was seeing.

Rather than helping him, however, he asked Jack a question in Spanish. "You have the payment?"

Jack nodded, pulling his eyelids up.

The man waited.

Jack could barely manage a whisper. "On — on the boat."

The man shook his head. "No señor. *Now.* You pay now."

Jack wanted to punch him in the head, but knew he barely had strength to prove he was who he said he was. He let the pack fall off his right shoulder again and swung it around, gripping it tightly with his left hand. The man grabbed for it, but Jack swatted his hand away.

Now *you want to help, asshole?* he thought.

The man looked offended, but Jack didn't care. *The last thing I need is you rummaging through my pack.*

He unzipped its top, then pulled the white brick out.

He handed it over. The man held it up, inspecting it under the sunlight as though it were a hundred-dollar bill. Finally satisfied, he nodded. He turned around and barked something toward the other two members of the crew, but Jack could barely hear over the noise of the engine and his own heartbeat, now pounding loudly in his ears.

The man held onto the brick of cocaine and left Jack on the dock to fend for himself.

Jack doubled down on this man being an asshole.

Cop or no cop, you suck. He forced his mind clear. *I just need to get on the boat.*

He hoisted the pack, felt the bandage on his right side finally tear, felt the blood pouring out freely now.

The pain was excruciating, worse now than it had been when the stick had first entered his side.

Stay... awake...

He gritted his teeth, tried to push back the tears and the pain and the blood.

Hold it together for a few more feet, Barr. You've got this.

He walked forward, seeing no opening on the railing of the boat. Its front end was level with the dock, and he stepped over to it, leaning over the rail and letting it hold his full body weight.

He dropped the pack first, letting it fall heavily to the floor of the open deck on the lower level. He saw that it was not a fishing boat but a tourist boat, one with rows of benches up and down each side. About halfway back, on the center of the deck, was a closed room with stairs nearby that led to the second floor.

He gripped the railing with both hands, then leaned forward. He tried to get a leg up and over but failed. Instead, his entire upper body slipped over the front of the railing, his legs falling harshly behind. He fell into a pile atop his pack, the wound now gushing blood once more. He rolled onto his back and looked up at the bright round dome light on the ceiling, blistering his eyes with its harsh brightness.

He squinted, narrowing his eyes to force the ache away.

The pain subsided then, and his eyes closed.

"WHAT'S YOUR STATUS, HEAVENS?"

Heavens wanted to throw the phone against a wall. His boss, Reynolds, was clearly getting antsy. He *really* wanted this CIA guy taken out for some reason.

He and Alameda had met up behind a small café on the southwest side of town. Joseph and Szymon were still working on the next phase of the mission — and they had met with resistance out in the western quadrant and were taking fire.

Heavens had not planned for this sort of op.

He had not planned to *fail*.

He took a breath. "Sorry to report... he slipped the noose, sir," Heavens said. "We're still tracking him, though."

Reynolds was a good boss, a decent guy. He had made a career running security teams throughout the South American region, and he was good at what he did. He was not explosive, not one to fly off the handle.

But if he were capable of it, it would be now. Heavens waited, wincing in anticipation.

Reynolds's voice came back on the line, even-tempered. *"I*

see. So what's the plan?" The way he spoke told Heavens even more than if he were to have lost his cool and started yelling.

It meant Reynolds was *beyond* pissed.

He was rightfully frustrated, but it also told Heavens that there really was more at stake for his boss. Whatever they had on the guy, Reynolds was in it up to his eyeballs. This couldn't just be about money.

"The plan," Heavens answered, "is to get back out there and find him. Joseph saw the asset inside a canopy tours tourist attraction, but they got pinned down by hostile fire."

"Hostile fire?"

"We're assuming *Vínculos* men. They pinned down Joseph, but Szymon was able to get inside, followed the CIA guy around the long way, and saw the asset stumble down the hill."

"And he couldn't engage?" Reynolds asked.

"Negative, sir," Heavens said. "He met up with some local cops."

"Local cops?" Reynolds asked. *"What's their role in all of this?"*

Heavens shook his head. "Wish I could tell you that, sir. Best guess is they're in on it, too, cartel men. Either working undercover or paid off, but it was clearly part of our asset's plan. Joseph reported that the CIA guy slipped him a block of what looked like cocaine. A big-ass block of it, too. Probably to gain passage on the boat."

He waited, but Reynolds didn't ask further questions.

He continued. "They got on a two-story riverboat. Counted three officers and our asset and took off right away. They're making a pretty good clip heading east on the main waterway. Best guess is they'll be in Manaus sometime early tomorrow morning.

"And you've got plans to follow them?"

"It set us back a bit, but yeah, Alameda and I are working on getting us a ride. The area's *hot*, though, sir. Lots of hostile forces trying to nab this guy as well. Any particular reason we shouldn't hold back, wait it out?"

"Yes," came the immediate reply. "I've got my balls in a vice over here, and the deliverable has not changed. They want this guy out of the picture. I've been told in no uncertain terms that collateral damage will not be an issue. But that extends to these cartel assholes who are trying to take him down as well. The more of them you can take out, the better, in my book. Most of these guys are low-level thugs anyway; no one's going to have recent information or intel we can use against them, so if you need to cut them to ribbons to get to the CIA operative, you have my full permission."

Heavens smiled. At least *that* was good news. His soldiers — his trusted team — were far better with overt guns blazing than stealth maneuverings. They weren't the kind of guys who wanted to sneak around, to take their time hiding out, to go undercover and wait for the opportune moment.

And we get to kill a bunch of actual *bad guys,* Heavens thought.

This just became a smash-and-grab — or, rather, a smash-and-kill. His team was more than capable of doing the smashing, and they had been raring to go at it since they landed in the jungle.

"Copy that, sir," Heavens said. "I'm not going to mess this one up again."

"Shit happens, Heavens, and the op's not over yet. I know it wasn't your fault. How did this guy slip the noose, anyway?"

Heavens chuckled. "He's some kind of badass or something, I guess. I don't know — these CIA spooks have a pretty eclectic library of training and skills. Pretty sure I could take the guy from a brute strength perspective, but he's a slippery one. We had him cornered, but he was high up on a rope bridge and literally sliced through the bindings and swung across the damn valley. My men couldn't get across quickly enough, so they had to go the long way around, shooting through the cartel. It was just dumb luck that he got injured on the landing, sliced his side or something, which slowed him down. We were able to get eyes-on just as he reached his ride at port."

"Jesus," Reynolds said. *"Sounds pretty atypical for an operative, but it's not out of the question. These guys are often military trained as well, and they go through the Farm. But they're not usually caught off-guard like that. Maybe he's missing his partner. He's only human. He's just a guy who wants to finish a job and get home. He has a weakness, like everyone else."*

"He certainly does, sir. And I'm going to find it. Between that and his injuries, I suspect we'll be able to get this over with sometime early morning, assuming we can catch up with his boat."

"Copy that, Heavens," Reynolds said. *"Thanks for the update. Let me know if you need anything else."*

"Sir — you still sending that second team?"

There was a pause. He heard typing, clicking sounds. *"Affirmative. Should be able to link up with you in Manaus. Closest drop zone I can get them to without drawing too much attention."*

"That'll do fine, sir. Thank you. I'm hoping we won't even need the guys, but if we do make it to Manaus without the CIA guy dead, they'll come in handy. Tell them to pack heavy — we can use the guns."

"Already on it," Reynolds said. *"Okay, I'm out. Talk soon."*

Heavens put the phone back in his pocket and glanced over at Alameda. They had a job to do, and though they had lost their prey once, the scent was fresh. The guy was bleeding, barely able to stand. Joseph even said he thought he saw him falling over the railing, basically passing out before he could get on the boat.

If that were true, he was as good as dead already.

"You ready?" he asked Alameda, who had been listening in on the phone call using his own comm system.

Alameda nodded back. "Always, sir."

"Alright, let's roll. We've got another squad to meet up with in Manaus, but I'll take it as a professional humility if we actually need their help. Let's circle back with Joseph and see if he's got us a ride yet. I want to run balls-to-the-wall to catch up with these guys before we even get close to Manaus."

Alameda smiled. "Sounds like a plan."

WHEN JACK AWOKE, the sun was very low on the horizon. Birds were chirping, looking around for their breakfast of insects.

Breakfast? What time is it?

Jack checked his watch. His jaw dropped. He had been asleep for almost a day, for well over twelve hours.

How is that possible?

He was on a cot erected inside the small single room at the fore section of the boat. The cot was set up next to a drawer-less file cabinet that had been filled with cardboard boxes. Across from him was a folding table on which sat a small coffee pot and a camp stove, with a propane tank standing in the corner. There were other small boxes lying next to that, and a large window with no glass stared down at him from above the table.

The entire space was no more than eight feet long per side, and it had been filled with storage items and cooking utensils. Two camp folding chairs sat by Jack's feet.

He rubbed his head, seeing his hand move slowly across his

face, like a comet with a blurry tail. He blinked a few times, each time feeling off-balance.

He had been drugged, and badly. Whatever he had taken had most definitely gone to his head.

He didn't feel bad — the pain had mostly subsided. He pulled his shirt up to inspect the damage on his side, the dried and caked blood causing his nose to wrinkle. He checked his handiwork but found that it was all gone.

Fresh white bandages wrapped his torso and new tape had been applied on top. There was only a single, round reddish-brown hole painting through the top bandage. Apparently someone had dressed and filled his wound. He sat up, noticing that there was more pain in his head than in his side.

The drugs are definitely doing their job.

He blinked a few more times, now shaking his head. He couldn't do it at full speed; it was like everything had to be slow motion.

They had given him some powerful painkillers, and likely some cocktail of other drugs he didn't even want to know about.

Shit. This would make him a little bit slower, a little bit woozy.

He knew he would not have to sail across a valley again, clutching the end of a broken rope bridge and landing on a stick, but that didn't mean he was excited to feel this strung out.

The door behind him opened. He turned and faced it as one of the men, still wearing the uniform of the Peruvian police officer, entered.

"Better?"

Jack frowned. *"Hablas... ?"* he asked.

The man smirked, shaking his head. "You are American. You speak English."

It wasn't a question. It was a statement, a command.

What the hell?

Jack's blood — at least the remaining portion of it — went cold. Who was this guy?

He tried again, the man cutting him off before he could finish the question in Spanish.

"I speak English, *pata*," the man said. "You bring the drugs, so you get your ticket. But you almost died. So I think that you still owe us."

Jack looked around frantically. He let out a sigh when he saw his pack at the foot of the bed, stuffed under one of the chairs. He finally pulled the folding chair up and away, throwing it halfway across the room as the man behind him chuckled. He pulled it close to him, unzipped it. He rifled around through it, felt the change of clothes. He pulled those out now, as well as the first-aid kit and the ammunition.

Then he stopped, puzzled.

No grenade. No Taurus. No phone.

He looked around his cot, finding neither there, either. He had been planning to toss the burner phone into the river, but apparently it had been done for him already.

"You think we will let you keep your weapons, *American*," the man said, his smile growing. "But you are very wrong."

The only thing that made sense to Jack was that Rudy's asset had been wrong — that these men were *actually* police who could not be persuaded to take a cartel member downstream. That he had literally handed drugs over to the DINANDROs, which meant they would not be going downstream, but *upstream*. Back to Iquitos, where they would place him under arrest.

He asked as much.

The man chuckled again. "Policia, DINANDRO, cartel, you pick. It is all the same to you, American."

Jack frowned, looking down. Where had he gone so horribly wrong? They knew he was American, but at least they didn't know...

"You think you are wise, coming here," the man continued. "You think CIA is smart enough to trick all of us, huh?"

Well, there goes that theory. This guy knew he was not just American, but CIA. All bets were off.

"You got in over your head, *compadre*," the man continued. "But it is okay, you still are going to get what you want."

"Yeah?" Jack asked, now in English. "What is it you think I want?"

The man walked fully into the room now, and Jack noticed he was holding the Taurus *Raging Judge*. The weapon glistened in the light. It hung at his side, pointing down, but Jack got the sense the guy was itching to use it.

"You *are* going to get to talk to Victor. Today, actually. So I suggest you rest, get your strength back."

Jack stared at the man as he turned back toward the open door and left the room. Just before he was out of sight, he called over his shoulder.

"Because you're going to need your strength, *pata*. I hear Victor is *very* excited to see you once again."

CHAPTER 46

JACK

JACK LAID BACK on the cot, his head staring straight up at the same style of oversized bulbous lightbulb that hung from the front deck. Bugs buzzed around it, even in the morning light.

Today was the day he was supposed to meet Victor, though not like this. He was supposed to watch carefully on their way to Manaus, try to get a read for the flows and drug trafficking route through the Amazon. Today, Victor's boss would be assassinated. Victor was primed to take the throne, ready for it like everyone else was.

And Jack was supposed to be there, ready to provide his organization with crucial information about Victor's whereabouts and gather intel on his movements. A sting operation would be set up then, and Victor's rise to leader of the Vínculos would end.

That plan had now changed, quite drastically. Who were these men, and why had he been sold out to them? The woman — Rudy's asset — had lied to his face. He remembered Rudy's words: *don't trust anybody but yourself.*

He had failed that small mission, and it had come back to bite him in the ass.

He sat up once again and shifted over to his pack. They had not changed his clothes, so he felt the bulge of the small vials still in his pocket, thankfully not smashed to pieces from his escape through the jungle, through the rope swing agility course, and then down the hill and onto the boat.

He changed his shirt, and he took the time now to take better inventory of what they had left him in his pack. They did not seem to care for most of the gear he had, but the block of cocaine he had been carrying was nowhere to be found.

He pulled open the inside pocket and felt around. His money was gone, too. They had stolen the wad of cash, but that was the least of his worries. There were still two other groups actively pursuing him. Had they seen him get on the boat?

It seemed these police officers were working with the cartel as well, working for Victor directly. By now, they would have told Victor they had him, so at least the cartel men chasing after him might pull back.

Or, on second thought, Victor might not trust these three guys to hold him, so he would just send the cartel scouts he had eluded back in the canopy bridges downriver as well, watching from the shore or tracking them on another boat.

He needed a plan, and none of his CIA training seemed to be helpful right now. His injury would slow him down, so making a run for it would not be as easy as simply running out the open door and diving off the side. Plus, he had no idea what sorts of creatures awaited him in the river, immediately picking up the scent from his wound as he swam to shore.

And what then? Iquitos was one of the most remote cities

on the planet, the largest one inaccessible by road. He couldn't simply trudge through the jungle countless miles upstream, hoping not to encounter any local tribes or predators lying in wait.

At least the man had said they were bound for Manaus, to meet up with Victor. Perhaps he should wait it out, plan his attack for later that day. Surely it was only a couple of hours more before they would get there, assuming they had been traveling all night while Jack slept through his drugged state. Perhaps it was best to rest, like the police officer had told him.

To just sit back and relax, biding his time and preparing himself for whatever move was next.

He pulled himself up out of the cot now, trying to listen for sounds of the men talking. He assumed there were still just the three of them on board. Under normal circumstances, Jack might be able to overcome one or two of them with his bare hands. But these men were armed, one of them with his own weapon. They hadn't taken his ammunition, but that was likely because he had no use for it now. What else were they packing? He wondered about what other weaponry they might have stashed away on the boat. Could he even get to it in time?

No, he needed to just sit back and be quiet to gather intel. At the very least, he could try to listen to their words, try to figure out what it was they were going to do with him once they got to Manaus. Would Victor be waiting at the docks for him? Would he just send a group of men to retrieve him? Would he even be there, or would Jack be tied to a chair again, waiting for Victor to torture him?

Jack pulled the three vials out of his pocket and rolled them around in his fingers. The heavy ceramic seemed impervious to anything but brute force, and for that he was glad. Glass would have easily broken open in his pocket as he tumbled down the hill, and it was still no small miracle that these had survived intact.

If they had not survived the fall, Jack would be dead now.

He had not had a chance to use them yet, but that time would come. He didn't know how, or when, but they were the only card he had left to play. He sat back down on the cot, rubbing the back of his neck and shoulders, trying to relax some of the stress there. It would be futile, but it felt good in the moment.

Nothing left now but to plan and wait, he told himself.

Trusting anyone else had been a losing proposition. Rudy had been more right than he could have ever imagined. It was now time to take matters into his own hands. It was now time to trust himself and no one else.

The problem was, Jack had no idea what to do next.

CHAPTER 47

JACK

THE POLICEMAN HAD LEFT Jack in the small room but locked the door behind him. The window was wide open, so it wasn't as though the men were terribly worried about Jack escaping. He poked his head out this window and immediately saw the same police officer who had spoken to him sitting in a chair next to the motor.

As if waiting for him.

He smiled at Jack, then waved Jack's Taurus in the air.

So that's why he's not worried about keeping me locked up tight. He'll shoot me as soon as I try to leave.

He took stock of his situation. These guys weren't too worried about keeping him wrapped up tight, as they hadn't bound his hands or feet. They likely *wanted* Jack to escape, so they could just shoot him dead and be done with it.

That was their first mistake. These guys had already underestimated Jack by cleaning and packing his wound. If they had been smart — if they had truly known who they were dealing with — they might have let him suffer a bit more, kept him weak. Instead, they had allowed him to regain strength, almost to his normal levels. He was still delirious from the drugs, but those would wear off soon. Even then, he wouldn't have to wait that long to attempt escape. He had already been working up a bit of a plan.

He had rummaged through the file cabinet, finding all the boxes packed with foodstuffs. Dried goods, cans, other nonperishable foods. He looked over the cans, wondering if it was worth trying to use one as a weapon.

But what would he do with it? Climb out the window, hope the police officer watching him didn't simply shoot him in the head, then toss the can at him? That was a lousy plan, one that would surely end with Jack dead.

No, he needed something else. Something more... permanent.

He once again felt the tiny vials of powder in his pocket. He pulled them out, examining them. So far, he had not had any great ideas as to how to put them to use against his pursuers, but perhaps here, with only time in front of him and the freedom to move around the small space, he could fashion something useful.

There was a microwave as well. He didn't have the ingredients for an improvised explosive device like the one he had used on the cruise ship six months ago while in pursuit of Victor, but still, it could be useful for another reason. He would let his inner MacGyver chew on it a bit.

He filed this away as a possibility, then pushed the vials back into his pocket. For now, he needed information. He wanted to gather whatever information from these men he could, sooner rather than later.

As he watched, another police officer strolled over to the man seated by the motor housing at the back of the boat. The engine was idling slowly, since the downstream current was swift enough to keep them moving with speed.

He heard another sound as well — another boat. This one was louder, moving quicker. Jack couldn't place exactly where it was, as all of the sound was coming to him from outside the open window he was listening through. He slid the table over a bit and pressed his back against the wall, listening while staying out of sight. He didn't want these men to know he was eavesdropping.

One of them whispered to the other, but the other responded louder. "Just a fishing boat," the man said in Spanish.

"They don't look like fishermen."

"What does a fisherman look like?" the man chuckled. "Just because they aren't holding poles or nets doesn't mean they are not fishermen."

There was a pause, and he heard footsteps as one of the men walked around the side of the small hut right outside Jack's door. Then he returned to the police officer manning the engine.

This guy must be the leader.

"They're getting too close. I'm going to tell Veracruz to be ready."

The man scolded him. "Be still. You worry too much. No one knows the CIA man is here, and no one needs to. If you go flashing your weapon, they will surely know what we are doing. Best to let them pass, even to let them ask us questions. If they are really not fishermen, we can urge them to continue down the river."

Jack waited a few more seconds. He heard the second boat idling down, then felt a bump as it came abreast of their own.

There were footsteps above his head — the third police officer.

A few frantic voices, Jack couldn't make them out. He waited a beat.

Suddenly a gunshot rang out. He didn't know if it was from his boat or the other, but the footsteps above his head quickened, now a stomping run. They were joined by the two officers at the back of the boat. He glanced out the window again and saw the police officer who had been guarding him begin to stand, looking around frantically.

Another gunshot, followed by three more. It sounded like they were shooting from all different sides. There were small arms, probably pistols. Jack heard the sound of his own Taurus, a louder and deeper *crack* than any of the others, and he knew he was in the middle of the battle once more.

Only this time, he was unarmed.

He felt confident that waiting here would only thin the herd. Letting the two armies battle it out above his head seemed to be the smart move.

But he didn't want to remain idle. He wanted to work on a plan of escape, knowing that eventually, somebody would prevail. Somebody would be left alive.

And that somebody would still be looking for him.

CHAPTER 48

JACK

THE SKIRMISH WAS SLOW, drawn out. Each faction seemed to be hiding, careful to take the shots only when they had a clean line of sight. The pistols' short range would make things even more difficult, their lower power and greater distance between the hiding spots almost nil against anything thicker than a sheet of paper.

Still, the battle raged on around Jack. He worked swiftly, doing his best to improvise while also listening to the shouts and commands of the police officers. He even heard a few new voices, their Spanish inflected slightly differently. Jack guessed that these were cartel men from somewhere else entirely.

He hadn't seen any of them yet, but he didn't know if he would recognize any of them, anyway.

Jack readied his pack, knowing he would need to leave quickly once this was all over. He placed it on the cot, making sure the ammunition was front and center inside. Still, he grabbed two magazines filled with his Casull .454 rounds and placed them into his pockets, zipping the cargo pockets closed.

He would grab whatever weapon he came across first, but he *really* wanted his prized Taurus back.

Escape now seemed possible. It would be only a fifteen-foot run to the back rail, followed by a dive into the dark green, murky waters of the Amazon, and though he still didn't trust his open wound to the nasty critters that lived in the river, he trusted the crazed gunmen fighting it out for his head above him even less.

If there was time, he could even come back for his pack.

He heard a man fall, the heavy thud ending with silence. The battle picked up only seconds later, and Jack knew one fewer team member was upstairs. He didn't know how many of the police officers had been taken out, nor did he know how many were there to begin with.

Time to move.

He needed to find the engine room, needed to sneak up there without being spotted. That, or he needed to get up to the top deck, find the dead police officer's weapon, and begin using it as his own.

He reared back with his good side, raising his left leg high and aiming at the spot just to the right of the brass doorknob. This boat had likely been renovated, this small room sandwiched between the first and second floors, held together with no more than a couple of sheets of plywood. The door, therefore, was single-core and would easily give.

He didn't give it a chance to fight back. He smashed the entire deadbolt and strike plate into pieces, the door flinging open and smacking against the outside of the room.

He was already in motion as it opened, and he shouldered the swinging door as it came back closed. He pressed to the left, knowing there was better cover against the long rows of benches near the front of the boat, and he prepared now to fight off any of the police officers that might still be on the first level.

There were none, at least not waiting for him here. There were, however, three men on the opposite side of the battle now aiming directly at him. The boat that had come alongside theirs was also a two-story, double-decker tourist boat.

But this one was filled with five cartel men.

And three of them were targeting him now.

Jack dove, groaning in midair as he realized he was going to come down on his damaged side just as the three men's pistols began firing.

CHAPTER 49

JACK

THE MERCENARIES that had been trying to kill Jack were the same ones who saved his life now.

Behind the three men on the bottom floor of the second boat, and the two men standing on top and firing over, Jack saw a third boat. Jack couldn't see the mercenaries on that boat, but he heard their gunfire. Immediately two of the men on the second boat fell, one of them on the top deck flying over the front railing and landing with a sickening crunch on the bottom deck. The boats separated for a moment, and the dead man slipped through and fell into the water.

Jack was crouched behind the end of one of the benches on the bottom floor of his riverboat, and he heard the sounds of the battle picking up between now *three* factions.

He was still effectively out of the fight, defenseless and unarmed, so he did not count himself as one of the groups fighting, though he was certainly fighting for his life.

He crawled toward the front of the boat, staying hidden as best he could behind one of the benches while the mercenaries' assault rifles ripped through the second boat. He heard cries of pain and shouts of surprise as the ambushers effectively nullified the five cartel men who had been crammed between the boats. They were not going last long, not with the two remaining police officers on his boat still shooting back.

Jack took the opportunity to crouch-run alongside the railing, toward the staircase on the outside of this deck. He took the stairs two at a time and rounded the top onto the upper deck, still crouched. The two policemen were still alive, both hiding behind benches similar to the ones on the first floor.

He needed to find the third man, the first police officer who had gone down. He knew it had happened near the front of the boat, so he crept along the back side of the benches to the front corner of the boat, farthest away from anyone firing back at him.

It didn't matter — one of the mercenaries, about twenty yards away on the top deck of his boat had spotted him. He could see the third boat clearly now and noticed that it, too, was a two-story tourism boat. These were the popular vehicles of the Amazon.

The mercenary fired three rounds toward him, peppering the area on the bench in front of Jack with bullets. He fell to the floor, his stomach flat against the fiberglass textured floor, and waited. He felt the pain beginning to throb in his side again, even his injured left leg joining in to alert him that he was exerting too much.

Great time for the meds to wear off.

He crawled forward a few benches, completely out of sight, hoping the mercenary would continue to pin him down in the corner, thinking he was still back there, and then he turned left.

He spotted the downed police officer's boot in the middle of the two rows of benches, exactly where he thought he had landed. He crawled forward, crouching once again as he came to a stop near the dead police officer. He examined the man quickly, found what he was looking for, and pulled it into his holster. He needed to get into a better position to defend himself before he decided to attack. The officer's pistol was smaller than his Taurus, a tiny snub-nosed thing firing .38 rounds, but it would have to do.

Jack was a good shot with anything this size, but it might take more than one or two rounds to down a grown man with it.

He checked the magazine before putting it in his holster, glad that there were nine rounds left with one in the chamber.

He fell back to his stomach as more shots rang out around him — lucky guesses from the mercenary firing over his head.

The battle had mostly moved down below, the officers, cartel men, and mercenaries deciding their best bet at staying behind cover was by heading back downstairs.

Jack took the opportunity to jerk his head up quickly, take a quick glance around, then back down.

He had spotted one mercenary, two cartel men crouched on their respective boats but on the side closest to him, and one police officer to his right, at the far end of this boat.

He crept toward this man. At the end of the rows of benches was an even smaller hut than the one downstairs — this was the engine room, and where the boat would be piloted. One police officer was just around the other side of this building, hiding behind the thick-walled railing in the corner of the boat. It was good cover, but only from one side. Jack ran around the side of the engine housing and fired three quick shots, catching the man in the back with all three. He was dead before hitting the floor.

Jack didn't bother checking the man for a pulse or to retrieve his weapon — he wanted *his* Taurus, so the last police officer alive must be the one who had taunted Jack earlier, who had stolen his weapon.

That was your second mistake, Jack thought.

The back stairs were right behind Jack, but he didn't want to reveal his feet and legs to the police officer downstairs in case the man turned around and caught Jack descending. Instead, he veered right once more and headed into the engine housing.

Inside, he found a veritable treasure trove — the exact stuff he had been hoping was here.

Two jugs of gasoline sat out in the open, red containers with yellow spouts on their ends. Each one was a fifteen-gallon jug, filled plenty high enough to handle the task ahead of him.

He ran out of the engine housing and grabbed the other thing he had seen. When the boat had been at shore the day before, in between fits of delirium and complete ineptitude, Jack had spotted a rubber hose hanging on a round holder on the backside of the engine housing.

He grabbed this, threw it over a shoulder, turning back again into the engine room. He navigated around the mounted pilot's chair, grabbed both jugs, and then exited again.

Jack needed to watch his back now — the police officer could potentially run upstairs behind him. However, he felt the man would be pinned down like everyone else, no one daring to poke their head up for fear of being shot by one of the mercenaries still on the third boat.

But he also knew he had to hurry — the mercs would be very interested in getting onto the cartel boat, and then the police officer boat, looking for Jack.

Jack was the ultimate goal, the ultimate prize. *Jack* was the reason they were all here.

HE WORKED QUICKLY, unscrewing the spouts from both jugs of gasoline, then stuck the hose down into the first one. He let it sit there for a moment while he worked with the other jug. This one would require much less fussing. He simply turned it on its side, the diagonal top corner where the spout was now fully open and exposed, immediately draining its contents onto the second-floor deck. He let the fuel wash out over the floor, the liquid spreading evenly and starting to drip down over the sides.

He hoped one of the men downstairs on either boat did not decide that now was a good time to light a match and take a smoke break.

He let the jug drain while he grabbed the first one with its hose sticking out. He needed to act quickly now, knowing he would only have seconds to pull this off. He left the jug upright on the second deck, pulling his body, the jug, and the hose along the textured floor to where the second police officer had been killed. He kicked the man's arm to the side and crouched in the corner where he had previously been hiding. From there,

Jack caught his breath, placed a hand on his side, and ensured he wouldn't accidentally bleed out all over the place.

Satisfied that his bandages would hold for at least a little longer, he ran through the motions in his mind.

Gunfire erupted from behind him — the mercenaries again, from the third boat. The boat had not yet come abreast of the second cartel boat, and Jack felt a slight bumping as it did now.

They're preparing to board the second boat, Jack realized.

He urged himself to move faster.

Jack examined the hose, satisfied that it had been coiled properly and hung over the holder on the back of the engine housing. He tried to arrange it so that he could hold the side still stuck in the fuel tank so that the rest would unspool evenly.

He grabbed most of the coil in his right hand, then stood up quickly. With one motion, he tossed the hose as hard as he could all the way *over* the second boat, watching as it unfurled and hung over each of the railings and then down, its end now on the first floor of the cartel boat.

He crouched once more, popping some seams in his bandages as he did so, evoking a cry of pain as the adhesive tape pulled away flesh and scabs. The wound itself was still throbbing, but he was afraid the bandage had ruptured, and blood would begin falling out.

He took a few breaths, hoping no one had seen what he had done. Hoping no one was now lining up a shot, waiting for him to perform the next set of moves.

He couldn't wait long. He grasped the hose with his left hand, doing his best to cover the rest of the hole where the spigot had been.

He shoved the smaller end of the fixture into the hose coupling, then covered it as best he could with his hand to try for an airtight seal. He groaned again as the throbbing increased in his body; his brain now unable to comprehend where the pain was coming from specifically.

Everything hurt. He wanted to just lay down, to sleep for three days.

But he was almost done. He stood up once more, this time gripping the handle of the fuel jug with his left hand, holding the hose airtight onto the end of the spigot. He began dumping liquid down the hose, gasoline bleeding through his fingers and dripping onto the deck. He ignored it; a few drips were not going to hurt anything.

He lifted the jug as high as possible, letting the hose fill with liquid and hoping there was enough force to push the air out and create a constant flow. He shook the jug a bit more, holding it up and resting it on the hard corner railing.

The jug was half empty already, and he sat back down in the corner, hiding once again. If anyone looked up now, all they would see were two hands, a jug of gasoline being drained into a green hose, and nothing else.

If they shot at him, the gasoline would likely not explode, but he would have other problems. There'd be no way to get out of this position without being hit.

Come on, he willed. He needed to ensure he got most of the gasoline onto the second boat. This plan only worked if that were the case.

He heard shouting now, in English.

The mercenaries.

One had seen the hose; the other was almost below Jack

now. He heard more gunfire, tried to place who was firing and where they were.

It sounded like a single pistol shot from the second boat — did that mean a cartel man was still alive there?

He also hadn't heard much from the police officer down below in a while. Perhaps the man was out of the fight, injured or dead already. Or perhaps he was hiding, biding his time and waiting for the mercenaries to come to him.

Or, if he were smart, maybe he was simply giving up altogether, knowing that the mercenaries were far better trained and better armed. Maybe he would simply surrender and let them take Jack down.

The jug emptied, and he tossed it over his head, hearing it land with a splash in the water downstream.

Okay, Jack. That was the plan.

He braced himself.

Time for phase 2.

CHAPTER 51

JACK

THE TOP DECK of the riverboat was slick with gasoline. He slid through it on his hands and knees, aiming for the pilot house again. He reached it, once more clutching the pistol he had grabbed off the dead police officer, but he wasn't planning to get into the fight.

His battle was elsewhere, and he needed to go down the stairs without being seen.

One of the mercenaries had seen the hose and was now shouting orders out to the rest of his men. They were now spread out along their boat and the cartel boat next to Jack's. He had not yet heard or seen anyone else step foot onto the police officers' boat.

But it was only a matter of time — they were all gunning for him.

Jack tripped and nearly fell down the stairs, the stench of gasoline fumes wafting up to his nose and landed on his back-side on the bottom step. The wound in his side nearly caused him to scream in pain, but he forced his lips closed, forced himself to stay quiet. Giving up his exact position now would ruin everything.

He gripped the pistol tightly, finger off the trigger, not wanting an accidental firing. It was possible for the spark inside the gun's chamber to ignite the gasoline fumes emanating up and filling the air around him, but it was highly unlikely. It was mostly for noise reasons — he still needed a few moments of stealth. Of course, he didn't want to take the chance of causing his own personal immolation.

The gun was more of a last-ditch effort if anyone happened to get the jump on him.

Two shots fired, both from different locations. Jack poked his head around the shack and saw two separate cartel men aiming for one of the mercenaries nearing the center of their boat. He was surprised to learn that two of the five were still alive. That meant the mercs had to battle through them before getting to Jack, but it would not buy him much time.

Jack reached the bottom floor of the boat and ran to the right, toward where the police officer had been sitting before.

The man was not there now, and Jack had not seen him anywhere else on the boat.

That left one place for him to be hiding.

Jack crept over to the window, crouching underneath it, then sprang up quickly. The man was standing exactly where Jack had been standing before, peering out the window inside the room.

Jack didn't hesitate. He reached through the window, wrapped his left arm around the man's neck, and yanked his upper body through the window. The man shouted in surprise, but it was quiet enough not to warrant any notice from the other fighters. He used the bottom edge of the window frame as leverage, wrenching the man's head out to the front of it while the rest of his body was inside. The man was large enough that clearing the window with the guy in tow would be tough, especially with Jack's injury.

But he wasn't trying to lift him out of the window... he was trying to kill him.

Jack left his feet, his elbow around the man's neck and his right hand clasped over his left wrist, performing a chokehold, with the added benefit of having two sheets of plywood between the guy's neck and the floor.

It wasn't even close to a fair fight. The man's arms flailed, and Jack caught sight of his own Taurus still in the man's right hand.

But the guy's hands were inside the small window, and he was too busy trying to pry off the man choking him, so he could not get a good shot off. Thankfully he didn't try. He was focused on keeping himself alive, but it wouldn't end well for him.

Jack needed this guy to die quickly, considering his right side was exposed to the cartel boat's edge. The mercs were still engaged in their own scuffle, and Jack heard footsteps pounding around the top deck above him. Either the mercs had finally boarded his boat, or the cartel men were here, spreading out their defense.

With a soft crunch, Jack felt the man's vertebrae pop as he wrenched his elbow sideways with a final thrust.

Jack let out a small yelp of pain as he let go, unable to stop it. He could feel a burst of blood coming out of the wound on his side, and he pulled a hand down to cover it. At the same time, the police officer's lifeless body thumped back onto the floor inside the small room.

Now it was his turn to try and get through the window. He didn't want to risk moving to the door he had busted open earlier — that doorway was facing the ongoing firefight. Jack heaved his injured body up and through the window, cradling his right side and letting the left side of his body do most of the work. It was not elegant, and he fell with a crash through the window, landing on the back of his neck on top of the dead police officer. His legs flew in behind him as he twisted around, and Jack somersaulted backward into the room.

Well, that's not going to win me any gymnastics awards.

His body was screaming in agony — injuries he hadn't known existed were now apparent.

He turned quickly, seeing his pack still on the cot.

He swung the pack onto his shoulders and then marched into the corner of the room to pick up his Taurus. He didn't have time to examine it, to check its magazine. He still had the magazines he'd stuffed into his pockets, so he shoved the *Raging Judge* back into its holster and turned around. He crouched in front of the man now AD, but he wasn't examining the police officer. Instead, he was rifling through one of the boxes next to the table and chair that were now laying in pieces in the center of the room.

It was trash, but that was exactly what he wanted.

He found what he was looking for almost immediately. He smiled, standing up and adding the glass object into his pack. Satisfied he was ready, he turned to the broken door, flapping quietly in the wind, and prepared to leave.

Jack knew it would have been smarter to climb back out the window, but he wasn't sure his side could handle it.

Besides, there would be no squishy police officer to land on this time.

He would have to risk moving out the door once more — calling attention to himself — but there was no other option.

He steeled himself, taking two quick breaths, then ran out the door, hitting it with his right elbow. He kept moving, using the swinging door as terrible cover for a few seconds, then ripping it completely off its hinges as he continued to the right. He ran as hard as he could despite his aching side, aiming for the back side of the boat. The slippery deck fought against his forward momentum, but his boots had enough traction to keep him moving in the right direction.

He aimed at the back-corner railing, reaching his left hand out to place a hand on the top of the railing as he lunged. His feet left the deck, his right hand still holding the strap of his pack, his left hand offering the only balance he'd find.

It was the most awkwardly executed swan dive anyone had ever attempted but, thankfully, no one was there to see it. Jack sailed over the railing headfirst, his body doing its best to calibrate so he would land in the water like a dolphin performing a perfect dive.

But he was hardly in a condition to jump over a three-foot railing with a 45-pound pack on his back. His boots clipped the top of the railing and sent him plummeting straight down toward the water's surface. He entered the water face-first, rolling over his front side as he did. His feet followed him down, turning his dive into an awkward somersault.

Once in the water, the pack carried him straight down, and he had to fight against the current as it immediately picked him up and pulled him away from the boats.

But he was in the water.

He couldn't see anything, though, so he smashed his eyes closed and swam in the direction he thought the shore would be. He blew air out his nose and twirled until he was right side up, fighting against the strain of the pack and the current.

Jack was pummeled over and over under the water, unable to right himself again, but eventually found purchase on the soft, muddy ground of the river. Taking advantage, he kicked up, aiming in the direction he believed the shore to be, suddenly realizing he was out of breath.

He panicked, his eyes bulging open and his arms flailing. One shoulder strap slipped off, and he panicked again while frantically trying to roll around and grasp onto the pack.

The river had mercy on him then, and he felt ground only a few feet below him. He kicked off once more, harder this time, now aiming straight up. He broke the surface of the water holding the pack with both hands wrapped around his chest, gasping for air.

There was an insane amount of gunfire behind him now, the tiny thumps turning into a hellish blaze of exchanging rounds as all parties decided to try to end the fight.

They wanted to end this as much as Jack did.

But they had no idea what Jack had prepared for them.

CHAPTER 52

JACK

JACK PANTED HEAVILY as he pulled himself up toward the tree. It was just a collection of branches and roots that slid into the water, stretching upward and twisting around a hidden trunk. The dirt around its base had long since eroded, and he had to work to keep his feet mounted on the branches and not let them fall through into the muddy bank.

His boots constantly slipped over the exposed roots, slick with algae, but he finally found purchase enough to lift himself out of the water, weighing twice as much now than he had before thanks to the waterlogged pack on his back. Jack forced himself up and over the ball of buttress roots.

He fell onto the base of the tree, rolling sideways and letting his pack come to rest next to him. He lay there for a few seconds, knowing that there was not enough time for him to catch his breath but still unable to move any limb.

He was beyond exhausted, beyond strained.

And that's when his attackers started shooting at him.

One of the cartel men had heard the splash, came running to the edge of the boat and saw Jack swimming toward shore.

Pieces flew around the trunk, off the tree and around him, and he knew he only had seconds to act.

He pulled out his gun and started shooting back. He had no way to get off a good shot, but it was enough to keep the man at bay.

Deciding he had run out of time, Jack leaned over, unzipped his pack without looking, and reached inside. He dug around, finding the object he needed in the inside pocket. He grasped the lighter and pulled it back out, his left hand reaching around his torso and holding it over the wound. His hand came away slick with blood. He knew he would need to reassess the damage as soon as possible, possibly even rewrap the wound again.

He was doing everything he could to prevent his body from healing. But it was either keep moving forward or die.

Die now... or die later.

He reached into the pack again and pulled out the latest object he had placed inside — an empty coke bottle he had found in the makeshift trash can, then reached into his pack a third time, water that had not yet drained sloshing around inside, and found the first-aid kit and his dirty shirt.

He fumbled with it, finally bringing it over his chest and setting it down on his belly as more rounds peppered the area around the water. These weren't aimed at him, which gave him hope that there were still people distracting each other, keeping each other occupied.

He could barely move, could barely stand, but he had to get a better perch. Jack pulled himself to his hands and knees, then up more, eventually sitting on his feet. He took out the large plastic jug of isopropyl alcohol from the first-aid kit, filled the empty bottle with it, then tore off a piece of the bloody shirt he had stuffed in the bag and shoved it over the opening and down into the bottle's top. The bottle was only half-full, but it was all he had. He hoped it would be enough.

He tipped and swirled the bottle side to side, waiting for the liquid to soak upward and cover the majority of the cloth, then he flicked the lighter open and lit it. He held the lighter out to the wet shirt, which smoked at first, but eventually a large enough flame caught that he felt satisfied with his tiny Molotov Cocktail.

He was right-handed, which meant this would strain his right side, but he could not wimp out and toss the thing under-hand. He needed the bottle to shatter, for the flame to spread as soon as it hit the air and release the alcohol onto the deck. And he couldn't toss it with his left hand and risk missing altogether.

He was surprised to see the boat he had jumped off of was now directly in front of him, only ten feet away. He saw three mercenaries on the second boat upstream. He thought he saw two other men, one of them likely cartel members on the second boat as well, somehow still alive and still in the fight.

But not for long. Jack waited another ten seconds, trying to time his throw properly. The men had seemingly forgotten about Jack for the moment, consumed by the other enemies firing back at them. It was an all-out brawl, each man daring a glance around their cover, firing wildly, then hiding away again to reassess or reload.

A firefight like this should normally last only seconds, but this one had extended minutes because of the amount of cover available to all parties. Only the mercenaries seemed to be gaining ground — all of the police officers and most of the cartel members were dead.

Finally, when the third boat was passing directly in front of Jack's face, he came around to the front side of the tree, gripping its trunk with his left arm around it, and heaved the bottle straight up into the air as hard as he could. It sailed in a high arc over the third boat, then landed with a heavy thump on the deck of the second.

And nothing happened.

Shit.

Jack had heard it land, but not the telltale sound of breaking glass. The bottle simply clattered around as it bounced around the deck. Apparently, the thing had not broken open.

And at some point, the flame must have died out as well, because Jack didn't see —

A massive fireball flew upward from the top deck of the middle boat. He heard one mercenary scream in surprise, followed shortly by agony as everything erupted around him. The gunfire ceased, replaced by screams of men as the boat was completely engulfed in raging flames in only four seconds. Thick, heavy smoke blocked out the sun.

Then the first boat in the line blew up.

CHAPTER 53

JACK

THE HEAT REACHED Jack's face, the intensity of the flames singeing his eyebrows. He needed to move. Though there was no fuel on the third boat — the one the mercenaries had come in on — Jack knew that it was only a matter of time before the flames leaped over and reached past the railing of the third boat, lighting it as well.

He reached down and grabbed his pack, shoving the first-aid kit in and zipping the whole thing closed. He swung the pack around his back and ran alongside the shore, precariously leaping from each larger root to the next, hoping his boots did not slip out from under him. Smacking his head and passing out would be a death sentence, as would slipping and falling into the river. He would be stranded here, unable to go upstream toward Iquitos or downstream toward Manaus with enough time to get help and care for his wound.

He was moving too slowly, but he couldn't bear the pain of pumping his legs faster, and he did not want to risk slipping and falling. He reached his target — a thinner magnolia tree with branches sticking out from all sides. There was barely enough space for him to crawl underneath two of the branches and begin climbing up, and he forced his legs to push him ever higher despite the grueling agony from his right side.

He reached his target height — about fifteen feet above the water, then found the branch he had been aiming for. It was thick enough — slightly thicker than his thigh — and he scurried out over it, holding onto the less sturdy branches around it until he hung out over the water.

The very tips of the branches of this tree had brushed the sides of the first two boats as they passed, and the third boat was no different.

He ran out of sturdy branch about five feet short of the boat passing by now. He needed to jump. Afraid to land on the hard railing and risk slipping to the deck below, Jack pulled the pack around in front of him, put his arms through both straps, and wore it like a fat suit as he tested the bend in the branch. There was some give to it, and he hoped it was supple enough not to snap and crack, sending him hurtling down to the earth and hitting every smaller branch on the way down.

He bent his knees, testing it like the tip of a diving board. Finally, he pushed down and jumped up as high as possible, propelling himself forward simultaneously.

The branch did its job admirably, sending him flying the last five feet toward the boat and another foot into the air. He aimed for the side railing; arms splayed out. He struck stomach-first, the pack thankfully taking the brunt of the impact, but barely caught the edge of the railing with his elbows locked over it.

Jack swung a bit, then finally settled. His upper body was straining, but for once, the laceration in his side was not the most painful thing he was experiencing.

He had pulled something in his elbow when he had landed, hitting a tendon or ligament that would soon cause inflammation and soreness. He ignored it for now, swinging his body left to right and hooking his leg up and over the edge of the railing. The pack made this difficult, so he had to roll the rest of the way and landed on his back on the second-story deck.

The impact was hard, and he cursed himself for not just wearing the pack like a normal person.

There was no more gunfire, but that was because everyone else was either dead or trying to escape the inferno engulfing both boats. He pulled himself up to his feet, then heard a splash. He looked over the edge and saw rippling circles of water moving outward, about the size of a human. He figured one of the mercenaries must have fallen into the water or jumped, hoping to make it to shore.

Whoever it was, they were still hostile and would still be trying to get to Jack.

He had sent the rest of their team up in flames, and he was not going to stick around to find out how they would take that.

The boat he was on now had an open engine console, which was still idle. Jack walked over to the pilot stand and found the throttle and wheel.

One hand on each, Jack slid the boat into reverse, separating it from the other two flaming hulls to his left.

He deftly pulled the boat forward around the fore of the cartel boat, swinging wide enough over the huge river to give it plenty of space. He sputtered by it, getting a feel for how the boat maneuvered, all while examining the wreckage of the two tourist boats next to him.

Both were sinking slowly toward shore, flames already

beginning to lick the tops of the trees hanging over this area of the river. Forest fires were not a major issue here since the rainforest got enough rain, even in the dry season, to offset any severely dangerous fires. Jack wasn't worried about burning down half the Amazon.

He was worried about why so many people seemed to want to kill him.

He had no idea how many he had taken out now, no idea how many had been sent after him in the first place.

And he had no idea how many were still trying.

He pulled the boat around the other two, then hit the throttle, pushing the boat up to speed. The gigantic vessel pulled forward quickly, accelerating with a speed that surprised Jack. The engine whined, and he pulled it back to about 75 percent, aiming down the river toward Manaus.

He was going to get there. Battered and bruised, fighting off death at every turn, but he was going to get there.

He was going to get to Victor.

JACK SLEPT IN FITS. He had tried to talk himself out of falling asleep, knowing he needed more than ever to be cognizant and aware of his surroundings.

The last thing he could afford was to crash the boat into one of the banks of the wide river or be asleep when a cartel or mercenary team snuck onboard. This last stretch of river that led into Manaus was wide, so he was not worried about crashing into the banks. And the man he had seen swimming away from the burning boats before wouldn't be nearby.

Still... he didn't want to sleep. He wanted to be alert.

But he simply could not keep his eyes open. He sat in the pilot chair, drifting in and out of consciousness. His body's exhaustion, fatigue, and terrible shape finally took its toll.

He had put himself through hell the last two days, and it seemed to finally be giving up.

His first-aid kit was useless, the rest of his gauze completely waterlogged with bacteria-infused river water. He considered that it might be better than nothing but opted instead to supplement his existing bandages with a few strips of an extra shirt he had found inside the lower room on the first deck. He just needed it to be tight, to hold the blood in while keeping the bacteria and infectious stuff out.

He had no more rubbing alcohol, nothing to clean his wounds with. He did a quick inventory of the boat but found nothing else useful there, either. While the police boat he had been on had been in use and seemed to be regularly occupied, this boat the mercenaries had taken or stolen seemed brand-new. Besides the requisite lifejackets and life ring mounted to a wall, there wasn't much on board for him to use.

He had no extra fuel, either, so he had stopped flooring the engine once he felt he was far enough away from the smoldering ruins of the two boats he had left upstream. The current was strong, keeping the boat in the center of the waterway, and for all of these reasons, Jack allowed himself to dip into sleep.

When he awoke again, a couple of hours had passed, and he could see the outskirts of Manaus alongside the river.

He started the engine again, watching the light of the city ahead break the darkness.

He eased the boat to the right, aiming for the large smattering of civilization that existed there. Other fishing trawlers and tourist boats passed him, and he waved at each pilot operator as they drifted close, as if he belonged there.

His body ached; he hadn't eaten in far too long, and he could use a couple of shots of whiskey, but he was otherwise in good spirits. For the moment, his injury had settled into a dull soreness. He did not know what lay ahead, only that Victor would be here. Rather than feeling the ominous reality that he was alone in hostile territory, multiple factions gunning for his life, he felt at peace.

He had escaped what he assumed would be the worst of it,

gotten away while taking out some of the enemies who wanted to stop him.

Now, he just needed to get into town, find a fresh change of clothes and perhaps some medication, then make his way to Victor's warehouse.

He wasn't sure how he would try to confront the man. He couldn't simply run in, guns blazing, and hope to live through it, but he also did not have time to wait him out, to try to catch him with his guard down. Victor would not have his guard down — he would be ready, expecting an attack.

He had left his waterlogged pack out to dry on the top deck, but the humidity and lack of clear sunlight had made that impossible. He did his best to wring out the clothes inside, so at least the pack wouldn't be carrying more water than necessary, but it still weighed ten to fifteen pounds heavier than he would have liked.

Regardless, he shoved everything back inside, placing everything where it was supposed to go, then placed it beside him at the pilot stand. He might consider ditching it in town — besides the ammunition, there was really nothing in it he couldn't find in Manaus. But he had no money, and the pack marked him as a traveler, an outsider. He understood now that anyone chasing him would describe him as tall, fit — *and* carrying a large rucksack on his back.

It was a dead giveaway, and if he wanted to hold anything and carry it with him he would need to find something different to carry around. Perhaps a tote bag or smaller backpack.

Jack checked the compass out of habit, not needing to know what it said. Based on the sun's position over the horizon and the way the river was traveling, he knew he was heading south-southeast. He aimed toward the long row of docks stretching out in front of him, hoping to find one that wouldn't question his arrival. Fishermen paid monthly fees for rental spaces, so he preferred to park, get out, and disappear into the city as soon as possible before someone asked him for his license or rental slip contract.

He found an ideal spot, farther south and away from the larger docks. It was a small inlet, only a marina gas station and restaurant appearing near it.

He could anchor on the shore, hop off and wade to the beach, then get lost. As good a plan as any, he turned the wheel slightly to the right and set the new target.

He checked his watch now, realizing that he would only have an hour to get into position before Victor's scheduled arrival. Jack wanted to be ready.

He didn't quite know what *ready* meant, but at least getting in place would be a start.

AS MUCH AS Jack hated to admit it, the reality was he was going to have to steal. His training in the CIA had mostly been focused on survival. Keeping him alive by parrying attacks with his hands, with weapons, with any number of improvised defenses, and survival against attacks from the environment itself. He had done short courses in wilderness survival, with a special interest and focus on the Amazon. He had met with experts and taken over a hundred hours of specific training exercises to feel comfortable when dropped into the rainforest. He had studied with martial arts experts, experts with knives, swords, and guns, and he had begun mastering all of them.

He had studied languages, the nuance and complexities of dialects in the Amazon region, Peruvian history and politics, and knew the history of the Shining Path organization and the Vínculos cartel.

In other words — he felt extremely prepared for this mission.

He was bleeding, his wound still not even close to healed, the pain from all of his scratches and scrapes and bruises coming to a head and making him regret every step he took toward Manaus, knowing that there were many more cartel members here as well, waiting for him to arrive.

And yet, of all the things that happened, what he was most concerned about was the fact that he was going to have to steal.

The CIA tried to recruit and train good people. Men and women, young and old, who could best serve the interests of the United States government. They were patriots through and through. They had the best interests of their home nation at heart. They were spooks, people whose job was gathering information, sharing intelligence, and performing operations in every corner of the globe.

For this reason, the CIA also trained its people on how to stay alive in a foreign country with nothing but the shirts on their backs.

Part of that training had included how to steal, to get what one needed, no matter how difficult. It had been drilled into his head — much like fighting itself — that this was a last resort, something meant to keep the operative alive to fight another day, to continue the flow of information and continue the mission itself.

No good person wanted to steal from other good people, from innocent people.

But that was exactly what Jack was planning to do. He had targeted the building set off the main road, on the outskirts of Manaus. He had observed, waited behind some bushes near a park bench, and sat on the ground, his pack stashed behind a tree. To the casual observer, he would look like a vagabond, a hermit, or a local homeless man. He had a week-old beard that added to the effect, and his face was smeared with dirt and grime, and there were crusty flakes of blood that had dried on his face and arms.

No one would cast him a second glance, and most would steer clear of him altogether.

The good news was, there were no other people here at the moment. He had chosen the corner of town due to the number of dilapidated and worn-down buildings that told Jack this was an aging industrial district of Manaus that would not have bustling markets and outdoor shops and vendors, as well that it happened to be close to where he had docked his stolen riverboat.

He had stumbled through a thick copse of trees, pushing sharp leaves out of the way, reopening thousands of small, microscopic cuts on his arms and hands, and finally reached the area near Ponta Negra, by the airport to the west of Manaus' downtown districts.

Here he had waited; he only had a few minutes to spare, but a few minutes was all it took. He had pulled the water-logged map out of his pack and examined it. The paper map was almost completely ruined from the damage it had taken over the past two days, but it showed enough of Manaus that he realized there was no way he was going to be able to scuffle all the way across town and get into position to await Victor's arrival on foot.

He would need transportation, and it wouldn't be free.

Stealing a car would immediately cause too much atten-tion, And the last thing he needed was for the Manaus police force to join in the fray.

That meant he had to resort to a lower level of petty crime: the theft of the corner store across the street and whatever lay inside its cash register.

He chose the mark just like he had been trained, aiming for a building that was set off from the rest of civilization a bit more than the others, the runt of the litter, an easy target. He watched and surveilled the place for two minutes, not seeing anyone come or go. There was a single car parked behind the building — the current sole employee in the store or the owner or manager.

He didn't want to risk breaking into a place that was locked up tight, so he wanted a place like this, a place where somebody was currently working. The doors would be unlocked, prepared for business.

He had also checked his waterlogged pistol, finding it still in working order. The ammunition should be fine, most of it had dried out on the deck of the stolen mercenary vessel. He preferred this weapon for that reason — it could take a beating, could be submerged under water for quite some time and still come out sparkling clean and ready for action.

And yet, he hoped he would not have to use it now.

Theft from an innocent civilian just trying to make a buck was enough. He didn't have any interest in killing them.

He pulled himself up from his seated position, his bones and muscles creaking with soreness and arguing against overuse, and he began walking toward the store. He had slung his pack over his shoulder again, but he only used one strap. He wanted to sell the appearance of a bum just looking for a handout — belongings over a single shoulder, strolling around looking for a handout.

He opened the door and was suddenly hit with an incredible smell. Some sort of local delicacy was being roasted in a tiny rotisserie oven in the corner, similar to how gas station hotdogs were cooked all day back in the States.

His stomach immediately lurched; he hadn't had a decent meal in so long he was starting to forget what they tasted like.

He was greeted by a warm hello, but he didn't want to make eye contact with the young man standing behind the counter. There was no way this guy was somehow connected to the mercenaries or the cartel, and they were far out of Shining Path territory.

But the CIA was not in the business of taking chances.

Jack sidled into the small store, narrow rows of chocolates and candies and snacks on both sides barely wide enough for his shoulders and pack.

The man repeated the greeting, then asked if he could help Jack find anything. Jack grunted a non-answer.

The man turned his head a bit, clearly intrigued by his patron. He didn't ask anything else, but Jack saw from a convex mirror mounted up in the corner that the man was eyeing him suspiciously during Jack's stroll through the shop.

He didn't have time to engage the man, to ask him questions to try to get him to look for something in the back, perhaps an item that wasn't stocked on the shelves. This man would know everything in the store, and there was nothing Jack could do to convince him to leave a dirty, suspicious-looking guy standing alone in the store while he went back to retrieve something for him.

And that only left one option.

Jack hustled around the small convenience store, grabbing a protein bar, a sports drink, and a bottle of water, and another burner phone. He grabbed the same brand he had purchased in Iquitos, a prepaid version with an unlocked card installed.

And on the bottom shelf... a brand-new first-aid kit.

He brought all this, wrapped under his left arm, up to the counter and dumped everything there.

The man tried hospitality once more. "Where are you headed?" he asked nicely.

Jack pulled the Taurus from its holster and shoved it into the man's forehead. The clerk immediately backed up, terrified, his arms raised.

"I — I mean no harm," the man stuttered in Spanish. "Please, sir. Please, don't shoot."

Jack grunted again, then quickly motioned with the Taurus toward the cash register. The man nodded, his face pale as a ghost.

Jack watched as the guy pulled the cash register open and dumped the measly collection of bills and coins onto the counter. Jack gave it all a quick count, deciding it was barely enough to get him a ride across town, much less anything else.

Good thing I'm not going to have to buy any of this crap.

"*Bolsa*," he grunted, the word for 'bag' in Spanish.

The man nodded quickly once more and pulled up a brown paper bag from behind the counter.

The entire time, Jack kept his eyes drilled onto the man's face, but his peripheral vision was focusing on the man's hands. If they dropped further behind the counter at all, Jack would have to take immediate action. He didn't want to shoot this guy. But if the guy pulled out a gun — a pistol or shotgun kept underneath the counter for the owner's protection — Jack would have no choice but to fire a few rounds, hopefully hitting something on him that wouldn't be fatal.

But the man didn't duck his hands. He was terrified, unarmed, and helpless.

And Jack had just robbed him.

JACK THANKED the man in Spanish, recognizing the irony in his words as he turned with the items in cash he had stolen from the poor young man. On his way out, he caught sight of a small rack of clothing against the wall. One was a Hawaiian shirt, triple-extra-large. On the shelf nearby, fresh, knee-high yellow socks.

Beneath that, a bathing suit.

Jack grabbed all three, then left the building. He noticed the man on the phone almost as soon as the door was swinging shut, but Jack wasn't going to stick around to wait for the cops to arrive.

He took his goodies back toward the park bench but kept walking deeper into the jungle between where he had parked the boat and this store. He turned to the left, traveling through the jungle toward Rio Negro and Marina do Davi, then stopped near a tree and sat down. He dumped the pack on the ground, ripped his shirt and pants off as well as his boots and old, soggy socks, then just sat for a moment, wearing nothing but his underwear.

It was an odd feeling, being stuck in the jungle with any number of critters and insects watching him, completely unclothed and vulnerable.

At the same time, it felt good. His entire body ached, but the wound on his side had settled into a low, throbbing sensation that didn't feel great but was nowhere near the pain from before. He had not seen any medication in the general store, and he was somewhat glad for it. He had already taken enough from the man, and though he was not proud of it, at least he would be able to put a fresh pair of clothes on, ones that weren't still damp or crusted with mud and blood.

After doing his best to clean his wound, pack it with an antiseptic gauze filler, and wrap it back up, Jack donned the swim trunks, ripping off his underwear and throwing it on the pile of his clothes next to him. Then he tore the socks out of their package and pulled them up, rolling them down over themselves so they didn't stick up to a ridiculous height on his legs. He stuck them inside his boots, which were thankfully dry enough not to cause extra discomfort. He tied them, then stood up, throwing the shirt over his back.

It hung off him like a bag, his thin frame completely lost inside of it. But it was *dry*. He buttoned it up, then stretched his arms out to his sides, doing a slow turn in the middle of the jungle, modeling the shirt for the forest itself.

This is absolutely ridiculous.

But it was cover, and it was far more comfortable than what he'd been wearing. The best sorts of disguises were those that would hardly seem like disguises. If he could somehow stumble across a fanny pack and open-toed sandals to throw on over his bright new socks, he might even complete the 'European tourist' vibe.

For now, this would have to do. He would be walking back through Manaus like a beacon, attracting all sorts of attention to himself. Hopefully, anyone from the cartel or Shining Path that may be around would simply dismiss him as some nut-job tourist dressed for a day in the sun.

Or they would just shoot him on sight and be done with it.

Jack donned the pack again as he picked up the sports drink. He tried to drink slowly but ended up chugging the entire bottle in two gulps. He tore open the protein bar next, devouring it. He threw the bottle and empty wrapper onto the pile of his old clothes, then bundled the entire thing together and stuffed it under his arm. He walked back over to the park bench, next to which sat a concrete-rimmed trashcan. He stuffed the clothes and trash into it and continued walking.

The street he was on featured some sort of factory on his left, a few cars parked in front, with a lot out back. He knew the general layout of Manaus — not as well as Iquitos, but he had studied routes through the city with Rudy.

He wondered if Rudy was watching down on him now, pushing him forward and urging him to continue his mission. He wondered if Rudy blamed him for his death — could he have stopped it? Why hadn't Rudy fought back?

Jack shook his head. He needed to find a car, but he also needed to get in touch with Rudy's handler, to keep the man posted on his progress. He tore open the packaging around the burner phone and tossed it to the street, then turned on the phone. The device was charged to 80%. He dialed the number on instinct and raised the phone to his ear.

Rudy's handler picked up immediately. *"Jack, where the hell are you?"*

Jack was surprised by the sudden intensity in the man's

voice. Had something changed? Had something happened back home?

"In Manaus, grabbing a cab to head to the opposite side of the city. Victor should be arriving in —"

"Jack, get out of the city. You're made."

CHAPTER 57

JACK

"I'VE BEEN GETTING all sorts of weird SIGINT and HUMINT red flags in your area."

Jack had been told the CIA did not have many watchers in the area; he had inferred that he and Rudy were two assets of only a handful in the region. It was typical CIA paranoia that they did not reveal the exact numbers to their own agents. For all he knew, every civilian he had passed *was* a CIA watcher. Much like the Shining Path watchers and informants he had come across so far, CIA watchers could be any age, any sex, and appear any way. These were not full-time or even part-time roles. Their job was to simply keep an eye on the surroundings, to provide the eyes on the ground for any assets that needed help in the region, only when the CIA required it.

As they weren't professional, it made it so that passing good intel around was nearly impossible — it was hard to tell who worked for whom, who was backstabbing whom, who was a double agent, or simply just collecting for the highest bidder.

The fact that his handler had told him he was getting

signals intelligence and human intelligence about his actions meant that the CIA did have its ear to the ground better than Jack had anticipated. While it didn't necessarily mean there were watchers who had seen him, it did mean that the CIA's network of information was unbroken. Signals intelligence was derived from tapped phone lines, Internet traffic and message boards, text messages, and any number of digital interference. Human intelligence, on the other hand, came not just from watchers but from listening in to local police radios, hacked cartel gear, and any intercepted human conversations.

"There's another group here," Jack said quickly as he walked. He was aiming for the block at the end of this street, one he saw cars traveling down. With any luck, a cab would be close by. "Mercenaries, best guess. You know anything about that?"

He waited for the handler to answer. *"Look, Jack. Things are getting heated up in DC. I'm being told that CIA assets are being pulled out of the region as we speak. Whoever wanted Victor watched has completely changed their mind."*

"Yeah, that much I gathered."

"I've got an exfil set up for you, but it will be three hours from now. I need you to head to the southeast side of town, near —"

"Negative," Jack snapped, his anger rising. "I've been shot at, nearly blown up, scraped and bruised, and they're *still* throwing guys after me. They're going to chase me there, even if I got there now and just wait it out. They're *going* to find me. Look, I came here to get eyes on Victor's new route, to gather whatever information we could about their operation."

"Yeah, Jack, I know the mission parameters. But your partner's dead, and you've been made. We can go back and regroup

later. We'll lose time, but we can't afford to lose another operative."

Jack wanted to argue, wanted to belabor the point. "What happens if Victor dies now? If there's another operation at play..."

"Hell if I know, Jack. The Venezuelan government wants the cartel to pull back, to stop operating in its jurisdiction. I'm guessing they called in a favor to the CIA to help take down the man they assume will come to power next."

"But I thought the plan was to assassinate the *leader* of the cartel — Victor's boss?"

"It was, yeah. The idea was to take out the head honcho, to let Victor slide into power thinking the coup was over, and to make him think he was safe. Hell, I've got intel that suggests the Venezuelan government itself helped Victor set up the upcoming assassination attempt. I know there are Navy intelligence assets in Venezuela, and they might have something to do with it."

Jack knew all of this already, and it was good to hear that much had not changed. "I don't get it, then. *What happens if Victor dies?* The whole point was that if we got eyes on Victor, watched him rise to power, we would be in a place to topple the cartel once and for all. If I exfil, I'm out. No one's here to carry out the *real* mission. Or am I missing something?"

"That would send things spiraling out of control," his handler confirmed. *"But we're just pawns in a larger game, Jack. The cartel may be running any number of illegal contraband through the region, but that's no longer our business. The Venezuelan government might want to take out the leader of the cartel, but for whatever reason, they reneged on the deal for Victor. They want us to back down. Or they've convinced whoever it is up on the Hill pulling the strings."*

Jack was fuming. "They sent me down here to *die*."

"That wasn't the plan, Jack. You understand how this works — you did it for twenty years."

Jack shook his head, gripping the phone tightly. "No, I provided intel; that was it. No one ever told me all these ops ended up blowing up in the operatives' faces. No one told me I was sending people on suicide missions."

"You can get out, Jack. Just be smart, play it safe. Stick to the isolated areas and stay hidden as much as possible, and I can get you —"

"Too late for that." Jack waved as he saw a yellow taxicab heading down the road from the east. "Victor's here, or he'll be arriving any minute now. If I'm made, that means he's already looking for me. And I'd like to meet him again, maybe give him an update on how *I've* been doing."

"Don't do that, Jack."

"Or what?" Jack asked. "What happens if Victor dies?"

There was a long pause, and he could almost picture the handler pressing his fingers against his temples, maybe pinching the bridge of his nose. Whatever nervous tic the guy had, he was certainly doing it right now. *"Jack, I don't have that information. I'm just... trying to get you out of there alive. The mission's off — we'll regroup and figure things out later. Let's just get you home, and we can debrief, then —"*

"You're lying to me." *Everyone* had been lying to him. Jack was starting to realize the ugly truth. Rudy, his asset, his handler. Everyone was playing a different game, and he had stumbled around in it thinking he was doing the right thing.

And, most ironically of all, Rudy had been lying to him as well. He had not been forthcoming. There was *something* about his death that plagued Jack — it wasn't just a Shining Path killing or a cartel hit.

Trust no one but yourself, Jack, he heard Rudy's words repeating in his mind.

What were you trying to tell me, Rudy?

Jack remembered working the desk job for twenty years, moving his way up through the Company. He had been good at what he did, he was good at looking at any amount of information that came across his desk, pieces of intel that seemed completely unrelated.

Unrelated until they weren't.

Eventually, the picture would appear out of the disparate pieces. Eventually, he would be able to see the point of all of it.

He was beginning to see the point of all of it now, with this mission. The trouble he was having was the realization that the point of all this — all of his moving around and trying to jostle for position down here... there *was* no point.

This was not about the cartel, and who was in power. This was not about the coup, not about Victor gaining control, only to have the US government backed by the Venezuelans topple the man's power by usurping his throne.

That was the lofty, idealistic assumption Jack had made. That was what he had thought he and Rudy were going into. Now, he knew that had not been the case.

This was just a game of politicians, of directors and owners and fear-mongers and tycoons playing craps with people's lives.

"Jack, I need to hear you confirm the order."

"I can't confirm that order," Jack said. "This ends *now*. I'm going to trust my own instincts on this one. Victor needs to be taken down."

"Jack, I'm warning you. I can't protect you, unless you follow orders."

"What happens if Victor dies?" Jack asked again. "*Who* doesn't get paid? *Who* is behind all of this?"

There was no answer.

"Guess we'll find out."

CHAPTER 58

HEAVENS

HEAVENS PULLED his body up and out of the water with a gasp and coughing fit. He had nearly drowned in the explosion and its aftermath. The blast had shot him fifteen feet away from the boat, face-up in the river, which had been his saving grace. He had floated, passed out, about fifty yards downstream, the current taking him wherever it wanted to go. If the boat Jack had stolen — the same one he and his men had arrived on earlier — had passed him, the CIA man had not bothered to check to see if Heavens was alive.

He had been outplayed, outmaneuvered. It was rare, but his respect for this target had grown immensely.

Heavens would still kill the man, but at least he would stop underestimating him.

Heavens had floated downstream a bit farther, getting his bearings and trying to lie still so as not to attract attention from any creature that might be lying in wait beneath him. He knew the stories of rainforest anacondas were usually fanciful, usually exaggerated.

But a hungry mother snake, looking for a quick and easy meal...

He had shuddered thinking about it. The last thing he wanted was to fight off a gigantic angry snake as it tried to wrap around his body, choking the life out of him.

He pulled himself out of the water and onto a low beach area. He guessed he was still an hour from Manaus at a full jog, even through the trees and thick forest. He would make it, which meant he would still arrive later that day. Whether or not that would give him enough time to track and find the CIA operative again, he didn't know.

But he could at least meet up with the other team Reynolds had sent to him. They would likely assume he was dead, taking on the mantle of leadership and running the mission themselves. They would be as well-trained as him and his other men, which was good.

What was *not* good was that Heavens had not seen any of his other men yet. He knew two of them — Alameda and Joseph — had been killed before the blast, from gunshot wounds. He had seen their corpses light up on the boat the police officers and CIA man had been on.

Heavens had been working through the boat filled with cartel operatives, carefully placing a bullet between each of their eyes to ensure they were dead, while he looked for the remaining one or two soldiers still in hiding.

When the first boat had gone up in flames, he had acted quickly, moving through the boat with more speed. He had known he only had seconds before the freak attack and surprise wore off, so he wanted to get ahead and behind whatever soldiers were still left alive there.

He had just stepped around a hose laying over the second

deck and hanging down to the first floor, his eye on the back of one of the soldiers crouched behind a railing, when the boat he was on simply ceased to exist. The blast had shot him upward and outward, and it was a matter of significant luck that he had not hit anything on the way down that might have prevented his body from leaving the boat.

But something had hit him after he had landed in the water, and he had gotten knocked out.

The last thing he remembered was seeing a piece of the large corner railing, curved on one side, heading directly for his head.

He had tried to dive out of the way, but he had barely just landed in the water himself when the railing struck.

He felt where the impact was, the small divot leaking blood from the side of his head, but he chalked it up to another battlefield injury. He would exact his revenge by finishing the mission, by taking out this CIA *asshole* who seemed so intent on eluding him.

How had the man managed to get past a boatload of cartel men, three police officers, and four well-trained mercenaries?

It had to be a huge amount of luck and some serious train-ing. The man had acted so quickly, had set the trap between the two boats and caused the explosion as if it had been planned weeks in advance.

It was some *serious* luck, but Heavens would make sure that luck ran out.

Manaus was the final play, the final battlefield.

He would meet up with his second team of four — make it into a team of five unless any of his men had survived and made their way to the city — and together they would go confront the CIA man at the place where he was supposed to be in an hour: a warehouse on the far edge of town that apparently the cartel owned.

He stood and checked his gear. He was traveling light, not intending to stay the night in the woods. Hopefully, that would still be the case, that he could make it to Manaus unchecked, so he disassembled his rifle and put it back together, ensuring everything was still in working condition. He repeated the process with his sidearm, a trusty old Glock, and he even pulled his knife out of its locking sheath strapped to his leg to make sure there was nothing surprising there, like a broken blade or dull edge.

Satisfied all was in order, he set his sights on the horizon and started his journey.

That was the last time you get the jump on me. You'd better be ready.

JACK GOT INTO THE CAB, and the woman driving asked where he wanted to be dropped off. The woman smiled, then began driving. Jack had the pack next to him on the back seat, his head hung down, his palms open on his knees. He didn't bother buckling the seatbelt. He was exhausted, wasted. He wanted to leave, wanted to take the handler up on his offer, but he couldn't.

He was beyond the point of no return now. He was in this to the end.

He had no idea what sort of butterfly effect-style of chaos he would unleash on the world if Victor died. Worst-case scenario, some bigwig politician or lobbyist would get pissed and throw a tantrum back in Washington; perhaps the Venezuelan government would be set back a bit.

But none of that mattered to Jack. Best-case scenario, the cartel would fall completely, allowing some other corrupt group to take over, and the cycle would continue. More assets would be wasted, more operatives burned, more Rudys killed.

He didn't care about any of that — he just cared about one thing.

He hadn't realized it until now, but he *did* have a hidden mission. This whole reason for being here was Victor. He thought he could do *only* the job they commanded of him; thought he could follow orders like a good little soldier.

He was wrong.

As he sat in the cab, staring at his legs and wishing to feel anything but the pain from his side and shoulder and knee and everything else, all he could picture were the faces of his daughters.

The faces of the thirty kids who had been crammed into the lifeboat. The same lifeboat Victor had laced with explosives, then sent out into the bay.

He pictured his wife's horrified face, watching from his own lifeboat as it arrived in port later. He couldn't imagine the shock and horror she had felt while she had watched the lifeboat explode. She had not seen the children inside, but the meaning of it all would have been obvious.

He remembered his own feeling of intense betrayal, of pure shock and macabre disgust as he had seen the lifeboat turn into a ball of fire right before his eyes.

Even though he had secretly corralled all of the children to safety just before that, asking the captain of the boat to help him, it was disgusting. Victor had actually gone *through* with it. Jack had saved thirty souls that day — young boys and girls — innocent and terrified beyond their wildest dreams.

And Victor had pulled the trigger purposefully, not knowing that Jack had already rescued the kids. He was performing a mass execution of children.

All because Jack had trampled his plans.

All because Jack had merely *existed* and had gotten too close to Victor's orbit.

He had sensed it at the time, but it was no more than a feeling. Six months had passed, and in that time, Jack had been able to recover a bit, had been able to regain his balance and focus as he moved from CIA desk jockey to CIA operative. He was still young and relatively inexperienced, but he felt confident a simple recon mission would be a great way to get his feet under him, earn his stripes as a spook.

He had thought he could perform this duty admirably, providing recon, getting eyes on Victor, then passing it up the chain.

But now he knew that was all wrong. He knew the *real* reason he had come here. He knew what he had been planning all along — it was a truth he had not been ready to acknowledge. The reality of it hit him like a ton of bricks while sitting in the back of the taxi, silent and completely still, like an animal in hibernation.

Biding his time, waiting.

He knew the truth now with an intensity he had felt only a few times in his professional career. This time, though, it wasn't just *professional*. It was *personal* as well. Jack knew what he was going to do, knew what his subconscious had been screaming at him ever since the plane had gone down over the rainforest.

He was going to find Victor, all right. He would miss his exfiltration point, but that was not a big deal. This was a civilized place; there were plenty of flights leaving, plenty of boats he could take, plenty of paths and routes through the vast jungle to neighboring cities and states and countries. He could become a ghost, disappear as long as he needed, eventually making his way back home. No, that was not the problem.

The problem was he was going to directly go against the orders he had been given. He was going to be at odds with the CIA, with his government. But he was tired of trusting someone else's judgment, tired of the backstabbing and counterintelligence passed off as intelligence, as truth. He was tired of the lies, the deceit.

He would find Victor today.

As the taxi drove over the crest of a hill and he saw the larger city of Manaus sprawled out in the distance, Jack set his eyes on the horizon, the exact direction where he knew the warehouse — and Victor, waiting inside of it — would be.

He stared at it, still not moving, still not speaking. Barely breathing.

He was going to find Victor, all right.

And then he was going to kill him.

"I NEED AN UPDATE, REYNOLDS." Wyman held the hefty receiver to her ear as she snapped her fingers at the door. Immediately, Kenneth Ma appeared. "I'm getting a lot of heat over here, and you know I *hate* heat."

She waited for the man's reply. It came a few seconds later. *"I told you I would call when I have an update, Wyman,"* Reynolds said.

She thought she sensed tension in his voice, unease. Had something gone wrong? Had the mission already failed?

"I understand you *said* that, but I'd like the update *before* the update, if you don't mind."

This time he heard she heard him sigh deeply. *"Look, Wyman. This is dirty business. You got me running a wet op in another country. The more words we share, the less plausible deniability I can promise you."*

"I'm not concerned with the number of words we share, Reynolds. I'm paying you to do a job, and I'm paying *dearly* for it to be done correctly. *Give me an update.*"

Ma waited by the door, and just as Reynolds was about to

speak, she pulled the phone back up over her mouth. "Hold that thought," she snapped.

She could almost feel the man's hatred and anger burning toward her from the other end of the phone. He was military, trained to take orders and follow hierarchy. She was a civilian, and though the power dynamic had shifted in her favor, she knew these military brats never liked to let old habits die.

Still, she had important things to do. "Ma, I need you to cancel my meeting this afternoon. I know the lobby is absolutely *dying* to hear from me, but they're just going to have to wait another day."

"But the vote is coming up, Diane. If we don't —"

"I understand *exactly* when the vote is happening, Ma," she said, her anger now directed toward her favorite intern. "But *I'm* in this chair, and *you're* standing at the door questioning my authority. What does that tell you about which one of us probably has better information, and therefore can make better assessments of the situation?"

It wasn't rhetorical, and she waited for an answer.

Ma's mouth opened and closed as if he were a dying fish lying on the dock. "I... I don't know, ma'am. Sorry, I'll let them know."

She snapped her fingers again, and Ma disappeared. "Sorry about that, Reynolds." She forced a smile. "Now, where were we?"

"I believe *I was about to tell you that I haven't heard from my men,"* Reynolds said, his voice dripping with vitriol. *"Which means there is no update, yet. Now, can I get back to —"*

"Not so fast," Wyman said. "I just had to cancel a meeting with wing nuts representing the gun lobby, but they're going to come knocking. And they're going to want to know a little bit more than 'soldier boy didn't answer the phone.' What was the latest you've heard?"

Another long pause, the sound of tapping as Reynolds did something on his computer. *As if he doesn't know exactly what the last thing he had said to them was.* His voice returned a long moment later. *"They found your agent in a marketplace in Iquitos. Bumped into him, actually. But they weren't trying to take him out at the time, so they just kept eyes-on and moved with him throughout the city."*

"Agent? Just one?"

"That's right," Reynolds said. *"Apparently the other one got himself killed in the woods."*

"Good." She hadn't necessarily meant it the way it sounded — she didn't *enjoy* hearing about American soldiers getting killed in the line of duty, but her problems *had* just been divided in half.

"Right, good," Reynolds said. His voice was dripping with sarcasm now, as well. She knew he didn't think highly of anyone on Capitol Hill, least of all a woman who was now in charge of passing legislation that directly affected American intelligence groups. Reynolds himself was not such a group, but he was far more aligned with their side than hers.

Still, the man made his money by working in the cracks between intelligence organizations and US-based military assets. He worked in the gray areas, the areas the US government did not want to say they had anything to do with. He was paid handsomely for that, as were the men he owned. So she didn't bat an eye at his response, it was expected. Of *course* he wouldn't appreciate the work she had done; he could hardly understand it.

She gave a slight shake of her head and then continued.

"Okay, so after this marketplace 'bumping into,' what happened? You were told the parameters had changed, and that the remaining asset was to be *removed* completely. *Eliminated,* I think, was your exact word."

"Yes, that's what I said. Elimination is the term we use. But he has not been eliminated yet, best I can gather. They planned to hitch a ride downstream, where they saw the CIA man jump onto a boat. Last I heard, they were preparing to hit the boat early the next morning while it was still dark, or at least dawn."

"What the hell happened? It's been hours since then. You haven't heard *anything*?

"Negative, they've been radio silent ever since the planned attack. But it doesn't necessarily mean the op went south. I would have expected an update from them by now either way."

"Then why haven't you?

"Listen, Wyman. I'll let you in on a little secret: these guys are professionals, as I am. You might call yourself one as well, but you're in a completely different world than the one I live and breathe in. We don't have to respect each other, but I need you to know right now that I'm running this op better than anyone on the planet could, with the possible exception of a few of those four-star generals that get to brush elbows with the president.

"So if I tell you that my men will report in when they have information, they will report in when they have information. I don't need you or anyone else breathing down my neck."

She waited a beat, then two. "You done?"

She knew he wanted to slam the phone down, to hang up on her and be done with the whole thing. But he had pride to recover, had his manhood to protect. *"Yeah, Wyman, I'm done. And I suggest we be done with this phone call. I'll let you know when I hear something else."*

She smiled wider now. "Very good," she said. "That's all I needed to know. I just wanted to make sure you were on top of things."

This time she took the opportunity to slam the receiver for him. The encrypted phone dinged the old-school bell built into the cradle, and she pushed her chair back, spreading her arms wide in a stretch. It wasn't *good* news, but it wasn't necessarily *bad* news, either. She could spin it, or have Kenneth Ma write something up that told the lobbyists what was going on.

Whatever she did, she was *not* going to lose this opportunity. The money was too good to pass up, and it was the best kind: completely untraceable and not reportable. No one would ever know it had exchanged hands and ended up in her wallet.

But it wasn't just the money this operation offered — it was also about the *power* she would gain from accomplishing this for the lobby. They controlled a good section of the voting population of her home state, and they could sway decisions with barely a word.

And the group had membership that included foreign nationals, as well. Though she was not in a position to take advantage of that sort of thing yet, it still felt good to know she had cards to play, should the time arise. There were some high officials involved in the government of Venezuela, as well as a few ambassadors of the country that she most wanted to please. They were technically enemies of the United States, but she remembered the old adage as she waited for Ma to return.

The enemy of my enemy is my friend...

If they wanted to keep this Vínculos asshole alive for a few more minutes, so be it. She would do her part.

And that meant she would make sure Reynolds would do

his part. She almost wished he had not gotten involved, but it was too late for that. These lobby idiots flip-flopped almost as much as real politicians, so by her wanting to get ahead of things, she had inadvertently gotten Reynolds' crew involved.

Now she had to backpedal, but she *was* an expert, like Reynolds had said. It hadn't taken long to find something to use — something even Reynolds thought was covered up.

Apparently the strait-laced, military-disciplined proprietor of a private security firm wasn't *perfect*, either.

Apparently, he had a thing for a much younger woman — a fact she had gleaned from the video footage Ma had dug up. And all it took was a gentle nudge, a mention of the hotel they had checked into, and Reynolds broke. He had pleaded, claiming to love his wife. She had listened intently, waiting for the blustering idiot to stop pandering.

When he did, she had made herself clear: this dirt gets swept under the rug, *as long as the CIA asset doesn't come home.*

It was a small price to pay to keep the world running smoothly, and now Reynolds was ingratiated to her side, as well. It was a win-win-win.

Well, the CIA operative was decidedly *not* going to win, but whoever they were, they had signed up for it. It was their job — these people all existed to serve their glorious country. She figured they all wanted nothing more than to die in the field, protecting and serving.

Happy to help with that, she thought.

JACK LEFT THE TAXI. He tossed the rest of the cash he'd stolen from the shopkeeper — a few dollars weren't going to be enough to purchase anything useful, certainly not passage out of Manaus. He figured he might as well go for broke, perhaps cash in on his thievery and pay this guy a little extra for his trouble. It wasn't *exactly* the 'pay it forward' approach, but perhaps it would help right a wrong in the universe or something.

It wasn't going to balance the scales — it wouldn't cancel out his debts with the general store owner he had robbed at gunpoint — but it was better than nothing.

Once again broke. And still far more beaten than he would have liked to admit, Jack heaved the pack out of the back seat and hobbled over to the building he had told the driver to drop him off in front of. It was an abandoned bookstore, and it would be the place where he would perform his recon and surveillance of the warehouse near it. The bookstore was three stories tall — plenty tall enough to see down to the warehouse and river next to it, and it had the added benefit of being just off a main thoroughfare through town. The streets weren't completely deserted, but if he could gain access to the bookstore building, he'd be able to stay out of sight well enough.

Jack ignored the expressions of surprise at his dirty, limping figure making its way down the street. He moved quickly, not wanting the stares to linger, but also knowing he was on the clock. He gained access to the old building easily, then took the stairs to the top floor. There, he dumped the pack on the ground next to a wide window. He had scoped out this building while in the taxi and saw that the windows on this floor were tinted, impossible to see into if he stood at least a foot back from them.

He took out Rudy's binoculars, then stood still by the window, examined the warehouse complex on the open land across the street. He checked his watch, already knowing the time but wanting to go through the motions anyway.

Two minutes.

He was sure Victor wouldn't be coming *exactly* two minutes from now — the man would either be fashionably late or he was already here, preparing. But from his talk with the handler, Jack assumed his presence here was not a surprise — there were other factions still after him, and if they all knew where Jack was headed, this place would be a party very soon.

Jack surveilled the warehouse and its surrounding outpost buildings. There were four in all: the single, flat warehouse, a support building connected to its southern side by way of a sheet metal roof, and two smaller shacks dotting the perimeter.

The main warehouse was a low, squat building the farthest away from him. Neither of the small shacks had windows, so Jack assumed they weren't guard outposts but rather meant for storage or maintenance. There was a barbed-wire fence running around the front side of the land that met up with the road, disappearing into the forest on the south. He assumed it formed the perimeter of the land owned by the cartel, surrounding the warehouse on all sides.

He didn't have time to walk a full perimeter — a move he would have done given more time. That would have allowed him to measure any guard movements; whether or not Victor had ordered his cartel men to do their own perimeter walks and examine the grounds, watching for intruders.

Instead, he had to resort to a sniper-like calculation — he would make do with what he saw here. It would have to be enough. He felt he could barely afford the two minutes, but without seeing what he was up against, there was no way he was going to just march onto the property and start shooting without knowing how many people he would meet inside.

He noticed at least four guards now, all wearing camouflage fatigues and holding assault rifles. They also wore something else.

Red bandanas. Around their necks.

Jack frowned. *Shining Path? Here?*

It seemed absurd, but they were dressed exactly the same way the two soldiers Rudy had killed in the forest had been dressed. He was too far away to see any markings on their person, but there was no other reason for them to be wearing bandanas — *or* to have them the same color as the *Sendero Luminoso*.

He saw five other men as well — these were not dressed like Shining Path soldiers, but civilians. Still, he knew the cartel would be hiding in plain sight, just as he had done in Iquitos. Victor's men wouldn't appear like soldiers but rather as plain-clothes civilians, harmless bystanders.

But they were inside the fence, so Jack knew better. He trusted his instincts, trusted his gut. These men were absolutely carrying weapons, either guns or knives, and they would all join in the attack as soon as Jack tried to gain entrance to the property.

He gave his reconnaissance a single minute, far shorter than he liked, as most of the guards on any patrol would take at least five times that long before changing positions and moving on to the next station. But he didn't see anyone else, at least not from his perch from the second-story window. Now, he focused on a route into the property. He had no sniper rifle, no way to take Victor out from afar, and he assumed Victor would be hidden well within the confines of the warehouse, safe from whatever happened outside.

He had no large explosives, either. There would be no way to take out the warehouse altogether, men and all.

Jack had feared this, but assumed it was inevitable: he would need to gain access to the grounds, somehow sneak past all of the guards, get into the warehouse, find Victor, and then kill him.

It was the longest of all long shots, but it's what Jack was trained to do.

Jack saw something out of the corner of his eye. He pulled the binoculars down from his face and frowned. From his right side, toward the southeast, was movement. A vehicle crested the hill just on the edge of town, the forest to its right and the river beyond that. It was heading down the very street Jack's building was on. When it came into focus a second later, Jack saw that it was no civilian vehicle.

It was a *tank*.

JACK

THE VEHICLE WAS a light artillery vehicle, capable of carting a handful of soldiers inside its reinforced hull. A massive 50-caliber gun was mounted on top of it, and Jack could see from here the clipped rounds rolling down into a pile on top of it — it was armed and ready for action.

The truck rolled down toward the front gate, and Jack immediately knew what was going on. The mercenaries had *also* found the location Jack was aiming for. They didn't care about Victor; they weren't here for the cartel.

All they wanted was Jack, and they had rolled up to the front gates, waiting for him to arrive.

It wasn't even a standoff; the men inside the gate simply watched as the vehicle parked a hundred yards away on the street. To them, it would look to be nothing more than the Brazilian military rolling through town. Not a common occurrence in Manaus, but not one completely unexpected, either. There were Army bases in the area, and there was plenty of illegal logging activity, drug running, and other criminal enterprises that required Brazilian military intervention. Having a few soldiers around was not going to startle anyone.

Whether or not he could get past the mercenaries was another question altogether. They were far better equipped than he was, with their M4 carbines and sidearms, as well as their fresh bodies that had not been through hell.

Jack only recognized one of the men — the same one he had bumped into in the market. He was now sitting in the passenger seat of the military truck, and his distinctive deep, hollow eyes stared out at the road ahead.

Jack cursed, then pulled away from the window. He shoved the binoculars back into the pack. He felt for the Taurus at his side, then walked back toward the stairwell. He did his best not to trip and die on the stairs, fighting against every urge to just sit down and take a nap. Thankfully the pain had been replaced by the pounding adrenaline he was starting to feel.

A plan was forming, one that would either get him killed immediately or help him gain access to the base.

He hoped it would be enough to get him past the first line of defense — the fence and the man standing guard behind it.

Jack reached the bottom floor, then pushed open the doors, no longer worried about being spotted — he was about to bring the fight to him, dressed in a ridiculous Hawaiian shirt and swim trunks. At least he still had his boots — the road ahead would be hard and grueling on his feet.

He turned right, heading up the street to the corner, then held back. There was a narrow alleyway set between the building he had been standing in previously and the row of one-story, dilapidated buildings next to the road where the vehicle had parked. He turned right here, adjusting the pack and tightening it around his shoulders as he walked over dirty puddles and bags of trash lying next to dumpsters. He counted off fifty paces, guessing this was the distance between where he had been previously and where the army vehicle would be. He looked to his left, satisfied to find another dumpster, this one with its lid closed. He reached out and forced his legs up and over the dumpster. He groaned the entire time, his side splitting and threatening to break his new bandages.

He pulled himself up onto his knees and then his feet, then reached up and grabbed the edge of the roof. It was corrugated metal and bent as his fingers held his weight. Still, he squeezed tightly on the edge, swinging his body from left to right. With a herculean effort, he swung to his right and brought his right leg up and over the side of the metal. He felt the edge of the sharp metal cutting into his pant leg, but ignored it, bringing his left leg up next and rolling to the side, on top of the flat roof. It sloped gently upward, reaching an apex that allowed him to latch onto.

He brought his Taurus up and held it out in front of him, then pulled his prone body toward the top of the shallow sloped roof. He saw the vehicle right in front of him.

He waited, watching as one of the Shining Path-dressed guards walked in front of his line of sight. He needed to make sure the path was perfectly lined up — he didn't necessarily need to hit the guy, but he needed to make it obvious where the shots originated.

He waited, satisfied when the man crossed in front of the end of his pistol barrel. It was an impossible shot, over 300 yards. But again, he wasn't trying to hit the man.

Jack aimed and fired, sending three quick rounds in the man's direction. All of them missed wide, but it got the man's attention. He brought his weapon up, hitting the ground but coming to his knees a second later.

The mercenaries also snapped into action, two of them jumping out of the back of the vehicle and coming around to Jack's side, using the vehicle as cover. Jack pushed back from the roof immediately, knowing that they would be looking up at him, knowing the shots had come from their side of the road.

But the Shining Path soldier did not think that at all. To him, the *army* truck had fired at him. Jack heard the soldier fire back, aiming directly at the front passenger window of the vehicle. He heard glass shatter, metal pinging as bullets hit the side of the truck.

The mercenary Jack had bumped into was shouting orders now, though he couldn't make out what they were.

The vehicle tore off suddenly, spraying rocks and dirt back as the two mercenaries left behind shouted at one another. He heard their voices approach from just behind the top of the roof, but they were merely seeking cover alongside the front of the shops down below Jack's perch.

More shots from the Shining Path side of the fence came, and Jack was satisfied to hear the sounds of gunshots, the battle kicking up and immediately raging.

He pushed back down the rooftop, almost laughing as he realized that the next part of his mission would be the hardest part.

He needed to jump down onto the dumpster lid once more.

His body was not going to forgive him for that.

RATHER THAN RISK jumping through the top of the dumpster with his full weight all at once, Jack pushed himself back on the roof, sliding feet-first on his belly. His feet fell over the edge, and he slowed his descent with his bare hands squeaking against the corrugated steel.

He let his feet dangle for a second, his side nearly splitting with the awkward stretch over the wound in his belly, but he held on. He waited for his feet to stop wiggling; then, he dropped the rest of the way.

The roof of the dumpster held as he landed on it, and he came to a crouch and then hopped off the side of it and back onto solid ground.

Jack was already moving; his feet pulled him toward the end of the alley, continuing in the direction he had come in from. He reached it, then turned left, nearing the end of the small strip center. To his left, back another fifty yards, he could hear the two mercenaries still firing onto the warehouse grounds.

He heard no alarms, but there would be more men coming now. Even directly in front of him, he saw a couple of men sprinting out from the warehouse and attached building, aiming toward the far fence on the south side of the grounds.

That was also Jack's target, though it wasn't going to be for the same reason.

Instead, Jack targeted a position diagonally across the street, one aiming directly into the thickest of the woods near the warehouse. He couldn't sprint, but he brought his legs forward as fast as they would work, holding the bandage to his side as he did so.

This would be the most vulnerable he had been in a while, and he needed the mercenaries not to pay him any attention.

Unfortunately, he was wearing a Hawaiian shirt, bright yellow socks, holding his side, and limping, all while holding a pistol in his right hand. He was basically wearing a flag that screamed, 'shoot me! I'm the CIA guy you've been trying to kill.'

He was halfway across the road when one of the mercenaries turned to do just that.

Fifty yards was easy enough for the assault rifle he was holding, but Jack was already in motion, and the man had not anticipated him to break free from the side of the buildings.

Jack dove forward, reaching a dense crowd of ferns at the far side of the road just as the bullet impacts hit the dirt road behind him. He felt the three vials in his pocket, miraculously still alive. They were heavy ceramic, but he had put them through hell. It was incredible they hadn't smashed to pieces while jumping around.

He pulled his body forward into the bushes, suddenly realizing that he had again torn his bandage and scab free. His side was screaming once again, the impact with the dirt on the side of the road tearing open the wound once more. Blood spilled down his right side, and there was nothing he could do to stanch it.

He was still wearing the pack, the added weight only helping to re-injure his wound as he landed, but he couldn't drop it just yet. By this point, it was a part of him, a part of the mission. He almost felt like leaving it would be like leaving a man behind.

He wanted to drop it at his feet and keep moving, but there might be something he needed later from it.

If I need to strangle Victor with a soggy map, I'm prepared for that.

The thought didn't console him, nor did it do anything to settle his nerves.

Laying in the weeds and ferns at the edge of this section of jungle, Jack swung around and dropped the pack next to him. He kept his Taurus up and aimed at the road where he had gone into the jungle. If the mercenary who had fired at him really wanted to get a good shot, he would be coming over now, chasing Jack into the forest.

Jack needed to reload. He used his left hand to open his pack and rustle around for ammunition. The box of rounds inside had spilled out everywhere, and he felt the cold metallic shells after every other thing he touched.

Finally, he found a preloaded magazine. He grabbed this as he ditched the old magazine, tossing it into the bag instead. He slapped the magazine into his Taurus.

The mercenary never appeared, and Jack took this as a

good omen. The battle was still raging beyond, the shots from both the cartel side and the mercenary side in full force. The mercenary who had ordered the truck to drive away had been smart; they had split the cartel's forces in two, and with the mercenary's longer-range weaponry and better training, each man might be able to handle three or four of the cartel's forces.

JACK'S TARGET was not the gate, where all of the mercenaries and Shining Path fighters were gathered. Nor was it any of the surrounding fence area around the warehouse. The barbed wire, perched atop eight-foot-tall fences all the way around, would be impossible for Jack to get over without killing himself, and it would leave him a sitting duck far too long.

No, his target was something much more subtle — an area he knew would be unguarded.

He ran through the forest and reappeared outside the fence on the southern property line, directly in front of a concrete pipeline.

The hole in front of him was barely larger than the width of his shoulders, but that was fine — Jack knew it wouldn't shrink. The drainpipe ran the length of the property from this side of the fence to the warehouse, an underground exhaust line for flooding and drainage.

Somewhere inside the warehouse would be a metal grate, heavy but not impossible to move. He would have to deal with whatever guards were inside Victor's base, but thanks to the commotion outside, he was hoping that would be easy enough.

He ran from the forest, nearly tripping over his injured leg, and fell onto his elbows and knees right in front of the pipe. There was a trickle of water standing in it, which drained out into a swampy section of forest floor that eventually met a small feeder stream.

There was nothing else in the pipe, and Jack hoped he wasn't about to stumble into the home of some predator that had taken up residence inside. With the heavy rains from the monsoon season almost past, he suspected this pipe was regularly flushed clean. Gutters and other feeds into the tube would make this an uninhabitable spot.

Or so he hoped.

Jack crawled forward, his knees scraping on the concrete of the bottom of the pipe, but he ignored it. He lifted his legs a bit higher both to cut down on the sound and any scratching that may rip his pants.

He proceeded like this for fifteen minutes, eventually reaching the pinprick of light he had seen from the beginning of the tunnel. The concrete tube was bisected here by a metal shaft, also circular, with a round metal grate covering its top. Jack stood up, his head barely hitting the bottom of the grate. He looked up and out through the slats and noticed that he was still outside. He crouched back down, then continued crawling.

Another ten minutes passed, and now he no longer heard gunfire. Either the teams outside had exhausted themselves, or he was so far away from where the battle was raging he could no longer hear them.

Five more minutes passed as he crawled on before he was finally met with another metal vertical shaft. He stood up in this one, but it was dark. He couldn't get a read on where he was until he let his eyes adjust. He thought he saw dim lights coming from somewhere up above and assumed he was somewhere inside the warehouse or the attached building.

Good enough, he thought.

He raised his arms, eliciting a sharp cry from his shoulder, and winced. *Not sure when I got* that *injury.* He proceeded more slowly now, his right side inflamed and hurting, but gripped the slats with both hands and pushed.

Nothing happened.

He tried again, finally finding that the grate was locked in place. He tried to get a hand up and out to feel around, but his wrist wouldn't fit through the thin slats.

He brought his hand back down, shook them to relax his muscles, and then tried again. This time he twisted to the left as if opening a jar from the inside out. He pushed with everything he had, trying to force whatever was holding the lid free.

It worked an inch. There was a loud groaning sound, and he pulled back, waiting.

He heard no sounds, no shouts of surprise or footsteps running over toward him, so he dared to try again. He twisted once more, this time pushing upward at the same time, and he felt a soft pop as the rusty metal grate finally came free. It was heavier than he thought, perhaps fifty or sixty pounds, but he didn't need to carry it far. He pushed it sideways, wincing again as the sound of the metal-on-concrete floor scraped and squawked and reverberated through the larger room above him.

He waited a few extra seconds, then, with a final heave, pushed the grate to the side.

But Jack's job wasn't done. He gave his hands one more break, then lifted his arms and pulled his upper body through the manhole.

He was inside.

JACK

JACK ASSUMED this was the smaller room that shared a roof with the warehouse, but was not technically part of the main building. Besides the concrete floor with its grate at the center of it, the room looked like it had been set up as an administrative office for an industrial or commercial enterprise. Cheap desks lined two walls, phones and computers on them that looked like they had not been turned on in years.

A healthy layer of dust and grime covered everything, and file cabinets stood looming against the walls in between. At the center of the room, near where Jack had emerged from his concrete pipe, were more desks. Only one looked like it had been used recently, a single laptop laying on its surface, closed. It was plugged into a surge protector on the ground that ran to an extension cord. The chair had been pushed back from it.

The grate itself sat dead-center in the room, and Jack looked in the direction the pipe traveled underground. The same concrete tube that ran underneath this smaller building would terminate somewhere in the main, larger space beyond.

That was where Jack wanted to go. He considered taking

the same route to the larger space — climbing back down into the hole and replacing the grate over his head, but he didn't want to take the risk of popping out a second time, this time in the middle of a group of pissed-off cartel grunts.

While the battle raged outside, inside would be Victor's domain, and he would likely have plenty of soldiers guarding him inside. If the warehouse was in fact going to be used for transporting the cartel's wares down the Amazon, it would also be filled with contraband. Drugs, ammunition, weapons. All of it would need to find a home here, at least temporarily, as the logistics chain collected the goods from the runners through all of their flows, which then were shipped out on boats in larger quantities to head down to their final destination at the port on the Pacific coast.

From there, the items would be dispersed around the world to whatever markets Victor's cartel operated in.

The main boss of the cartel now was mostly a figurehead position — all of this was Victor's work. The Vínculos had grown marijuana and poppy plants in the jungles of Venezuela, eventually growing large enough to attract the attention of the Venezuelan government. Bribes were made, corrupt politicians were paid off, and the cartel was allowed to operate unchecked for fifteen years.

When Victor rose to power, ingratiating himself with his leader, he had carved out a chunk of the empire for himself and built the Vínculos into what they were today.

Everyone expected the leader of the cartel to die soon — either by way of assassination from within or outside the operation — or from natural causes. The man was in his late eighties, and rumors were that he never left his house.

Victor, therefore, was next in line.

Jack couldn't figure out what had changed. What possibly could have happened that would have changed the minds of those pulling the strings back in Washington? Why would Victor now be their golden boy, marked as safe from whatever power struggles plagued the region? Why the sudden one-eighty — in the middle of Jack and Rudy's intelligence operation? What had caused them to change course to make sure Victor did *not* get killed?

Jack stood in the dark room, pondering everything, realizing suddenly that he was going to be totally exposed if someone opened either the door leading further into the warehouse or the door leading outside. He moved to stand behind the desk, finding safety behind the metal slab. He had his Taurus in his hand now. The first person coming through either door would get a bullet to the head.

He stepped forward now, making his decision. His body was falling apart, his muscles tired and weak, but he still had a job to do.

Victor would be here soon, if he wasn't already inside the warehouse.

He tried to imagine what he would find inside. If it were a drug operation only, there would be workers there, packaging and preparing loads of cocaine. Even with the additional contraband he knew the Vínculos engaged in — weapons and ammunition — he imagined rows of tables set up in the larger space, dozens of paid cartel staff counting and collecting, tracking every item that needed to be shipped in or out. The operation would be massive, once it got up to speed.

But it was quiet. There was no noise coming from the other, larger space. Victor had not set all of this in motion yet. Their intelligence report said that Victor would arrive first, preparing the warehouse for his needs, getting in tight with local Manaus officials as needed. Then, in the weeks and months to come, he would ramp up production, hiring cartel men and women to staff the warehouse and get things running smoothly.

It was no different than the massive distribution centers for merchants back in the United States. Usually, they would buy cheap land outside of town, hire at minimum wage an army of employees, then drive them hard to extract every ounce of output from them before burning them out and moving to the next wave of recruits.

This warehouse would be much the same in short order.

And he intended to stop Victor before it got that far.

Burning down the place would have no effect — Victor had plenty of money to build a new warehouse. It was all sheet metal and cheap construction materials, anyway. It would barely set him back. And with the powers of the Vínculos in the region now, Jack assumed they wouldn't even need a warehouse to hide inside of — they could simply operate an open-air market, dealing in black-market drugs and shipments of drugs, free and clear thanks to their clout, or the officials would be paid well enough to look the other way.

Unless I can stop this at the source, Jack thought.

And he knew that source well. He just needed to find him.

CHAPTER 66

JACK

JACK FLUNG the door open and stepped through a narrow five-foot-long hallway. He heard noises, a clattering of metal, from farther within the larger warehouse. Another door sat at the opposite end of this hallway. The space was like an airlock, obviously built later and connected. Jack held the Taurus with both hands, now feeling more vulnerable than ever.

He had left the pack behind as it wouldn't fit through the tube, but it had done its job. Now, it would just weigh him down.

He cursed himself for not bringing an extra magazine but quickly realized that he would be in significant trouble if there were enough targets inside the warehouse to even *warrant* an entire clip.

He waited by the opposite door for a minute, listening. The sounds inside were rhythmic, likely caused by some machine. But the mere fact that he was hearing it meant he was not alone in this larger building. He didn't know how the warehouse would be split up — if it would just be a long, open room with columns holding up the roof, or if it had been subdivided into smaller sections. Their intel had not given him anything useful about the building aside from its location. They just knew that the Vínculos — specifically Victor — owned the land that this building had been constructed on.

He took a few breaths, checked the handle of the door, then twisted it open carefully. His back was against the wall next to the door, and he eyed the space through the widening crack. It seemed the area beyond was smaller than the overall warehouse building, and he let the door fall open a little wider. He quickly brought his gun up and centered, glancing around in the room, letting the pistol follow his eyes as he cleared the space.

This room was empty, save for boxes and crates stacked up inside. Shipments, most likely. He saw a garage door along the wall he had just been hiding on the other side of. It was possible this would be a staging area where trucks would be loaded up and driven to the port at Manaus, taking all of the crates and their contents downstream.

Jack pressed against this wall, eyeing the room to find the next doorway. Another garage door sat opposite the one he had seen, and next to that, a smaller interior door.

He hustled to this door and pressed his ears against the wall next. He heard the clattering sound, louder now, and thought he could pick out voices in there as well. He tested the handle again, then twisted it. Just as he had done before, he let it open a crack, then peered inside.

He had been right. This larger space in the center of the warehouse was where the magic happened. Rows of tables stood near the center of this room, shelves along the walls. It was a high-ceilinged room with a catwalk running around the second level. He could see a few more doors on the opposite side of the large space.

And he saw guards.

The three guards he saw were pacing along the catwalk, AK-47s in their hands. They watched below as about a dozen men and women sat or stood at the tables, processing all sorts of contraband.

It was exactly as he had imagined, but he didn't relish in the discovery for long.

There were at least as many guards on the side of the room directly above him — the side he couldn't see, and he knew he needed a better plan than to just run out the middle of the room and start firing in every direction.

He snuck out this door, not bothering to close it behind him, and kept in the shadows underneath the catwalk on his side of the room. All the people working at tables far away were heads-down in their work, and no one looked up, or even glanced in his direction.

Jack kept his back pressed against the wall, the Taurus in both hands, watching the guards and darting his eyes from one to the other, then down to the main floor and back.

While he was not a fan of cartel men who had devoted their lives to crime and murder, he had no specific beef with any of these guards. Attacking them would only get him killed — there were more of them, they were better prepared and armed, and they had the upper hand.

Unfortunately, he would have to get through *them* to find Victor.

One of the guards turned and began walking the catwalk directly over Jack's head. He fell silent, not moving, hidden next to a post holding up the wall and roof of the warehouse.

He waited for the man to pass, but instead, the guard stopped, waiting directly above Jack.

He held his breath. Another few seconds went by, and the man started pacing again, heading back in the other direction.

Jack let out a breath and picked up his speed. To move was to invite attention, and to invite attention was death. But to stay still was to just postpone the inevitable.

Jack was aiming for a door at the end of the room, on the wall to his left. There was nothing special about this door — it just happened to be the next-closest one to him. He assumed he could not make his way around this central area through the smaller rooms around the perimeter, but he could at least poke his head in and try.

Or perhaps he would get lucky and find Victor behind this very door, sitting down and watching TV.

Jack smiled at the thought. *If only it were so easy.*

Jack held his breath once again and made his way toward that door. Finding it unlocked as well, he twisted it. He winced as he pushed, suddenly realizing his mistake.

The other two doors had not created any noise whatsoever when he had opened them. This one, however, was *very* squeaky.

A loud sound pierced over the low din of the metallic clanging of the workers inside and their voices from the larger space.

He felt the air in the room get sucked out, all noise suddenly seizing.

A shout, then another. Gunfire erupted from above him.

He had no choice now. He pushed his shoulder through the door, swinging the weapon and his upper body around as he did so. More gunfire reached the doorway, splintering the frame right where he had previously been standing.

Inside this room, he found more crates, more boxes. But it was also devoid of human life. He rushed over to one of the boxes and lifted the lid. Blocks of gleaming white cocaine, triple-wrapped in cellophane, stared back at him.

"Dammit," he whispered. He tried another crate, this one right next to the first one. Also full of bricks of cocaine.

He strode over to the far side of the room, wondering if maybe the crates were grouped together by what they contained. He pushed the lid off this one as he heard footsteps racing down a metal staircase along this wall outside in the main room.

More drugs.

"Way to go, Jack," he told himself. "You had to stop in the room with the *drugs*, not in the room with the *guns*."

Jack had no idea what was inside the crates back in the previous room, but if all of the crates in here were full of cocaine, he had to assume one of the other rooms would contain useful weaponry.

Whether or not those weapons would be loaded, or if ammunition was nearby, he did not know either.

All he knew was that he couldn't kill somebody with a brick of cocaine.

CHAPTER 67

JACK

HE FELT the Taurus heavy in his hands, once again glad he had returned for the old friend. He wouldn't last long against multiple assault rifle-toting mercenaries and cartel soldiers, but at least this room didn't have any rear entrances. He could put up a stand, at least die with his back against the wall.

There was a lot of commotion coming from outside the doorway as the workers beyond reacted to the gunfire. Screams from women and men alike reached his ears, as well as the battering sound of rifle fire on the outside of the doorway.

The gunfire seized shortly after that, and Jack lowered his body behind the two crates he had just checked inside. He waited, knowing what was coming next.

He heard their footsteps long before they reached the doorway. They had stopped firing because their leader had likely told them to let two guards rush the door to check inside and find whoever was sneaking around.

The first man rushed into the room, and Jack fired twice. He didn't need to — the first shot hit the man just above his nose, immediately sending him flying backward, his head sporting a new hole.

The second man hesitated, but his body was almost through the door already.

Jack fired low, hitting him in the hip, and the man stumbled forward. Jack finished him off with two more rounds to his side.

Okay, Jack. Time to move. He only had a few seconds before the doorway would erupt in gunfire again as the soldiers upstairs realized their two men had been taken out by the enemy combatant inside.

Jack slid across the room, one leg tucked underneath the other like a runner sliding for second base, and he stopped as his foot impacted the first of the dead guards. Jack lowered to his back and laid there for a second, feeling around with his hands.

He found the man's weapon and pulled it away from the soldier's grip with his left hand, the Taurus still in his right.

He stuck the pistol back into its holster and pulled the AK up with both hands, still lying on the floor as a smattering of gunfire found the doorway. He kicked off the dead man's side and slid backward again, farther into the center of the room, away from the doorway.

More shouts and commotion fell into the room, joined by more footsteps of men stomping down the stairs.

Jack sat up and crouched, not aiming for the doorway but instead the space right next to it.

He waited, counting off the seconds.

His ears told him the men coming downstairs were down by now and were silently making their way to the doorway, pausing there and waiting for Jack to emerge, or for one of them to toss a grenade inside.

Jack didn't want either option to happen.

He fired the AK-47, quickly reacting and fixing his aim with the sudden kickback, emptying half the magazine into the sheet metal wall next to the doorway.

He stopped, then heard two distinct *pops* — two bodies smacking hard onto the concrete floor.

Four down.

He had counted at least six guards in the room outside, but there were likely more around the rest of the warehouse's room spaces. He had gotten lucky in not finding anyone in the rooms he had entered so far, but his luck was bound to run out.

For that reason, he needed to level the playing field. Staying inside this room would not end well for Jack. Eventually, his magazine would run dry, and his gun would be useless. At that point, Victor himself could walk in and put a bullet between Jack's eyes.

He rushed over to the first of the dead soldiers that had fallen in the room, the man whose gun he had stolen, and felt around the man's pant pockets.

He pulled out a single flashbang grenade.

The Vínculos cartel was obviously well-funded — thus well-equipped — but he was still surprised to see a flashbang grenade on a non-military unit. Usually a flash grenade would be more useful if the tables were turned — throwing it into a smaller room was a better use for the explosive, as the *bang* part would happen in an enclosed space.

But Jack didn't have the luxury of ordering the remaining guards into a small room so he could take them all out with one throw.

Therefore, he would use the device not as it was intended — not to blind and disable his enemy — but more as a *distraction*. It would affect anyone in the larger room — even the workers who might still be there — but Jack didn't have a choice. While the stun grenade emitted a pop at nearly 170 decibels, this would be diminished in the larger space.

They would all heal.

He pulled the pin and tossed it sidearm out the door. He had to use an angle to throw so he wouldn't reveal his position and frame to the shooters outside. Nevertheless, the throw was on target, clanging off the wall outside and bouncing back toward the center of the larger space.

And there, it exploded.

Jack had squeezed his eyes shut after the count and turned his head in the opposite direction, but he still felt the effects as the grenade popped in the opposite room. The effects he felt were nothing compared to what everyone out there would be feeling. Jack was already in motion, bringing the AK back up as he ran out of the room.

The attackers would not be incapacitated for long, if they were at all. Those on the second floor would have been affected the least, and while the white flash would be blinding, it wouldn't completely incapacitate them.

Jack didn't have the standard five to seven seconds — he only had one or two.

He sprinted as fast as he could, aiming for the smoking remains of the flashbang's metal-oxidant explosive smoke wafting from the center of the room.

He rushed toward one of the tables just as he noticed movement from the second floor.

One of the guards had fallen but was recovering quickly,

swinging his AK-47 around as he tried to stand. Jack fired wildly, spraying from one side of the man to the other, hoping that one of the bullets stuck.

At least one did, but Jack knew the men would be wearing body armor. If they had stun grenades and AK47s, they would have armor as well. The man stumbled backward, hitting the wall behind him, but he was still alive.

Jack didn't have time to wait around. He knew the other guards would also be homing in on his position. He kept moving, hitting one of the tables with his butt and left hand as he bumped into it from behind. Jack used his hand to pull the table up and over onto its side, then crouched behind it, looking up at the wall in front of him. He saw one more guard over to the left side of the room, rubbing his eyes but beginning to stand.

It was a long shot, but Jack steadied his gaze, took a breath, and fired a quick burst.

The man went down. Shots rang out over Jack's head, starting from behind over his left shoulder. He flung himself to the ground, pressing his belly flat onto the concrete.

He was pinned down now, exactly in the position he had hoped *not* to get into. When he had left the previous room, he had taken the risk that there were still guards on the left-side catwalk, ones that had remained upstairs while some of their cohorts came downstairs to fight him. He was hoping that the four men he had already taken out were from this side, and with his back up against the table, he would be able to see the remaining attackers. He had taken two of them down, killing at least one, but there were apparently another two or three behind him now.

Far too many.

Jack lay on the ground, clutching the AK-47 above his head, knowing that his luck had officially run out.

CHAPTER 68

JACK

JACK WAITED, still pinned to the floor. The cartel soldiers behind him were spreading out — he heard the man directly behind his position on the second level shouting at his two counterparts. These two had spread out from their central position and were now making their way around the perimeter of the room. He winced, knowing they would be shooting from both directions — and if he popped up, all three.

He couldn't exactly run in the opposite direction back toward the edge of the room, either. The tables were the only cover around and leaving them now would mean instant death.

He had sorely miscalculated — his adrenaline had gotten the best of him, caused him to stop thinking. He knew he could take out one, perhaps two of the guards if he could catch them off-balance, but the third — and fourth, or more, if they entered the room — was the issue. He swore he had only seen three guards on one side of the upper catwalk and assumed three more would be on the other side.

He had killed six already, so how were there three more remaining? At most, he guessed there would be eight.

When had he gone wrong?

Well, he argued with himself, *coming here in the first place, completely alone with no backup, was likely the first mistake.*

Perhaps the battle outside had waned, and the mercenaries had been overwhelmed and killed. Perhaps a few Shining Path or cartel members had come back inside.

He still couldn't figure out how the Shining Path was here, seemingly working with the cartel. Were they only *dressed* as Shining Path soldiers? Why?

All these thoughts and more flashed through Jack's mind as he lay prone on the concrete floor. He noticed, ironically, a metal grate next to him. If he had only come in this way, leaving the grate open as he had done in the small, attached room next door, he would have a hole to escape through now.

He wouldn't have made it without being seen by one of the workers or guards, but at least he could have had a chance at retreat.

Jack heard a voice again, but it was lower, quieter.

It was directed toward him. "Hello, Jack."

Jack's blood went cold.

"You got here right on time, my friend. I wasn't sure I was going to get to see you again. You've been busy, it seems. Many of my men are dead because of you."

Jack squeezed his eyes shut. It seemed the pain from his injuries was returning in full force, all at once. He felt his leg tightening, his side aching. His shoulder and wrist even hurt, new injuries he wasn't aware he had. His feet were tired as well, overextended from having to push the entire length of his body through the wet concrete tube.

"I would ask to what I owe the pleasure," Victor continued, "but I believe I already know. It seems you and I have been involved in a game played by our governments — but one you may not have even been aware we *are* playing. Trust me, Jack, it gives me no pleasure to tell you that this sort of thing annoys me to no end.

"However, it does not change the fact you are here." He paused, then raised his voice a bit. "You *are* here, meddling in my affairs once again, Jack."

Jack breathed evenly, focused. He had no ideas, no plan. There was no more left in the tank. He was exhausted, worn down, beaten.

Dying.

He felt his side, and his hand came away covered in blood. His bandages were no longer able to keep his blood in, and it had not been nearly long enough for him to have created more. He was losing it by the pint — how long would it be, then? Would he even last long enough for Victor to kill him?

He guessed he would be completely bled out in a matter of hours unless Victor decided to bandage him up *before* he killed him. *That would be a sick twist of fate.*

"Jack, the last time we met, I was arrogant. I assumed I had you figured out. You were better than I thought, taking all of us by surprise. That will not happen again."

Apparently he was not *going to bandage him up before killing him.*

"Santiago, Cruz, spread out a bit more. Make sure you have a shot lined up."

Victor had directed this order at his men, and Jack heard them shuffling further along the catwalk. He looked up, craning his neck and tensing his back which only caused his side to ache even more, and saw one of the men, either Santiago or Cruz, aiming his AK-47 down at him.

It was a clean shot, an easy one. Less than twenty yards, with a rifle built for far greater distance than that.

"Jack, please stand up."

Jack felt tears coming to his eyes. *This is not how this was supposed to end. This is not how any of this was supposed to go.*

He thought about Rudy, about his death in the woods. Every step of the way, Jack had been beaten, had been bested by the environment itself, scared forward by invisible forces like the Shining Path regiment that chased him through Iquitos.

He had come out on top with his life, but every battle had caused him to lose something.

Now, he was losing the war. He would lose his life completely if he didn't think of something quickly.

"*Now*, Jack."

Jack got to his knees, leaving the AK47 on the floor. He knew his head was in full view. Victor didn't take the shot.

Jack rose to his feet, stood slowly. His hands brushed against his Taurus at his back. He tried to fight away the pain, to fight away the blood pouring from his side. He turned, now facing the wall Victor was standing above. He looked up to the catwalk, met the eyes of the man who had tried to kill his children.

Jack had the gun in his hand now, but there was no way he would get it up fast enough to get off a shot. Certainly not a *clean* shot, and Victor was just far enough away that it would be tricky to try to use a pistol against him.

"Don't bother dropping the gun, Jack," Victor said.

Jack saw it then. Hadn't noticed it before. Victor had his own weapon, a pistol, but he was aiming with two hands as he pulled the weapon up and out in front of him. He had the high ground, too — for him, it would be an easy shot.

Jack reacted too late. He tried pulling the Taurus up, tried falling to the side, but his body was stiff, too worn to react quickly.

Victor fired one shot. Then another.

Both of them hit Jack.

He fell backward, caught himself with his back foot as one bullet shot through his shoulder, just beneath his collarbone, while the other landed in his upper arm. He was spun around, then pushed forward again by his own momentum. He stumbled over the table.

The last thing he saw as more blood surged from his body and more pain erupted throughout his entire right side, was the concrete floor as it rushed to meet his face.

Jack's torso fell over the table and smacked against the concrete floor inside Victor's warehouse.

His eyes shut, and they did not reopen.

CHAPTER 69

JACK

JACK WASN'T DEAD, but he wished he was.

He had never felt pain like this, never felt as if every breath would hurt worse than the last.

He staggered his breathing, not on purpose but because his body demanded it, sucking in tiny sips of air between sobs and clearing his throat. There was blood in his mouth; he could taste it.

He spat, but it only fell over his chin and stuck there.

He blinked, lifting his head. He was still lying on the warehouse floor, this time on his back. The table had been moved out of the way, and four men were standing over him.

"Santiago, Cruz, go check what's happening outside. It's too quiet."

Two of the men — mere shadows — left Jack's vision, and he tried focusing on the two remaining ones.

He picked out the man talking — Victor. "Good to see you are still with us, Jack," Victor said. He smiled, but there was malice behind it. "You have heard the stories about me, I am sure. People like *you* who tried to come in the way of *my* plans, of *my* business — they do not just get to leave. Even if it is in a casket, they do not just get the satisfaction of a quick death."

Jack's eyesight returned, and he saw Victor silhouetted in the dark, dim light of the warehouse. The man's hair had grown out a bit, but Victor kept it held in place with some sort of product. He wore black, but not the same black camo outfits his cartel soldiers wore. He wore a button-down shirt and black slacks, sharp snakeskin boots poking out from underneath them.

Jack tried to speak, tried to move, but none of his appendages seemed to be working. He felt blood pooling out over his chest, warm and comfortable. At the same time it calmed him down, he could feel it sucking the life out of him with every drop that left his body.

"It would normally be enough for me to let you bleed out here," Victor said. "*Normally.*" He paused again, then turned to the other man standing next to him, extending a hand. "But today is no normal day, is it, Jack?"

Jack saw what the man held now, what he handed to Victor.

A rope.

The end was hooked — no, a hook was tied to it. Jack couldn't tell, he squinted at it. He tried to shift, suddenly realizing his legs weren't unresponsive — they had been tied together. His hands as well.

Terror rose in Jack's body. The tears began streaming down his face.

Victor reached down and placed the hook between Jack's feet. He felt tension, his feet smashed together tighter as the hook caught the bindings holding his feet.

He had been out long enough for them to tie him up, both

hands and feet. His arms were in front of him, but they had also been tied around his waist. He couldn't move them left or right, nor up and down.

Victor snapped his fingers, stepping back. Immediately the man next to him stepped back as well, and Jack saw a small box in his hands. It was connected to a string or cable that reached up to the ceiling, near where the rope had been hanging down. He pressed a button on the device, and Jack felt his feet raising in the air.

No, no, no, Jack thought. *No, not like this.*

His feet kept moving, the blood on his chest now trailing over and around his neck. Jack looked side to side, growing more frantic by the second.

"This warehouse used to be a meatpacking plant," Victor explained. His voice was calm, as if taking visitors on a guided tour. "I considered having them tear *everything* down and rebuild, but for what? All I need is a rectangular space, somewhere I can hide my teams and set up my logistics chain."

He stepped back toward Jack as his feet hung in the air above his torso. The rope kept pulling, kept ascending. Jack looked up and saw a pulley system high above his head, at the top of the warehouse.

"As you can see, I left a few of the implements in place. There was no reason to take them all out, since it would cost money and time. I wanted to get started with our new route as soon as possible. A route that would open up the *entire* South American continent to the worldwide black market for weapons.

"Drugs, too, though they are a bit more finicky — more localized government police forces seem to be sniffing around for drugs. But weapons dealing — now *that* is the future.

Something I was never able to convince my boss of. Hopefully, this will do the trick."

Jack listened, unable to block out the man's voice, as his body was pulled upward, upside down. Already more blood was moving to his head, now bursting forth from his two gunshot wounds on his right side. Even the wound on his lower torso seemed to be joining in the party, and he saw the bandage there was now just a dark maroon rag.

"Consider how symbolic this is, Jack. You have interrupted my *entire* operation, and for that you will be killed. However, I also find it serendipitous that you ended up right here, by your own accord, in the center of my empire. My teams will return to this room, the tables will be set back up once more, and business will continue.

"This time, however, they will have something dangling above them — a reminder both of what disloyalty brings, and a reminder of what we are all working toward."

Jack's eyes went wide.

"Have you ever wondered, Jack, who it is I *really* work for? Who *you* really work for? Have you ever considered... it may be the exact same people?"

It was horrifying, but he knew exactly what Victor was describing. He felt his body lifted now, his arms pulling against his waist but the bindings keeping them still there. His head was still on the ground, scraping against the concrete. He was being lifted all the way to the ceiling of this warehouse, where he would bleed out — upside down — and die.

"My men found your entrance route, as well," Victor said, changing the subject. "Smart move, Jack, entering through the drainage system. In a sense, I guess you will be *exiting* through that same system, as well."

Jack felt the grate scraping on the back of his head as the rope pulled him toward the immediate center of the room. His head was heavy, his eyes stained red with blood that continued pouring over his face.

And still he rose, unable to move.

THERE WAS gunfire from somewhere far outside the building. Victor snapped his eyes up and nodded at the man who had been holding the box. He handed it over to Victor, and he stepped close to Jack and looked at the man. "Go check," he said in quick Spanish.

The man hustled away, and Jack was left with Victor, now alone in the warehouse. It would have been a strange sight, had anyone else stumbled in. Jack was dangling by his feet, swaying gently as the rope pulled him straight up to the ceiling of the warehouse, a good forty feet above.

Victor was standing directly beneath him now, holding the box that controlled the pulley mechanism. He was smiling, apparently nonchalant about the war his men were waging outside. "I trust you are still with me, Jack?" Victor asked.

Jack tried to nod, his eyes almost closing. But the blood seemed to invigorate him, seemed to have a little bit of fight left. Not that he could do anything with it. "I'm harder to kill than you think," Jack mumbled.

"Apparently so," Victor responded. "Tell me, Jack, while we

have time. How was it you were so qualified to come down here, to sneak in right under my nose and play cartel man for a day?"

All of this, Victor had asked him in Spanish. Jack replied in Spanish equally quickly. "You inspired me to change," Jack spat. "To *grow*. Turns out the CIA is quite capable of training operatives quickly. Nothing like being in the field, though."

Victor laughed, throwing his head back and dodging as a trickle of blood finally made its way around Jack's ear, through his hair, and down to the floor below. "That must be true," Victor said. "And I am positive this field training is giving you the experience you will need to carry out a long and illustrious career as an operative."

Jack choked on blood, then spat a wad of it out. "If you're going to kill me, just kill me," Jack said.

"No!" Victor snapped. "Have you not been listening? Do you not know who I am? I am a man with power, but that power comes from *legend*. From the *myth* that I have worked to build for *decades*. And what are legends but stories? All of the stories my men tell of me — ones I'm sure you have heard, as well — they are all stories. Some elaborated, but all are true. *They* are what give me my power. The fear — you cannot manufacture that."

He looked up at Jack and cocked his head to the side. "*This* will incite fear like nothing else, Jack. To leave you swaying high above their heads — can you imagine the legend it will create?"

"The only legend I've heard is that you're an asshole," Jack said. His voice was nothing but a mumble.

"Surely you can give me more credit than that, Jack," Victor said, his voice icy. "I have been working very hard, for a very long time, for all of this. He raised his voice as Jack rose higher and higher through the warehouse center. "Ultimately, you failed. I expected that, but it is interesting to me the spectacular *manner* in which you failed. You see, Jack, this game is very similar to any game of strategy. Sleight-of-hand, manipulation, all of it plays a role in our organization. Both of them — that's why you and I are actually similar. I believe I told you that once, and you didn't believe me.

"It's why your government has been playing games with mine. It's why *you* were sent here. It's why my *brother* was sent with you."

Brother? Who the hell was Victor talking about? "I am *nothing* like you," Jack shot back.

Victor chuckled. "You did not know, did you? He turned on me long ago — on all of us. The three of us grew up together — me, my brother, my sister. But it was clear from a very young age that I would be taking over the family business. He never liked that, never could accept it for what it was."

Jack frowned. *Why was Victor suddenly changing the subject? Was he reminiscing about the past?*

"He and I never saw eye to eye, but I never thought he would betray me like this. When we had a chance to move the family business into cartel business, he had a choice to make. I thought we could get through to him."

What is he talking about?

"I thought he could change, understand. I was wrong, and it almost cost me my business numerous times. It took Olivia some time — they always had a better relationship. I knew she would be able to track him down. As it turns out, family ties *are* always the strongest."

Jack shook his head now, completely missing Victor's

point. Still, his skin was crawling. Victor Elizondo was not a man to ramble, to get off topic. "Who — who is Olivia?"

"You met her in the city, actually. Surely you remember? She was trying to help you. Or that's what *you* thought. I was impressed you were able to escape those men, but the other group that you brought to my doorstep — the ones out there fighting my men now — probably helped."

Jack recalled the fight between the three boats, recalled how it had ended. That must mean... "Olivia," he whispered. "The informant. Rudy's asset."

"My brother told you about her, didn't he?" Victor continued. "He must have — he must have said you could trust her, since *he* had recently come to start trusting her?"

It suddenly hit Jack, in that moment, dangling upside down.

He hadn't just been played by his own organization, his own government.

He had been played by *everyone*.

CHAPTER 71

JACK

OLIVIA IS VICTOR'S SISTER. *And that means...*

"And Rudy Estrada," Jack whispered. "Rudy was your brother."

"Rudy?" Victor asked, a smile on his face. "Is that his *under-cover* name? How quaint. 'Rudy' was a great uncle of ours, a favorite of his. I had to kill him about twelve years ago, so it's no wonder my brother took his name. Carlos was always a bit of a softy, always willing to trust people just because they told him to.

"That was his downfall, you see. He actually *believed* Olivia wanted to make amends. I told her to find him, to see where the CIA would put him. He left for America more than two decades ago and has been ingratiating himself with your superiors ever since. It took her a while, but she finally found him and convinced him she wanted out."

Jack nodded. It made perfect sense. Olivia had told Rudy — Carlos — that she had swapped sides, that she wanted to help him take down the cartel that had caused so much grief in his life.

And everything else began to make sense, as well.

Trust no one but yourself, Jack thought. The words Rudy had used. He realized now it was a warning. He had *wanted* to trust Olivia — his own sister — but knew it wouldn't be smart. He also knew he could not tell Jack who she was, or it would put both of them in danger.

Jack realized in an instant that Olivia had killed Rudy. The man was a trained operator, hardened underneath his softer-looking exterior. Jack knew better, and he had seen the man in action. The only person on the planet who could have gotten that close to him — close enough to put a bullet between his eyes — was his own sister.

Jack wanted to sleep now, wanted to close his eyes and shut it all out for good. But he couldn't help himself — Victor was talking, giving him information.

"All this time..." Jack said, his words now nothing but a mumble. "All this time, it was *you*. Pulling the strings."

"I wish I could take *all* the credit, Jack," Victor said. "But my sister is as cunning as I am. It was her idea to lure Carlos here. She made sure the right information was fed through the right channels, made sure that your government knew about our actions down here. I had no idea they would send you as well, but when my men saw the aircraft, saw that it was the same aircraft two agents had gotten into back in Colombia, I figured it would be easy enough to remove both of you from the playing field.

"You both survived, somehow, but again, I shouldn't be surprised. Rudy was very well-trained, I hear. And you have proven to be equally as hardy."

"*Your* man?" Jack said. "We were shot down by Shining Path rebels."

Victor nodded, his smile growing. "Yes, yes. That old communist cult started by Guzman. The resurgence in recent years has been taking its toll on the region, yes? It's all the Peruvian government can talk about, and the Brazilians are just as scared that they will bleed over into *their* territory. As it turns out, this sort of unrest is *exactly* what is required for someone like me to lay the groundwork and foundation for a new route."

"You *used* the Shining Path to further the cartel's interests?"

"I didn't use them," Victor said. "I *created* them. That was my genius behind all of this. My boss will be dead soon — the whole world knows, including him. Either from natural causes or my own hand, *he* will die, and *I* will take control of this entire operation. We needed this route, and we needed a way to get it set up fast.

"I wasn't sure if it were a viable path to take, so I began ordering my men into Peru, into the same territories where the Shining Path Maoist rebels had a base of operations. I kept splitting my forces, sending more and more men to act the part of Shining Path. Everyone here was terrified of them, so no one ever got close enough to ask questions."

Jack swallowed.

"It all worked *too* perfectly, I think," Victor continued. "Some of my men even seem to believe that they are now fighting for a higher cause, a higher power. They've even bought into it. Whatever — it allowed me to sneak into the region unnoticed, to at least get people in place and build enough of a stronghold here before the Peruvian government could really do anything about it. At the drop of a hat, I can have the entire Army sent to fight off my little Shining Path iteration. It's all sleight-of-hand, Jack."

CHAPTER 72

JACK

THE PULLEY STOPPED MOVING, and Jack's feet were now only about a foot or two away from the ceiling of the warehouse. He pulled his eyes upward, actually looking down, and saw that he was about forty feet off the floor. To fall from here would be death. It was too far of a drop to attempt, even without considering he would be dropping headfirst and would not be able to whip his body around.

Not that he had a way to escape, or the bandwidth left in his muscles to attempt something like that.

He swayed gently, listening as Victor talked below him. They had switched to English at some point, likely all part of Victor's power play — not only had he anticipated Jack's every move, but he could also communicate better than Jack in both languages. "You think this is a game between two *men*, Jack," Victor continued. "It is not. It is a game between two *nations*. Mine and yours. Most governments say that they wish cartels like mine do not exist. They will even mobilize armies to guard their interests, then tell the public they are afraid of us.

"But you should know the truth by now, Jack. You should

understand it intuitively, since you are here now, you have seen what has transpired. Do you think your government *really* wants to take me down?"

"My government wants you dead," Jack said. "*I* want you dead."

"*Think*, Jack," Victor said. "My boss *will* die. I *will* take over. Your government wanted to kill me as well, to throw my cartel in disarray. But they forgot that they were not dealing with just the Vínculos, with just me. They were dealing with my *government*, the people of Venezuela as well. Our livelihood depends on providing the things I sell to places around the world. Places *your* government can't touch.

"As such, the livelihood of my people — the Venezuelans themselves — relies on my organization doing this. My government has no money, but you and I both know they cannot simply turn to the United States for a handout. They cannot beg for help from countries like yours, who are too greedy and too caught up in their own self-interests to lend a hand. They *want* Venezuela to fail, because it will be proof to them that their idealistic society is somehow better than ours. That's the real reason.

"So governments like the United States are conflicted: on the one hand, they want to hold up Venezuela as proof of a system that doesn't work. They want us to fail. But on the other hand, there is a *lot* of money to be made in keeping armies fed and armed. More money than you can imagine — and money, it turns out, equals *power*. There's nothing your government wants more than that, Jack. So I ask you: who is the *real* enemy here?"

Jack's mind raced. He had a hard time processing everything he was hearing, knowing that Victor was mostly just waiting for his men to return, to receive word that the job outside was finished.

After that, he would kill Jack. He had options, too. He could certainly shoot him again, but blood was almost completely covering Jack's face now, dripping steadily directly down into the drain beneath the warehouse. Victor could also press a button and drop Jack straight down onto the floor, cracking his skull against the grate beneath him.

Jack knew it was over. Victor's man would return soon enough, deliver the news that the cartel had won, and Victor would finish the job.

Hanging upside down in a dirty old warehouse, Jackson Barr, Jr. would die.

Jack felt something shift in his pants pocket, then nearly fall out. He had completely forgotten about the vials he had stolen from back in the market in Iquitos. One of them had almost slid out of his pocket while he was upside down, but he pressed his hands forward over his crotch and the ropes used to tie them around his waist to hold the things in place. He shifted now, having trouble moving since he had no hard surface to push back against, but eventually got the ropes worked around to the side.

Jack was able to slide his hands to the left, eliciting more pain as the ropes ground against his right-side injury. The bullet wounds on his shoulder and arm were excruciating as well, the pain throbbing through his entire body as blood was expelled through the holes. He could reach the pocket now and used his left hand to slide his fingers inside. All three vials were right there, barely inside his pocket.

He wrapped his fingers around them, feeling the cold

ceramic surface with their tiny cork tops. He pulled them into his hand as Victor laughed.

"This is ironic, Jack," Victor said. "When we first met, you had me talking, had me explaining myself. I *swore* I would never do that again, that I would never be in a position where I had to stoop to your level in order to explain my dealings. I will leave it at that, Jack. You deserve nothing more from me except death, so I will give you that now."

"Victor."

Jack said the word calmly but tried to put some gravitas behind it. He needed to delay him, to get him confused — or at least interested — for a few more seconds.

Jack had grasped the three vials in the band of his knuckles, holding them upright, so their tops faced the ceiling. He would have to use extreme care now, as the contents inside could easily kill him.

Phyllobates terribilis, or the golden dart frog, was a tiny creature endemic to the jungles of Colombia. For centuries, indigenous peoples used fluids from the frog's skin glands on their arrows. The batrachotoxin, widely considered one of the most lethal poisons on the planet, was used by some healers in extremely small doses.

They would leave the toxin to dry in a specially crafted fluid, which would oxidize and turn into a fine powder.

That was the very powder Jack held inside the vials.

In Peru, products like this were tightly regulated, as they were in all developed nations. But it was also a culturally important medication. Open-air markets, like the one Jack had been passing through, would sell any manner of similar potions and formulations, as well as the natural ingredients that made them up.

Most of them were as good as snake oil, but a few — like the powder Jack was holding in his hands now — were actually good for something. Mixing a quarter teaspoon of the already diluted powder with water into a watery paste, then spreading it over skin, acted as a medicated salve, a topical pain killer.

But any more than that in an isolated area, and it could cause significant harm. Emptying a whole vial onto the skin, or otherwise ingesting it, could kill a grown man.

And Jack had taken *three* vials of the stuff.

He was using his right hand now to pull off the cork lids. They were on tightly, but he was able to wriggle them free and hold them with his right hand.

He did not want to drop either the corks or the vials. Dropping the corks might end with them landing on Victor's head, alerting him to Jack's motivation and Victor simply moving out of the way.

Jack felt his body swaying gently, and he pulled his head upward as hard as far as it would go to get a good view of Victor. Everything was strange, unnatural, from this vantage point. He was upside down, his head pounding with the flowing of blood passing through his body. His heart was working overtime, his lungs ready to explode. Even without his considerable damage, Jack would have had a hard time aiming properly.

He pushed his feet and shins against the current of the hanging rope, feeling his body sway in ever-larger arcs. He continued this, swinging upside down as Victor came into and left his view over and over again. Finally, at the apex of the arc, Jack upturned all three vials at once and shook their contents free.

The powder fell out of each of the tubes, holding their

compact cylindrical form for a while, only dissipating when each of the tubes had fallen about halfway to Victor. At that point, when they met resistance from the air, they began to expand into a cloudy puff of smoky powder.

Each of the particles was still heavier than air, however, and they all fell.

...directly onto Victor's upturned face. The cloud covered his head, and Jack heard him choke and gasp for breath as it enveloped his face. Particles landed in his eyes, his mouth, even some in his nose as he sniffed, trying to hack through it.

He stepped away, stumbling backward. "What — what is this, Jack?" Victor mumbled. "You are trying to hurt me? With... what?"

He clutched his chest, trying to cough.

No air would come.

"What... is this...*Jack*?"

The last word came out only a mumbled syllable. Jack continued swinging, growing dizzy as he watched Victor fall to the side, still trying to breathe.

The cartel boss gasped again, then coughed wildly. It seemed as though he could get air into his lungs now, but the damage had been done. Victor dropped his mouth open, eyes wide. He gripped the sides of his head and rocked back and forth, then fell to his knees.

Victor tried to speak, tried to plead. The alkaloid batrachotoxins acted fast, especially since they had unfettered access to Victor's insides by way of his nasal cavity and eyes. He began foaming at the mouth, eventually falling face-first onto the floor.

He writhed in agony for over a minute, dying far more slowly than Jack would have thought possible. The man held on, somehow able to breathe through it all, somehow able to fight until the last faithful second.

And, with Jack swinging upside down high over his head, blood dripping out and draining from his body, creating a puddle of slick black on the grate in the floor far below, Victor Elizondo died.

THROUGHOUT HEAVENS' military career and the time he had spent in private security for Stonefire, he had seen and done a lot of things. He had also come to expect certain things.

He had *expected* to fire his weapon, for example. He had certainly done that now in spades, and the final results of his outburst were outside this warehouse, lying haphazardly on the ground.

He wasn't sure the exact number of men his team had taken out, but it was all of them. No hostiles remained in the area, at least outside. Szymon had been downed in the riverboat fight, and Joseph and Alameda had been killed in the blast.

His new group had fared better, but only slightly. The only other remaining member of his new four-man team was performing a perimeter check just inside the main warehouse building, and Heavens had decided to head inside the main space, where he had heard gunfire earlier.

He had moved slowly, cautiously, and tightened up when he came across the other thing he had expected to find today.

Blood.

There was lots of blood, and Heavens knew in an instant that the massacre outside had continued inside, as well. He had taken the stairs outside to enter the warehouse on the second floor, opting for the high ground in case the battle continued inside.

Now, he saw the bleeding corpses of three men who had fallen to the left of his position, heard the drips of blood spattering against the concrete floor down below. He swept his eyes to the right and saw a few more lumps – more corpses.

The CIA man had certainly been here. Whether he was *still* here — and whether or not he was still alive — remained to be seen. It was too dark to see anything clearly, and he had entered from the easternmost side of the warehouse, which meant that the rectangular shape seemed to put him on the side of the wall opposite where most of the fighting had occurred.

Heavens began walking around, the catwalk clinging loudly under his boots. He saw something swinging out above the center of the space — again, just a shadow. His eyes narrowed as he focused on it and tried to discern what he was looking at. He picked up his pace, turning the corner and aiming for the descending metal stairs that led to the bottom floor.

He heard his radio crackle three times quickly — the all-clear from his new teammate outside — and he picked up the pace even more. As he reached the stairs, the dim light revealed what it was he saw swaying.

A body. Swinging from a hook.

Of all the things Heavens *had* expected to find inside the warehouse, this was absolutely not one of them.

It was a human, male, hanging upside-down, arms and hands bound together and tied around his waist. There was not enough light to see the person's face clearly, but a thick painting of blood completely concealed it, anyway.

Heavens had a hunch he knew who this was. He looked like a pig gone to slaughter, the man hanging lifelessly from the ceiling.

There was a control box laying on the floor next to a drain, into which thick rivers of blood were now disappearing.

And next to the drain, another man.

But *this* man had died in a far more gruesome way, it seemed. His eyes were bulged open, the whites visible even from the bottom of the stairs now, and one hand was wrapped around his throat, as if trying to prevent it from opening up enough to let something slide down it.

He frowned, examining this new find. The man's other hand was splayed out to the side, palm up. His features were contorted, matching the positions of his legs. It seemed he had stumbled around a bit, grasped at his throat, and then perished before falling backward. The lifeless corpse stared straight up.

Straight up at the CIA man.

Heavens smiled. Somehow, the CIA asset had managed to kill the guy. Somehow, while dangling helplessly from the ceiling, he had *still* tricked everyone and pulled it off. Against all odds, the man had managed to finish one more job, one more mission.

Heavens hardly had the full story; he was well aware of that fact. But he never did — his job wasn't to know the full story; it was to *act*. To move, to kill.

If he was forced to guess, this CIA asset had been deployed

to this region to kill the very man that was sprawled out next to the grate and beneath the horrific torture scene above. That he had accomplished his mission successfully before perishing himself was incredible.

The radio squawked something again, but Heavens was focused on the CIA man's face.

It seemed to be twitching, moving. Heavens walked forward, now only ten feet away from the two dead men in the center of the warehouse floor. He looked up at the CIA man, then down at the control box. He saw what it was and understood it immediately.

A single rocker switch. *Up or down.*

The dead man had lifted the CIA agent, hanging him by his feet, likely then torturing him and forcing whatever information out of him he had wanted.

The poor guy had suffered greatly before dying, but it was still nothing compared to what the man next to the grate had endured.

He looked like he had been poisoned, but how?

Heavens strode over, ignoring the whiff of sharp iron stinging his nostrils as he stepped through the thickening swamp of blood near the grate, then reached down to pick up the control box. He lowered the body until he was face-to-face with the man.

And then the man coughed.

Heavens nearly dropped the control mechanism as he reeled backward. He caught his balance, eyes wide. "Holy shit," he whispered.

His teammate entered the room, also opting for the second floor. He was standing on the balcony, up above Heavens. The CIA man's body swayed between them.

"Hey," he shouted. "This guy's alive. Get your ass down here and help me get him out."

He wasn't sure why he'd said it. Heavens' mission — the entire point of his being here — was swinging in front of his face. He should just kill the guy, stab him in the chest, and be done with it.

But something in Heavens had caused him to rethink his mission. Everything he had learned so far — Reynolds' weird attitude and change of heart, his admission that there was *some* sort of leverage holding him hostage, and the sheer fact that the guy swinging in front of now *seemed* like the good guy.

He had done nothing wrong. He had toppled the cartel's leader here in Manaus — surely that was a *good* thing, right?

The man above had burst into action, but Heavens focused again on the swinging man's face. His eyes were closed, but a new trickle of blood had appeared from somewhere near his mouth, draining off the side of his face.

He frowned deeper. "You okay, brother?"

No answer.

He used the control box once again to lower the man even more, cradling his neck with his free hand as the man neared the ground. He rolled the head upward onto his knee, kneeling down to accept the weight of the man's upper body as he came to rest flat on his back on the warehouse floor.

His teammate was by his side now, and Heavens wasted no time explaining what he thought had happened here.

"We need to get him out, need to get him help. Let's untie him."

As they got to work, Heavens stood and stepped back once more. He had felt a soft buzz in his pocket. His cell phone.

He pulled it out and looked at the number.

His frown intensified, now reaching his brow and fore-head. *Odd timing*, he thought.

He was getting a call from Reynolds.

JACK'S FACE FELT HOT, stifled. He coughed, then his eyes shot open. He tried to still himself; he was shaking.

No. *Everything* was shaking.

"Woah, buddy," a voice said. It was distorted, amplified.

He felt his ears. There were cups over them. Headphones?

He tried speaking. "Where — what's happening?"

"We're in my chopper," the voice answered. *"You're laying down, and I'd bet you've got a hell of a headache pounding. Stay horizontal, for now."*

"I'm alive?"

The man chuckled. Jack's eyes cleared a bit, and he saw the other speaker. He sat across from Jack, sideways, since Jack's head was lying flat against a makeshift bed. His face was dark, but it looked dirty, muddy. His eyes were wide, watching Jack.

"Barely. Thanks to my new buddy here, you've got the best field medicine absolutely no money can buy."

Another voice chuckled, but Jack didn't see the man.

"Anyway, we scooped you off a hook hanging from the ceiling. You apparently took out their leader — poison?"

Jack nodded.

"*Cool.*"

"Who are you?" Jack asked. He recognized the man now but didn't know his name. It was the mercenary, the man he had run into back in Iquitos, and the same one who had followed him to Manaus.

"*Name's Heavens. Up until very recently, I was with the South American branch of Stonefire, a private security firm.*"

"You quit?"

"*Something like that. Look, I know we got off on the wrong foot — you know, with me shooting at you and all that — but I want to make amends. Figured the best way to do that was to get you out of that warehouse, loaded up into my exfil unit, and patched up best we could.*"

"Thanks," Jack said.

"*Don't mention it. But if you want, you* could *mention how the hell you came to be getting chased by private mercs, cartel assholes, and your own government?*"

Jack frowned.

"*I've got my reasons for leaving, and I figured you did, as well. Who'd you piss off?*"

Jack didn't respond.

"*Look, you don't have to tell me everything, but I really am trying to make sense of this. Act of good faith: here's what I know: I was sent to watch you, to keep you on task, but somewhere along the way, wires got crossed and* both *our missions changed, right? Mine was to take you out, no questions asked.*"

"I'm assuming you asked questions, then," Jack muttered.

"*I did. Still am. You're Jackson Barr, Jr., yeah?*"

Jack nodded.

"*Got a call from my recent boss a few hours ago. He told me*" *who you were and told me what's been going on. Can't help me anymore, so he certainly can't help you now. But I think we can help each other."*

"How so?"

Now, Heavens frowned back at Jack. He tried to pull his head up, but the pain was severe. He felt the throbbing behind his eyes, the blood ready to surge out. *At least there* is *blood in there,* he thought.

"Hmm, I would have thought you'd know at least that. Suffice it to say, whoever you pissed off went really *high up. They put a hit out on you, which got to* my *ex-boss. I don't know why they did, but I guess killing off that guy in Manaus sent them over the edge. They want you dead, my friend."*

"Dead?"

"Like, six-feet-under dead. Dead, dead. Yeah, man. They weren't happy to hear what you did, and apparently that gave them a perfect excuse to turn them against you."

"Them? Who?" Jack was still reeling from what he remembered of his encounter with Victor, so he couldn't begin to understand what was happening now.

"Navy and Army Intel. FBI, should you end up stateside. And, of course, CIA."

"Wait," Jack said. "They're after *me?*"

Heavens shrugged. *"As I said, you pissed off some people in high places, and they need a scapegoat. Brother, I don't think you're going to be wanting to head back home anytime soon."*

Jack swallowed, and even that was painful. *Home* was *exactly* where he wanted to go. He said as much, but Heavens silenced him.

"I'm feeling you, but it's not a good idea. We're headed to Colombia now, and then I'm jumping back to Brazil. Rio, then

maybe São Paulo. I suggest you tag along, at least until you're walking again. I can't protect you forever, but for now, our interests are —"

"Protect me?" Jack asked, incredulous. "You're telling me that my own organization wants to bring me in? To interrogate me?"

Heavens chuckled again, then held up his phone. Jack squinted at it, trying to understand what he was seeing. After a few seconds, he saw that it was a message board-type site, something internal that Heavens had access to.

He saw his own face there — the clean-shaven look Jack sported the last time he had taken Company directory photos — and saw the markings underneath his name.

"Red is 'dangerous suspect, detain.' 'Green is person of interest.'"

Jack saw that his were three black diagonal lines. "And... black?"

Heavens' head fell to the side; his voice lowered through the speaker in Jack's ear. *"Black is 'KOS' — kill-on-sight.' Whatever you were into down there, you royally screwed up. Sorry, man."*

Jack's mouth fell open. *How could this be? What had he done to deserve this sort of treatment? And from his own government?*

It didn't make sense.

"I need to see my family," Jack said suddenly. "My kids."

At this, Heavens' eyes fell. He grabbed the phone from Jack, swiped around, and held it back up to Jack's face.

Jack read it, the blood cooling and draining more with every word. *No. There's no way...*

Whoever was behind all of this, they had acted *fast.*

He was staring at a news station's website, one from the municipality he and his family lived in. It was their obituaries page.

And he was reading *his own* obituary.

"They'll have told your family by now," Heavens said. *"Surely sent a spook or two out there to talk through it with your wife. They'll be helping her plan, your, uh, funeral."*

"I'm *not dead,*" Jack grunted. He tried to sit up, but the pain was too much.

"I'm sorry, man. They did it to me, too. Whoever's behind it got to all of us. They want us gone. Wiped. Eliminated. And they're thorough, working quickly. I hate to be the guy to tell you, but you can't go back."

It didn't make sense. He couldn't see his wife again? His daughters?

But one thing *did* make sense, and that plagued Jack even more.

As he lay on the chopper's floor on the bed of dirty shirts and clothing, trying to recover from the whirlwind last three days, he remembered Victor's words to him:

Who is the real *enemy here?*

AFTERWORD

Thanks for reading! If you liked this book (or even if you hated it...), write a review or rate it. You might not think it makes a difference, but it does.

Besides *actual* currency (money), the currency of today's writing world is *reviews*. Reviews, good or bad, tell other people that an author is worth reading. I'm hoping that since you made it this far into my book, you have some sort of opinion on it.

Would you mind sharing that opinion? It only takes a second.

Nick Thacker

Jack Barr Thrillers

The Caribbean Affair (Book 1)

The Peruvian Exchange (Book 2)

Six Assassins Thrillers

Primary Target (Book 1)

Subtle Target (Book 2)

Unstable Target (Book 3)

Captive Target (Book 4)

Vendetta Target (Book 5)

Final Target (Book 6)

Mason Dixon Thrillers

Mark for Blood (Book 1)

Death Mark (Book 2)

Mark My Words (Book 3)

Harvey Bennett Mysteries

The Enigma Strain (Book 1)

The Amazon Code (Book 2)

The Ice Chasm (Book 3)

The Jefferson Legacy (Book 4)

The Paradise Key (Book 5)

The Atlantis Artifact (Book 6)

The Book of Bones (Book 7)

The Cain Conspiracy (Book 8)

The Mendel Paradox (Book 9)

The Minoan Manifest (Book 10)

The Napoleon Job (Book 11)

The Embers of Siwa (Book 12)

The Epsilon Event (Book 13)

Harvey Bennett Mysteries - Books 1-3

Harvey Bennett Mysteries - Books 4-6

Harvey Bennett Mysteries - Books 7-9

Jake Parker Thrillers

Containment (Book 1)

The Patriot (Book 2)

False Allegiance (Book 3)

Standalone Thrillers

ABOUT THE AUTHOR

Nick Thacker is a thriller author from Texas who lives in Hawaii and Colorado. In his free time, he enjoys reading in a hammock on the beach, skiing, drinking whiskey, and hanging out with his beautiful wife, two dogs, and two daughters.

For more information and a list of Nick's other work, visit Nick online:
www.nickthacker.com

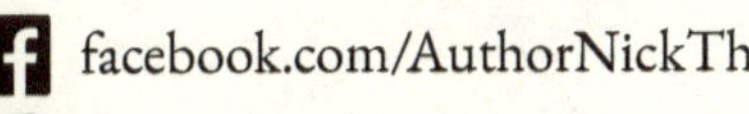

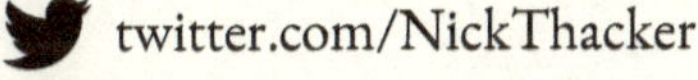

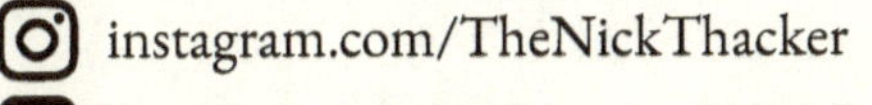

www.ingramcontent.com/pod-product-compliance
Lightning Source LLC
Chambersburg PA
CBHW050923220726
48290CB00018B/1344